Baked Goods and Bad Blood

THE FERNWOOD MYSTERIES
BOOK TWO

ASHLEY SAMUELS

TCA PUBLISHING

One

Today was going to be a good day. I could feel it.

Stepping out of my car downtown and into the warm sunshine, I shut the door and glanced around, practically giddy over the idea of having an entire Saturday off. That never happened.

It wasn't supposed to today, but the wedding I had on the books cancelled at the last minute. The bride's mother called me yesterday evening to tell me they wouldn't need the cake. Her daughter caught her groom in a compromising position with a bridesmaid, so the wedding was off. I offered to still bring the cake—they had paid for it, and it was done, after all —but the woman told me to donate it somewhere because her daughter didn't want any reminders. I thanked her for her thoughtfulness and wished the bride well.

Monday, I planned to re-frost the four individual layers and take them to a daycare center, the nursing home, and the local domestic violence center.

Today, though? Today was all mine.

After I talked to the bride's mother, I called Scarlett and asked her if she wanted to go shopping. I still needed an outfit and a present for Daphne's bridal shower. She immediately called her employees, asking if anyone wanted extra hours. Ella—the saint—had snapped them up.

Practically skipping over the sidewalk, I made my way to Scarlett's boutique, The Whispering Fern. She'd worked the morning hours since we agreed to meet for lunch and then shop. Plus, I wanted to look at her selection. She carried some amazing pieces, like the one I wore today.

I smoothed my hand over my sundress. The white frock with its small pale-pink and green flowers was perfect for today's warm, sunny weather.

The bell over the door tinkled as I entered.

"Hey." Scarlett smiled from behind the counter.

"Hi." Returning her smile, I walked further into the store.

"Ella's not here yet, but it shouldn't be long."

"That's fine. I'll browse." I was a few minutes early, anyway.

"Go check out the skirts I just got in." With a knowing smile, Scarlett pointed toward the far corner. "I think they'll look great with those tall boots you have. Or even the wedge sandals you have on."

I lifted a foot, twirling my ankle. "Aren't they great?" I bought them at The Shoe Boutique just down the street.

"They are. You're lucky your feet are bigger than mine."

I was lucky I was bigger in general than Scarlett. When we were young, before I hit my last growth spurt, we were the same size, and she used to constantly borrow my stuff. Now, the only things she borrowed were some of my sweaters.

"Joe had smaller sizes." I wagged a finger at her, smiling, as I started toward the clothing racks.

Her nose wrinkled. "I'm sure, but I don't need more shoes. My closet is overflowing as it is."

So was mine, but that didn't stop me. "There is always room for more shoes." Laughing, I turned away.

It didn't take me long to find the skirts Scarlett indicated. The rich, mahogany leather miniskirts were simply stunning. The gold rivets and zippers only added to their opulence.

Finding the tag, I checked the price and winced. It shouldn't surprise me that the skirt was expensive. It was real leather.

I still lifted my size off the rack. This was for my sister's bridal shower. I couldn't go in just any old thing.

Skirt in hand, I wandered around the store. It wasn't until I had another skirt, two blouses, a dress, and a jacket in my arms that I realized I'd been there fifteen minutes and Scarlett hadn't joined me.

I walked out from behind a rack, looking toward the front of the store, but stopped when I saw the space behind the counter was empty.

"Scarlett?" Frowning, I turned in a circle. Had she decided to tidy up and I just didn't notice?

But she was nowhere to be seen.

Still glancing around, I walked over to the counter and set down the armload of clothes. Backing away, I meandered toward the employee-only area at the back of the store.

"Scarlett?" I called again as I walked through the door to the back room.

Like the front of the store, it was empty.

Where on earth did she go?

As I neared the rear exit, a raised female voice reached my ears. Curiosity got the better of me and I walked forward. Resting my hand on the door handle, I slowly turned it and peered through the crack.

The back door to Scarlett's shop sat recessed by about thirty feet. Just at the edge of the building, I could see the back of her flowy white shirt, waving in the air as she gestured with one arm as she spoke.

She turned, taking several paces into view. It was then I

saw the phone pressed to her ear. Anger darkened her face. "If that's the way you want to speak to me, don't bother coming back." Pulling the phone away from the side of her face, she stabbed at the screen with one finger, hanging up.

"Everything all right?" I pushed the door open and stepped into the doorway.

Scarlett jumped and looked up. The frown on her face smoothed out. "Yes." She rolled her eyes. "Sorry. I didn't mean to abandon you." Putting her phone away, she started toward me. "Did anyone come in?"

"No." Backing up, I moved away from the door. "Was that Ella? Is she not coming?"

"It wasn't Ella." The frown from before returned, but rather than a sharp frown of anger, this one was more concerned. "She's not here?"

I shook my head, my own frown forming. And not just because Ella was late. Scarlett hadn't said who was on the phone. She was entitled to her privacy, of course, but usually I was the first one she turned to when something upset her. We always talked it out. It helped calm her down and see things in a different light. Today, though, she wasn't talking.

"That's strange." Scarlett glanced at her watch. "She should have been here almost ten minutes ago. Let me call her."

The bell over the front door jingled, interrupting her. She heaved a sigh. "Sorry."

I waved a hand. "It's fine. You call her. I'll go out there."

"Are you sure?"

"Yes," I said, already backing toward the door. "I know how the register works."

Scarlett's head bobbed. "Okay."

Leaving her to find out where Ella was, I turned away and pushed through the doors to the main store.

"Hello." Pasting a smile on my face, I greeted the middle-aged woman who'd come in.

She smiled back.

"Let me know if I can help you with anything."

"I will, thank you."

Taking up residence behind the counter, I picked up the items I'd chosen and removed them from the hangars, folding them neatly as I rang them up. Once I had all the items scanned, I dug into the small, brown leather, cross-body purse slung over my torso and checked myself out.

The receipt printer whirred. Scarlett emerged from the back as I tore the paper off.

I glanced over. "Hey. Did you get ahold of her?"

She shook her head with a frown and laid her phone on the counter, sighing. "No. Hopefully, she's on her way and didn't answer because she's driving. We'll wait another ten minutes or so, then I'll try her again. If she doesn't show up, I'll have to stay." She wrinkled her nose with an apologetic look. "I'm sorry."

"It's okay. This was last minute. I can go wander, then bring back what I bought, and you can give me your opinion. I already picked out a few things." I waved the receipt, then gestured to the neatly folded pile of clothing to the left of the register.

Scarlett smiled. "Nice. I see you found the new skirts."

"I did. And I might very well wear it to the shower." I tipped my head, running an assessing eye over her face. Though she smiled, she didn't look happy.

"Are you sure everything is all right?"

"Yes," she was quick to answer. "It'll be fine. I don't want to talk about it right now."

"Okay. Well, if you change your mind, you know I'll listen."

This time, Scarlett's smile was more genuine. "I know, and I'm grateful. But really, everything is okay. Or it will be, anyway. Soon."

More confused than ever, I just nodded. We talked regularly, and I had no idea what could be bothering her or what that phone call was about. But I wasn't going to press the issue. She'd tell me when she was ready.

That wouldn't stop me from worrying about her, though.

Two

E lla never did show up.

I stuck around The Whispering Fern for about forty-five minutes, chatting. Just before I left to venture out on my own, Scarlett received a text from Ella that said she'd suddenly fallen ill and was sorry she wouldn't be able to make it in. Food poisoning, she said.

I didn't let the lack of a shopping partner get me down, though. It wasn't long until my hands hurt from toting packages. Christmas was a few months away, but I found several things I knew my sisters would like. In addition to an elegant blouse to wear with the skirt I bought at Scarlett's boutique, I also bought another bridal shower present for Daphne.

Did she need the super-soft alpaca wool blanket?

No.

But I bought it, anyway. It was big enough for two and would look great in Daphne and Morgan's living room. Scarlett agreed with me when I showed it to her later.

Home now after helping my friend close up for the day, I thanked my lucky stars my bright blue SUV came equipped with a self-closing hatch. I poked the button and backed away from the vehicle. The hard part would be getting my front door unlocked while holding all these bags.

With the handles pinching my fingers, I walked up the path. Fumbling with my keys, I got the right one to stick out and shoved it in the keyhole. With my fingertips, I turned the knob and let myself inside.

My cat, Millicent—Millie, for short—trotted toward me, meowing loudly.

"Hi, sweet girl." Smiling down at her, I took care not to step on her as I headed for the dining table to deposit my things.

Millie hopped up beside the bags and stuck her face in the closest one.

Chuckling, I stroked her multi-colored back. "They aren't for you."

She chirped and backed up, moving to explore another bag.

I left her to it and went into the kitchen. Somewhere, I had a batch of Dad's chicken soup. I hadn't mentioned it to Scarlett, but I thought I would take it to Ella. Since it was frozen, she could put it in the refrigerator and, hopefully, by the time it was thawed, she would feel like eating again. The soup was gentle on the belly and what I always reached for when I was ill.

Under a bag of homemade mini-pancakes, I found the container of soup. "Victory." Smiling, I closed the freezer door, then went back to the dining room to get my purse and keys.

"Millie, I'll be back again in a bit. Please don't knock everything off the table." Some of the bags were on the heavier side, but my cat loved sacks and bags of any kind. Any time I brought one into the house, she had to sit in it.

For a moment, I debated emptying them all, but I didn't buy anything breakable. Even if she knocked one to the floor, it would be fine.

So, I left them be.

With a quick scratch under Millie's chin and the frozen soup container in hand, I walked out the door.

The drive to Ella's was a quick one. She lived in an apartment complex about five minutes down the road.

I hoped I could remember which unit was hers. I'd only been there once. Scarlett had been out of town and asked me to take Ella home from work once when the young woman's car was in the shop. That had been in the early spring.

I thought I knew which one it was, though.

Turning into the complex, I let muscle memory guide me and stopped in front of building D. The little yard sock flying out front of unit seventeen looked familiar. I was pretty sure Ella was in unit eighteen.

Now to find a parking spot…

Leaning forward, I scanned the lot, looking for the telltale "Visitor's Parking" signs. Most of them were occupied, but I found one near building C and parked.

Ella's complex was alive with activity. School had started and the pool was closed, but that meant nothing to kids on the weekend. They were out in force, enjoying the warm weather.

I couldn't help but smile as I watched a group playing on the wide sidewalk across the parking lot. Two little ones sat on the path near the grass, drawing with sidewalk chalk while three older children ran around with a ball. A sixth child stood by herself with a bottle of bubbles, blowing through the tiny wand and giggling as the bubbles popped on her face.

It brought back many happy memories from my own childhood. Some days, I wished I could just sit and draw on the ground and pretend my problems and worries didn't exist.

Reaching Ella's door, I rapped my knuckles on the steel.

The door pushed inward slightly at my touch.

"What the heck?" Frowning, I unfurled my hand and lightly pressed on the door, pushing it open. "Ella?"

Boy, I hoped I had the right apartment. If not, someone was about to be rather startled by my presence.

"Ella?" I called again, pushing the door open far enough I could step inside. I peered into the dim interior.

All the lights were off, but there was enough sunshine streaming through the windows for me to see well.

The living room I entered was clean, but obviously lived in. A basket of unfolded laundry sat in front of the couch. On the middle cushion, Ella had a stack of folded towels.

She must have been in the middle of laundry when she began feeling unwell.

"Ella? It's Delaney. Scarlett's friend? I brought you some soup." I walked further into the apartment, getting a view of the small kitchen now. A half-empty pot of coffee sat on the warming plate of Ella's coffeemaker and a dirty skillet was on the stove, but there was no Ella.

I glanced up the staircase.

Maybe she was upstairs sleeping?

I didn't really want to wake her if that were the case. Perhaps I would just put the soup in her refrigerator and leave. I could leave a note on the counter.

Lengthening my stride, I turned into the kitchen and quickly stowed the soup in the fridge. Now I just needed to leave a note.

Except it bothered me that the door was open when I got here.

Biting my lip, I debated what to do.

Maybe I would just go up and check to make sure she was all right. If she was sleeping, I'd leave her alone and write a note. It could be she stepped outside for some reason and just didn't realize she didn't close the door all the way since she wasn't feeling well.

Changing course, I walked back through the living room

and rounded the banister to go upstairs. My feet made soft thumps on the cream-carpeted steps. At the top of the landing, I paused, taking in the three doors, one at the end of the hall and two on the right.

All three were open, and I could see into the one directly to my right. It appeared to be a workout room-slash-office and was unoccupied. I moved to the next door, which led into the master bedroom. Like the one before it, it, too, was empty.

That left the door at the end of the hall that was slightly ajar. Light spilled from around it, and I could make out the edge of a bathroom vanity.

My heart sank. The poor girl must be tied to the toilet.

I knocked softly but didn't push the door open in case she wasn't decent. "Ella?"

"You can come in, Delaney."

My face morphed into a fierce frown. That wasn't Ella's voice.

It was Scarlett's. And she sounded upset.

I pushed the door inward. "Scarlett? What—oh my goodness!" My hand flew up to cover my mouth. Disbelief rooted my feet to the floor.

Sitting cross-legged on the linoleum, Scarlett cradled a lifeless Ella in her arms.

"Delaney." Scarlett looked up at me with watery eyes, tear tracks staining her face. "She's dead."

Three

D ead?

I blinked as my brain stuttered, unable to process the sight before me.

What did she mean, Ella was dead? The girl had food poisoning.

Right?

But food poisoning didn't kill. Not this fast.

I blinked again, taking in the milky white pallor to Ella's skin and the blue tint to her parted lips.

Oh my.

The first tears sprang into my eyes and my hands covering my mouth quivered. Some of the starch left my knees, and I sagged into the doorframe. "Have—have you called for help?"

Scarlett shook her head. "My phone's in my car with my purse. I didn't plan to stay long. I just wanted to check on her before I went home. Make sure she didn't need anything. Then I found her like… like… this." Her voice broke, and she swallowed hard. "I couldn't bear to leave her."

Scarlett's confession spurred me into action. My brain now had something to do. "Are you sure she's dead?" Once more,

I ran an assessing glance over Ella's pale skin and still chest. She looked pretty dead.

"Yeah. She's cold."

I would take her word for it. I'd already touched enough dead bodies to last me a lifetime.

A shiver went down my spine as I remembered pulling Phil Brunswick from his car and his wife, Felicity, from the depths of the lake just a few months ago.

No.

I refused to let those memories invade. I'd done fairly well dealing with them and the emotions associated with the murders. Backsliding to the nightmares that plagued me for the first couple of weeks wasn't something I wanted to repeat.

Turning away from Scarlett and Ella, I dug into the smaller purse I'd exchanged my massive tote bag for that morning and pulled out my phone.

The 9-1-1 call I made was quick. Despite my desire not to touch Ella, I confirmed for the dispatcher that she was cold to the touch when the woman asked us to start CPR. There was no bringing her back from that.

Less than five minutes later, the ambulance crew arrived and confirmed it.

Ella was indeed dead.

To give the crew room to work, Scarlett and I moved downstairs and huddled together on the corner of the couch, awaiting the police's arrival.

Numbness invaded my mind while we sat there. I couldn't believe this was happening again.

At least this time, the death was natural. No stab wounds or bullet holes marred Ella's body. There was no blood on her clothes or on the floor. It was nothing but a horrible tragedy.

The clomp of booted feet and the creak of leather brought me back to reality. I looked up to see Scarlett's cousin, Isaiah Roberts, walk through the door in full uniform.

Right behind him was Jack.

My heart stumbled over itself in its haste to beat faster. I hadn't seen Jack lately—several weeks, in fact—but he was no less handsome than I remembered.

He stepped over the threshold, scanning the room and looking much like he had the first time we met. Khaki tactical pants encased his muscular legs, and a black polo with the police department's logo hugged his broad shoulders and chest. That dark hair that called out to my fingers looked as gorgeous as ever and complimented the dusting of black beard stubble on his jaw.

Those rich brown eyes landed on me. Only their slight widening gave away his surprise before his brows slammed together. "Delaney?" He propped his hands on his waist, just above the gun and badge strapped to his hip. "Again? Why?"

I shrugged. "I told you before, I'm apparently a magnet for death." Which was a habit I needed to break. Natural or not, I didn't want to keep finding dead people.

He huffed a quick breath. "You said you were a murder magnet. I'm hoping that's not what this is."

I frowned. "Then why are you here?"

"It's a death investigation." He headed for the stairs. "You two sit tight."

Not a problem. The numbness might have receded somewhat, but I wasn't sure my legs could support me yet.

Sinking back into the cushions, I crossed my legs and waited silently. Scarlett seemed to be in the same mood and didn't initiate any conversation. Huddled together, we watched medical and law enforcement personnel come and go.

About twenty minutes after he went upstairs, Jack returned, alone this time. The cream carpet that continued from the stairs and into the living room muffled his footfalls as he walked over and sat down in the chair adjacent to the couch.

"You two holding up okay?"

Scarlett lifted a shoulder, not meeting his gaze, while I tried to offer him a small smile, grateful for his concern.

"Probably as well as can be expected," I said.

He nodded once. "Well, how about we talk about what happened and then the two of you can go home?"

"Yes, please," Scarlett said.

Jack withdrew a notebook from a pocket in his pants and pulled the pen out from where it was clipped between the buttons on his polo. "All right, so let's start with how you know Ella."

"She works for me," Scarlett said, softly.

"Okay. What brought you two over here today? Did she not show up for work?"

Scarlett and I shared a quick glance.

"Sort of," Scarlett said.

"We were supposed to go shopping. Scarlett and I, I mean." I gestured to my friend. "I had an unexpected cancellation today, and since it was a wedding, I didn't book any other events. Suddenly, I had an entire day free. So, I called Scarlett and asked if she wanted to go shopping. I needed to get an outfit for Daphne's bridal shower next weekend."

"I was supposed to work," Scarlett continued. "But I called my employees and asked if any of them wanted the hours. Ella said she did." She glanced away, blinking furiously. "She was supposed to come in at noon." Her voice had turned into little more than a whisper.

"She never showed, though." I laid a hand on Scarlett's shoulder and picked up where she left off. "We tried calling her but didn't get an answer."

"She, um, she did send me a text, though, eventually." Scarlett turned bleak eyes on him. "She said she had food poisoning and couldn't come in after all."

"Do you still have that message?"

Scarlett nodded. "My phone's in my car."

"Okay, before you leave, I'd like to see it."

Again, she nodded.

"So, what brought you here?"

"I just wanted to check on her. See if she needed anything. I tried calling before I closed the shop, but she didn't answer, so I decided to swing by on my way home. I found— found…" She trailed off, her face crumpling, and waved a hand. "I can't," she whispered around a sob.

My heart clenched and tears threatened to spill over. I blinked them back and wrapped an arm around Scarlett's shoulders, squeezing.

Jack got up, returning a moment later with a box of tissues. He held them in front of us, and we both took some.

"Thank you," I murmured.

Sitting back down, he looked at me. "What brought you here? Did you come with her?" He nodded to Scarlett.

"No. I ended up shopping on my own. Before I went home, I stopped off at The Whispering Fern again to show her what I bought, then I left when she closed. When I got home and went over the day in my mind, I decided to bring Ella some of my dad's chicken noodle soup. It was frozen, so I figured by the time her stomach settled enough for her to want to eat, it would be thawed."

"Okay. How did either of you get in? Scarlett, do you have a key?"

"No." She brushed a lock of her auburn hair out of her face and sniffed. "The door was unlocked."

"So, you just went inside?"

She nodded. "I was worried. She wasn't answering calls or texts, and she didn't come to the door when I knocked."

"All right. Walk me through what you did once you came inside."

Drawing in a shaky breath, Scarlett pressed her lips flat. "I called her name when I entered and looked around downstairs for her. When I didn't see her, I went upstairs. The light was on in the bathroom and that's where—" She stopped, hiccupping around a sob. "It's where I found her. She was on the floor." She pressed the back of her hand to her mouth. "In front of the toilet."

"What position?"

"Um, on her side."

Jack jotted a note down. "What did you do next?"

"I went to her. As soon as I touched her, I knew something was wrong." She closed her eyes and a tear slid free. "She was so cold. Not, like, you've been outside too long, chilly. Just… cold." Her nose wrinkled. "I don't know how else to describe it. She just felt… different."

"Did you check for a pulse?"

Scarlett dashed the moisture off her face. "Yes." She sniffed. "More than once and on both sides of her neck. I just —I couldn't believe it. And I couldn't bear to leave her alone to call for help, so I just sat with her."

His brows dipped with a small frown. "You didn't call for help right away?"

She shook her head. "I couldn't. I couldn't leave her. She died alone, you know? I just didn't want her to be alone anymore." Her words ended on a broken whisper and more moisture gathered in her eyes.

"How long did you sit there?"

Dabbing at her eyes, Scarlett inhaled a breath. "Um, I'm not sure. Not long. Delaney showed up a few minutes after I found her."

"And you called for help, then?" He looked at me.

"Yes. And I agreed with Scarlett that there was no point in trying to get her help faster. She was quite… quite, um, deceased." The memory of Ella's open-mouthed face and the lifeless flop to her body was enough to turn my stomach.

Jack made some notes, then glanced up again, his eyes on Scarlett. "Did you notice anything strange or out of place when you arrived?"

Scarlett's eyebrows twitched with a tiny frown, then

smoothed out. "No. Not that I can remember. Other than the door being unlocked. That surprised me. But I thought maybe she'd been on her way into work when she suddenly felt ill and just didn't lock the door as she ran back inside."

He turned to me. "What about you? Anything strike you as odd?"

"No. Everything just looked like she'd been interrupted." I gestured to the pile of laundry beside Scarlett and then nodded to the kitchen and the dishes on the stove and in the sink.

Jack's gaze flicked to the laundry. He clicked his tongue softly against his bottom lip. "Okay. Scarlett, could you go out and get your phone, please? I'd like to see your messages with Ella."

"Of course." Slipping away from my light grasp, she stood.

I folded my hands in my lap and watched her leave.

"How are you really holding up?"

With a quick blink, I looked at Jack. "I'm all right," I said, my voice quiet. Truthfully, I was still in a bit of shock.

His dark eyes studied me intently, but I didn't mind. I appreciated his concern.

"You're certain you didn't see any signs of foul play? Was Scarlett really only here for a few minutes before you?"

"What?" My eyebrows drew together. "What are you getting at? You think Scarlett had something to do with Ella's death? That's insane. Why would she want to hurt her?"

He shrugged one shoulder. "You tell me."

"There's nothing to tell, Jack. Not only does she not have a reason to hurt Ella, she would never do something like that, anyway. Scarlett wouldn't hurt a fly."

Unbidden, the cold, angry tone she'd used on the phone earlier filtered through my thoughts. I had to admit, that was out of character for her. I'd never heard her sound like that before.

But it wasn't Ella who'd been on the phone.

"What?"

Startled out of my thoughts by his sharp tone, my gaze snapped to his. "What?"

"You thought of something."

"Huh? No."

"Don't lie to me, Delaney. I could see the shift in your expression. What were you thinking?"

"Nothing. Not about Ella, anyway."

"But it was about Scarlett?"

My gaze slid away. "It wasn't anything important." Guilt soured my stomach. Why would I even think such a thing about my best friend? Angry or not, I knew she would never hurt anyone.

"Something sparked the thought. I'm not saying it's important, but it could be."

I looked at him again. "Why does it matter? Ella wasn't murdered."

"We don't know that."

When I opened my mouth to tell him how preposterous that was, he held up a hand.

"It's highly unlikely, I'll give you that, but so is dying of food poisoning. I don't want to miss anything because I made assumptions."

That brought a frown to my face. I could see his point, and I still thought he was barking up the wrong tree, but I knew him well enough by now to know he wouldn't let it go. "It's just something I overheard her say on the phone earlier." I let out a sigh. "When I got to the shop this afternoon, Scarlett was busy, so I browsed for a bit. I got caught up in shopping and when I got through the racks, I realized she wasn't behind the register anymore. I thought maybe she was in the back, so I went looking for her. In the back room, I heard a voice outside the back door. When I peeked my head out, she was twenty or thirty feet away on the phone. Whoever it was, she told them not to come back if they were going to speak to her like that. Then she hung up. That's all." I lifted my hands for a brief moment.

"All right. What made you think of that conversation?"

"She was angry. Her tone, her posture—everything said she was really mad at whoever was on the other end of the phone. I couldn't help but think just now that if she were to hurt anyone, it would be the person she was talking to." The guilt returned, eating away at my stomach. It was so ridiculous to think Scarlett could hurt someone. "Anyway, like I said, it wasn't important. It wasn't Ella on the phone."

"You're sure?"

"Yes. I asked because Ella was late, and she said no. Then she called her."

"But you didn't actually hear who she was talking to that made her angry?"

My frown deepened. "No." I didn't like what he was implying. "She didn't lie to me, Jack. It wasn't Ella."

He just raised an eyebrow. "What time was that, again?"

"Noon."

"Exactly?"

I huffed. "No. It was a little after. And no, I don't know the exact time. I got there around noon, shopped for ten or fifteen minutes, then went looking for her. Would you also like to know which direction she was facing when I spotted her and which hand she held her phone in?"

His lips twitched and a touch of amusement sparked in his eyes. "No. I think I'm good for now."

Crossing my arms and my legs, I sat back and glared at him. I knew he was just doing his job, but it was still irritating. Even if Ella was murdered, Scarlett didn't do it.

The front door opened, readmitting my friend. My heart broke all over again for her. She still wore the same look of utter devastation as when she stepped out.

"Here you go, Detective." Scarlett woke up her phone screen, letting it read her face, then handed it to him.

Quickly, he scrolled through the messages. "This is your only communication with her today? No phone calls?"

She shook her head. "Just the ones I made when I called this morning to see if she could work. Otherwise, it was just those texts."

I continued to glare as Jack watched her face.

Once more the front door opened, effectively ending his line of questioning. We all glanced over to see a man in his mid-fifties enter, carrying a silver case and wearing a tie. I recognized him as Dr. Callaway. He was a local physician and also the coroner.

Jack stood. "Excuse me." With a nod and a polite smile, he handed Scarlett her phone and walked away.

She sank onto the couch beside me.

My ears strained as I tried to listen in on Jack and Dr. Callaway's conversation. Their hushed tones were too quiet, however, and soon it didn't matter because they went upstairs.

I thought about asking Scarlett again who she'd been so angry with earlier, but she looked in no mood to talk. Staring at the staircase, she slowly twirled her phone in her hands.

So, I sat back, staying silent, waiting on Jack to return and tell us we could leave.

About ten minutes later, he and Dr. Callaway came back downstairs. The doctor walked out of the house, his stride purposeful and quick. Jack rounded the banister.

One look at the seriousness on his face and the bottom dropped out of my stomach.

He walked into the living room, stopping by the chair he recently vacated. "Scarlett, I'm going to need you to come to the station for some formal questioning."

I shot to my feet. "You've lost your mind! She didn't do anything." Scarlett rose to stand beside me.

Her eyed me, giving away nothing. "Maybe so, but Dr. Callaway smelled almonds the moment he examined Ella's body."

"Almonds?" My glare turned into a confused frown. "What does that have to do with anything?"

"An almond scent on someone is associated with cyanide poisoning. It seems you really are a murder magnet, Delaney."

Four

The television played as background noise while I baked a batch of lemon blueberry macarons. They weren't for any particular event. I just needed the distraction. Tomorrow, I would take them to Mom and Dad's. They would eat a few and set the rest out for their guests.

Sifter in hand, I poured the last of the almond flour and powdered sugar inside and squeezed the handle, adding the dry goods to the whipped egg whites. With a spatula, I folded and pressed the batter together until it ran off the spatula in a smooth ribbon.

Gathering my baking trays, I filled a piping bag with the mixture and piped inch-and-a-half circles on parchment paper.

Millie, my cat, glared at me and ran off as I banged the trays on the counter, extracting the air bubbles from the cookies.

"Sorry, Mills." I spared her a quick glance and vowed to give her some extra treats later.

The last smack of the tray hit harder, and I frowned, staring at it for a second before I realized it was someone banging on the front door.

On my way out of the kitchen, I glanced at the oven clock. It was a bit late for visitors, but after the day I'd had, it wouldn't surprise me if word got around to my sisters or parents. I hadn't bothered to call anyone after I left Ella's apartment. All I really wanted at that time was to be alone and process what had happened.

Reaching the door, I peeked through the peephole.

It was Scarlett.

With a quick flick of my fingers, I unlocked the door, then twisted the doorknob. "Hey," I greeted her with a bright smile, glad to see her free from Jack's clutches. "He let you go. I told him he was barking up the wrong tree."

To my surprise, she glared at me. "That wasn't all you told him." Fire flashing in her eyes, she stormed past me into the house.

What? Deep confusion knit my eyebrows together. I turned, closing the door and relocking it. "What are you talking about?"

"Oh, don't play dumb, Delaney. You know exactly what I mean."

Hurt made me snappy. "No, I don't, so how about you enlighten me."

She rolled her eyes. "You told him you overheard me arguing on the phone. That it might have been Ella."

Surprise rounded my eyes. "I never said it was Ella. He asked me if I was sure it wasn't, and I said no because I couldn't hear the other person's voice. But yes, I told him I overheard you arguing."

She glared at me again. "Why? That call had no relation to Ella's death. None."

"It wasn't intentional. I didn't say, 'You know, I overheard her arguing on the phone with someone. You should check that out.' He asked if you had a reason to hurt Ella. I said no, and that you would never hurt anyone. *Then* the memory of how angry you were on the phone crossed my mind. For half a second, I doubted that, and apparently, I couldn't keep that expression off my face. He called me on it. And, well, you know what he's like. He just doesn't quit."

"So, you told him something private?"

"You never said it was private. Just that everything was 'fine.'" I air-quoted. "It's not fine, or you wouldn't be so upset. What is going on? Because you didn't come here to rake me over the coals for telling Jack you were angry on the phone."

Some of the fire leached out of her eyes as her shoulders slumped. She walked into the living room and set her purse on the floor by the couch before sinking into the cushions.

I moved to sit beside her, but kept some distance, not wanting to crowd her when she was upset with me. We'd hug it out when she was ready.

"What's wrong?" I asked softly. "Who was on the phone?"

Rolling her lips inward, Scarlett pressed them into a flat line, turning them white. "My dad."

Immediately, my mouth dropped open and my eyes widened. "I'm sorry, what?" Scarlett's father left her and her mother when she was two. I'd never met the man as he hadn't been a part of my friend's life after he left.

"Yeah. I know. Crazy, right?"

"Slightly."

"Today wasn't the first time he's called. We, um, we actually met a couple of times."

I felt like my eyes were going to be permanently the size of saucers. "You did? When? Why didn't you tell me about this?"

"I was going to, but something…" She trailed off and glanced away for a moment. "There was just something holding me back. I think… I think I wanted to make sure he was going to stay before I integrated him into my life."

That made sense. "Okay, so what happened?"

"He called back in June for the first time. About the same

time the whole thing with the Brunswicks happened. That's part of the reason I didn't say anything to you. With all that craziness, you had enough going on. You didn't need to worry about me and my estranged father."

"You're my friend, Scarlett. I wouldn't have cared." I reached out, squeezing her hand quickly before letting go.

She offered me a small smile. "I know. But I didn't want to burden you. Anyway, I agreed to meet with him." She lifted a shoulder. "I was curious. Who wouldn't be?"

I nodded. That was understandable.

"He apologized for leaving and not maintaining contact. Said he was 'messed up in the head' and didn't want to put that burden on me or my mom."

"Do you believe that?"

Her expression soured. "No. Not now. He seemed sincere enough at that first meeting, so I agreed to have lunch with him. Do you know what he did?"

I shook my head.

"He claimed he forgot his wallet. At first, I didn't think too much of it. Because it happens, right?" She lifted a hand, looking at me expectantly.

I nodded.

"Anyway, we made plans to get together again, so at that point, I figured I should probably tell my mom before someone spotted us together and she found out."

I winced. "I bet that didn't go over well."

"No. Not at all." Scarlett sighed. "Not only was she upset that I had met with him, but she was angry that he was up to his old tricks still."

"Old tricks?" I frowned.

"Yeah. So, you know Mom never talked much about my dad. He just wasn't around."

"Right."

"Well, apparently, he didn't just leave. Mom kicked him out and said if he wanted a relationship with either of us, he had to get a respectable job and stop scamming people. She said Dad's a con artist."

Her gaze dropped to her hands. "I still wanted to give him the benefit of doubt, you know? I mean, he's my dad." She lifted a shoulder and looked up. "So, I met with him again. This time, he said he was strapped for cash because his paycheck was late."

My eyebrows rose. "Where does he work?"

"One of the local resorts. So he says." She rolled her eyes. "I'm not sure I believe him."

"I'm not sure I would, either. What did you do?"

"I told him I would pay the bill, but this was the last time we'd be meeting. I mentioned the conversation I had with Mom about him." Her expression hardened, her cheekbones jumping out in stark relief as she clenched her teeth. "He told me my mother was a lying sack of"—she paused and flip-flopped a hand—"you know."

"Ouch. Yeah, no. She's not even close to that."

"Exactly. And I told him that, too, as I threw some cash down on the table. I also told him to lose my number."

"Except he didn't, did he?" I said quietly.

Picking at her nails, Scarlett shook her head. "I know I should have blocked him, but—" She paused and glanced away, chewing on her bottom lip.

"He's your dad."

"Yes." She turned back to me, the corners of her mouth turned down in a pained look. "I didn't answer. The calls or the texts. I just let everything roll to voicemail or left it unread before deleting it."

"So, why did you answer today?"

"I didn't recognize the number. And with Ella not answering her phone, I thought maybe it was her and she'd had car trouble or something and was calling from someone else's phone." She scoffed. "I should have let it go to voice-mail, then called her back if it was. The first thing out of his mouth was, 'Finally! Don't you know it's not nice to ignore your own father?'"

Disbelief made my eyes round. "Seriously?"

"Yep. I should have hung up on him then and there, but I was dumb and didn't. Instead, I baited him with, 'Oh, you mean the way you ignored me for twenty-eight years?'"

I couldn't help it. A grin broke out on my face. "Nice."

Scarlett chuckled softly. "Yeah. I was hoping it would shut him up and he'd hang up, but it just made him angrier. He told me I was a" —she flip-flopped her hand again—" just like my mother. At that point, I told him if he was going to speak to me that way, I never wanted to see him again."

"That part I heard."

She blew out a long breath. "I'm sorry I didn't tell you all of this earlier. I was upset, and frankly, I was embarrassed. Both by how I got bamboozled by the jerk and by the fact that someone like that could be my dad." She reached out and covered my hand. "I'm sorry."

I shifted closer and hugged her. "I'm sorry too. For airing your dirty laundry."

Scarlett gave a watery chuckle as she pulled back. Dabbing at her eyes she shook her head. "It's okay. You're right in that Jack is tenacious. He'd have found out no matter what."

"Yeah, and I didn't want him to make your life miserable trying to find out what I overheard. But I also didn't expect him to haul you into the station."

"It wasn't that bad, actually." She leaned back, pulling a tissue from the box beside the couch. "He asked about the phone call and where I'd been all day." Her mouth pulled down. "I might have a bit of a problem, though."

"Why?"

"I was alone all morning and last night. I don't have an alibi for Ella's murder. And I didn't call the police right away." She grimaced. "I know he doesn't really think I'm a likely suspect, but I'm still on the list."

Oh, that just wouldn't do. "Well, then, I guess we'll have to do something about that."

Apprehension sharpened her gaze. "Delaney…" She shook her head. "What are you going to do?" Her eyebrows raised. "You're going to stick your nose in things, again, aren't you? Like you did with the Brunswicks' deaths?"

Keeping my expression carefully neutral, I flicked a hand in the air. "I don't know what you're talking about. I was just going to offer her family my condolences at church tomorrow. Or take them some baked goods and do that if they aren't there."

Scarlett groaned. "You're never going to snag Jack for your own if you keep inserting yourself into his cases."

My expression fell, and I gave her a dirty look. "Who says I want to snag him?"

"Seriously?" she said with a laugh. "I've seen the way your face lights up when he walks into a room or when you mention his name. You like him."

I huffed. She *might* be right.

Maybe.

Five

"Delaney!"

I looked up from pouring a cup of coffee for Mr. Barber at the hushed excitement in Carol Prosser's voice. She approached the coffee bar with a wide smile that transformed her plain face.

"Hey." I smiled back. With a quick glance at Mr. Barber, I handed him his coffee and he wandered away.

"Good morning." Greeting Carol, I picked up a cocktail napkin. With a set of tongs, I placed a mini cinnamon roll on it, preparing to hand it to her. She loved them.

"Good morning," Carol echoed. "So, I was wondering…" She sidled a little closer to the counter, still smiling. "Can we set up a time to discuss wedding cakes?"

Before I could process her statement, she whipped her left hand up to show off the sparkling half-carat diamond solitaire on her ring finger.

I gasped. "What? Carol!" Excited for the woman, I put the roll down and hurried around the coffee bar, enveloping her in a hug. "When did this happen?" In June, I had steered Morris Beach in her direction, hoping the man would find a more appropriate target for his affections. I was not the sort of woman he wanted for a wife, but Carol was perfect.

It seemed I was right.

"Friday. Morris took me on a hike and asked me to marry him while we were watching a young eagle family. Can you believe it? I'm getting married. Me!" Her delighted laughter rang through the church lobby.

"I'm so happy for you. Of course we can talk wedding cakes. But first, I have one question. What does your mother think?" Lucile Prosser was famously overprotective of her only child.

A little of the happiness disappeared from Carol's eyes. "She thinks it's too fast. That we need to date longer." She huffed. "If she had her way, I'd be fifty and still single. But you would be proud of me. I put my foot down. I love Morris and want to marry him. She can't stop me. Even if we have to elope, I'm marrying that man."

"Well, good for you." I was glad to see her finally standing up to her mother. For too many years, she'd let that woman rule her entire life.

"I think so." The happiness returned to her eyes. "As such, however, Mother is refusing to pay for anything, so Morris is footing the bill. We'll need to keep the cake simple. There are so many costs involved. It's mind-blowing. I'm hoping she'll come around and pay for my dress, though." Consternation brought a soft frown to her face.

"We can certainly discuss options."

An idea struck me. "You know, I could use a hand with my mobile bakery. Would you be interested in working for me a few hours a week?" It wasn't an offer made out of pity. I'd been contemplating hiring help. Several of the weddings I'd catered this summer had led to more opportunities. I was rapidly approaching the limit of what I could do alone.

"Oh, I don't know. Mother and Morris don't really want me to work."

"Well, you've already told your mother that she needs to let you live your life. As for Morris, just tell him you're learning useful skills for marriage." A lopsided smile graced my face. "He loves my cinnamon rolls as much as you do."

Intrigue lit in her hazel eyes. "That's true." She answered my smile with one of her own. "So, what did you have in mind?"

"How about a few hours of work each week in exchange for your wedding cake? And once you've worked off the cost —which, for you, will just be materials—I'll pay you. You can put it toward other wedding things or just save it for a rainy day. When is the wedding, anyway?"

"You'd really do that?" Moisture gathered in Carol's eyes. "You'd bake our cake for free?"

"Not free." I shook my head. "You're working for it."

"Oh!" In an unexpected show of emotion for the reserved woman, she threw her arms around my neck and hugged me.

Chuckling, I hugged her back. "Is that a yes?"

She eased back. "Yes!" she said, laughing. "Oh, you just made my day."

"It's mutual. I'm drowning and could really use the help." Hiring an assistant would eat into my profits and delay my goal of buying a building for a brick-and-mortar storefront, but I would still make more than I had been just a few months ago. And it would save my sanity.

"Then you have a deal." Carol beamed.

"Perfect. You still haven't told me when the wedding is."

"Oh." She chuckled. "In the spring. April or May, most likely. The venue isn't an issue. We decided to have it at one of the shelter houses in the forest, since we love it there. Bookings for next year open January first, so we still have some time to nail down the date. I need about six months to get a dress and have it properly fitted. Those are the big things. I can make the food ahead of time and hire some people to serve it. You're making the cake. I can make my bouquet too."

I wanted to ask about attendants but didn't want to make her feel bad if she didn't have any. Lucile kept her from having many close friends.

"That all sounds lovely. If you need any help, please ask. My family and I will do what we can." I was certain Dad would happily help with the food if she even hinted at the desire for assistance. My sisters and I would help decorate or with anything else she needed.

"Really? That would be great. I'm trying to keep things simple. We won't have many guests. People from church, and some friends of Morris's from work."

"What about my friends from work?" Morris walked up and put an arm around his fiancée's waist.

Carol smiled up at him. "I was telling Delaney about our wedding plans. She offered to help and said her family could too."

Morris turned to me, surprise on his face. "You'd do that?"

"Of course," I replied without hesitation. "And we've also struck a deal for your wedding cake. But you're going to have to be okay with her working a few hours a week."

His forehead wrinkled with a small frown. "Oh, I'm not sure—"

Carol patted his chest. "It'll be fine. She's going to teach me some of her special recipes. And anything I earn past the cost of the cake we can put toward the wedding or the honeymoon."

"You don't need to worry about paying for anything for the wedding." Morris looked at her, a tender look in his eyes. "I told you, I have it covered."

"Maybe so, but this is my day, too, and I want to contribute."

His frown stayed in place, but he didn't argue further.

I reached for one of the macarons I baked last night and held it out to him, hoping to sway his opinion. "She'll learn things like this."

"What's that?" He frowned at it.

"A lemon blueberry macaron."

Tentatively, he accepted the cookie and took a bite.

I knew the moment the flavors burst over his tongue. His eyes widened, brightening with delight. "This is delicious, Delaney."

"Thank you." I beamed.

Morris side-eyed Carol. "Maybe it wouldn't be too bad of an idea if you spent some time in her kitchen."

Carol chuckled. "She promised to teach me how to make her cinnamon rolls too."

"Oh, well. That would be… I'd like that."

I resisted the urge to fist pump. "Good. It's been decided. Carol, when can you start?" I wanted to lock this in while I had Morris's taste buds in my clutches.

"Oh, wow, um, Tuesday? I could probably do Tuesdays and Thursdays for now. Would that be all right?"

"That's fine. Do you mind early mornings? I start at five a.m. most days."

Carol's eyes widened slightly, but she shook her head. "I'm usually up early. Not that early, but I can do that. In fact, it might be best. Mother won't be awake yet."

"That sounds like a plan. I'll see you bright and early right here on Tuesday morning."

"Thank you, Delaney. So much."

"No, thank you, Carol. You're saving my sanity." Grinning, I turned and picked up another macaron and the mini cinnamon roll I plated when I saw her coming. "Here. Get a taste of what you'll soon know how to bake."

"Oh, yum. Thank you." Carol accepted the treats and immediately took a bite of the macaron. Like her fiancé's expression, hers also brightened with surprise. "This is amazing. What made you bring something so different? We've never had these." She glanced at Morris. "Have we, honey?"

He shook his head.

"Oh, I just needed a distraction last night." Some of my joy at Carol and Morris's news faded as memories of yesterday intruded.

She frowned. "You look upset. What happened?"

"Did you hear about Ella Kerns?"

Carol frowned, but Morris's eyes widened.

"I heard some rumblings as I mingled just now," he said. "Did you know her?"

"She worked for my friend Scarlett at her boutique. We—Scarlett and I—found her body."

Carol gasped. "Body? What?"

"Do the police know what happened?" Morris asked.

"I'm not sure," I hedged. I didn't know if Jack had released an official statement about Ella's death and didn't want to give away details he wanted to keep private. "Have either of you seen any of her family here? I wanted to offer my condolences."

"No," Morris said.

Carol shook her head. "I haven't."

I hadn't, either, but I'd been busy too. It wasn't wholly unexpected for them not to be here. I'm not sure I could go out into public—even to church—so soon after something like that.

"Okay." I offered them a smile I hoped was cheery, but I had a sneaking suspicion it didn't quite hit the mark. "I might stop by their house later, then. Take them some of what's left." I nodded to the array of baked goods on the counter.

"I think that would be lovely," Morris said. "You have such a good heart, Delaney. And I have to say, one day, some man will be lucky to call you his wife. I know I once hoped that would be me."

Carol's eyebrows slammed down.

Oh, boy. I prayed he'd amend that statement.

"I would have been honored to be your husband."

Carol stiffened in his arms.

Man, this just kept getting worse.

"But I'm quite happy you turned me down. We just weren't a good fit."

Phew! I stiffened my knees, so I didn't sag into the counter. Thank goodness he saw the light.

Morris looked at Carol, a wide, happy smile on his face. "You're the only woman for me. I love you, my little bird."

"You're so sweet." She beamed up at him. "I love you too."

"Thank you, Morris." I pasted a smile on my face, happier than ever he took my advice and wooed Carol instead of me. I couldn't handle all the sickly sweetness. Or the macho attitude. Why did I have to get married someday? Maybe I wanted to stay single.

At that moment, irony laughed in my face.

The church's front door opened, and Jack walked into the lobby.

I clenched my teeth together. There was no chance of a relationship there. Not after I showed up at *another* murder scene.

Jack paused just inside the door, letting his eyes adjust to the lighting. It only took him a moment to scan the room.

Then he turned toward me. Our gazes locked.

Swallowing hard, I looked away. My sleep-deprived brain couldn't handle his intense stare today.

"Oh, well look who's here." Morris glanced toward Jack. "Maybe he'll have some information to share on Ms. Kerns's death."

I hummed a noncommittal noise and fussed with the remaining baked goods. It was almost time to head into the sanctuary for the service. He might, but that didn't mean I'd be asking.

Not because I didn't like him or want to get to know him better. I just didn't want him to suspect my plans for after church. He'd stop me, and someone needed to clear Scarlett's name.

"Good morning."

My eyes slid shut at the sound of his deep, rich voice. It itched my brain so good.

Morris was the first to greet him. "Detective, good morning."

Carol also murmured a greeting. I looked up long enough to toss Jack a quick smile, then kept shuffling pastries around.

"I hear there's been some trouble in Fernwood again," Morris said.

"A bit, yes, but we're on it."

I could hear the distance in Jack's voice. He didn't want to talk about the case.

"Do you have any cinnamon rolls left, Delaney?"

At the sound of my name, I looked up and immediately wished I hadn't. Dark brown eyes met mine. It would be so easy to get lost in his gaze.

"Delaney?" His brows drew together.

I blinked. Apparently, it was even easier than I thought. "Um, yes." Picking up the tongs, I put a roll on a napkin and handed it to him.

"You should try one of her macarons too," Morris said. "Delightful."

A knowing smile spread over Jack's face as he lifted the cinnamon roll, his eyes still locked on me. "Oh, I know."

Heat crept over my cheeks as the memory of his flirtation at his friend's wedding resurfaced.

"When did you have her macarons?" Carol asked. "She doesn't typically make them." The woman propped a hand on her hip and turned to me with a curious stare. "Are you holding out on us, and the two of you have been secretly dating?"

Jack choked on the bite of roll he just took.

"You all right, Detective?" Morris thumped him on the back.

The fire in my cheeks reached new heights. "No. No, nothing like that." Carol's newfound spine suddenly wasn't so appealing. The mousy woman who used to let her mother do all the talking was much better for my sanity.

"A wedding." Jack coughed, patting his chest.

"His friend got married, and I made the cake and party favors. They were macarons," I elaborated.

Morris nodded as if that's what he thought all along. "Good. You're not her type."

Jack frowned, and his gaze sharpened. "Oh? Who is? You?"

I groaned.

Carol sent me a sympathetic smile. "Morris is my fiancé. I assure you, Delaney is very much unspoken for."

"Carol!" I hissed.

She turned a wide-eyed innocent look on me. "What?"

Music swelled from the sanctuary.

Oh, thank goodness. "Look at that. Time for the service to start." I took a step back and tugged on my apron strings, then whipped the heavy fabric over my head and laid it on the counter. "Excuse me. I'm going to join my family."

Not waiting for a reply, I made a swift exit. Glancing upward as I hurried toward the sanctuary doors, I said a quick prayer of thanks.

Six

I sure hoped I was doing the right thing.

Glancing around the neighborhood, I let the warm sun soothe a bit of my nerves. A bird squabble near the front of the light blue two-story house drew my attention to the bright pink roses lining the flower beds.

I walked up the driveway of the Kerns's house, watching two finches duke it out over a seed. One finally won and flew up into the large oak in the front yard. The other pecked at the ground beneath the feeder again. Others joined it.

It shouldn't be such a nice day. Not for this family.

If it were me, I'd want the weather to match my mood. A good, soaking rainstorm to blend in with my tears.

Mounting the two concrete steps to the porch, I shifted the bakery box I carried to one hand and rang the doorbell.

A few moments later, the white door swung inward, revealing a young woman bearing an uncanny resemblance to Ella.

"Yes?"

I had to blink twice before I could speak. I knew Ella had a sister. I'd even met her a few times. But I'd forgotten how much they looked alike.

Wetting my lips, I offered her a kind smile. "Hello. My name is Delaney Fowler. Do you remember me from church? I'm also a friend of your sister's boss, Scarlett. I brought your family some treats. It's not much, but I hoped I could brighten your day just a little." I presented the box.

"Oh." The young woman eyed the box, frowned slightly, then glanced over her shoulder. "Um, you can come in."

"Thank you." I stepped over the threshold onto the gleaming dark wood floors. A quick glance around revealed a well-appointed living room to my right. The gray sectional looked like the type of couch a person could sink into with a good book. A cream and light-blue rug covered part of the floor in front of it, and abstract art in soft colors graced the off-white walls. It was a cozy room.

To the left was a formal dining room. The walnut table and eight matching chairs gleamed in the sunlight streaming in through the window. White china with tiny flowers sparkled behind glass in a solid-wood hutch.

"My parents are on the back patio." The woman—Allie, I remember now—turned and led me down a hallway beside a set of stairs and into a kitchen that looked like it belonged in a magazine. Brilliant white counters and cabinets shone in the sun. A crystal chandelier sparkled over the center island, bouncing prism rays off the equally white walls. The only pop of color was a vase of roses in the middle of the island. They looked like they'd come from the plants out front.

Allie walked around the island to the door set into the back wall. She twisted the knob and walked through, leaving it open for me.

"Mom? Dad?"

An older couple in chaise loungers glanced back.

My heart broke at the sight of the mother's face. Puffiness rimmed bloodshot eyes and dampness still shone on her face.

"This is Delaney. Scarlett's friend."

"Oh!" The mom covered her mouth.

Ella's dad stood, his eyes locked on me with an intense stare.

I squared my shoulders, unsure what to expect. "Hi. I'm sorry to intrude. I just wanted to offer my condolences and bring you this." I gestured with the box in my hands. "It's pastries from church this morning. I noticed you weren't there and thought you might like to have some."

The dad's face softened. "That's very kind of you." He took the box when I offered it to him. "Sit down, please." He gestured to a chair opposite the one his wife occupied.

"Oh, that's okay. I—"

"Please," the mother said, her voice husky. "The police said you were there."

My eyes widened for a fraction of a second. I hadn't thought this through. While I wanted information about Ella and who could have a reason to hurt her, it didn't occur to me that her family would have questions about what I saw yesterday.

But I couldn't turn them down. They were hurting and wanted answers just as much as I wanted to clear Scarlett's name.

So, I sat.

The father set the bakery box on the small table in the middle of the group of chairs, then leaned across and offered me a hand. "I'm Dave. I know we've seen each other at church, but I don't think we've ever been formally introduced."

"Nice to meet you." I shook his hand.

"You too." He sat down, then looked at his wife. "This is Paige. And our other daughter, Allie." He gestured to the young woman as she came around to sit in the chair beside me.

"Hello." I nodded to them both.

Allie murmured a hello, but her mother just stared at me tearfully.

"Can you tell us what happened?" Dave asked.

"I don't know what happened. What have the police said?"

"Just that they think she was poisoned." Allie crossed her legs and folded her hands over her knee as she spoke softly.

"That's what I heard too. I'm so sorry for your loss."

Paige sniffed and gave a jerky nod. "Thank you. Do you— do you think she suffered?"

I bit the inside of my lip, trying to hold the memory of Ella's face at bay. "I don't think so. It looked like it was quick." I didn't know if that was true or not, but there was no way on earth I would tell them that.

"Good. I hate to think that—that she suffered." Paige's face crumpled, and she dabbed at her eyes with a tissue.

Rolling my lips in to press them together, I nodded. "Yes. Me too."

Silence thicker than the molasses I used for my gingerbread cookies descended. Their grief weighed them down, adding years to the elder Kerns's faces.

After several beats passed, I softly cleared my throat and turned to Allie. "I suppose the police asked, but do you know who would want to hurt Ella?"

Rather than tearing up more or looking confused, I was surprised to see a fierce anger leap to life in the woman's eyes.

Her jaw worked, and she glanced at her parents. Dave had gone still, and a muscle ticked in his face.

"We know who did this." Allie's voice rang with conviction.

"Allie—" Paige started, but Allie cut her off.

"Stop protecting him!" She stood up so quickly that her chair rocked, skittering back several inches. "I don't understand why you insist he's innocent. Leo is a manipulative jerk. One day, you'll see that I'm right." Glaring daggers at her mother for another moment, Allie stormed away.

What just happened?

Who was she talking about, and why did the family seem to have such differing opinions about him?

My gaze bounced between Dave and Paige as I tried to gauge which one would be more likely to answer my questions.

Neither of them wanted to make eye contact, so finally I just threw the question out there. "Who is she talking about?"

"Ella's ex-boyfriend, Leo Stanhope."

Oh.

"Is he not nice?"

"Allie seems to think he's not." Paige's gaze cut toward the door where her daughter disappeared. "We never had a problem with him."

"Why did he and Ella break up?" Maybe there was more going on that the parents didn't know about.

"She just said they had a difference of opinion on what they wanted. We took that to mean Ella didn't want to get married."

My forehead wrinkled as I blinked in surprise. "*Ella* didn't want to get married? But her boyfriend did?"

"That's what we assume, yes." Paige picked at the tissue clutched in her hands. "He was much more serious than her."

"Why does Allie think he's a jerk?" Asking her sister to marry him wasn't a jerk move. If anything, it was green-flag material.

Her wording rang out in my mind. She'd called him a *manipulative* jerk. Maybe he was trying to coerce Ella into marrying him.

"She says he was controlling. We never saw it." Paige motioned between herself and her husband.

That was interesting. How was it that Allie saw it, then? Did Ella confide in her? Or was the woman just more observant than her parents?

My gaze flicked toward the door. I needed to talk to Allie.

But I wasn't finished with her parents yet. "Can either of you think of someone who would want to hurt her?"

"No," Paige said, a crack in her voice. Her face crumpled once more.

"Ella was a good kid," Dave said softly. "She didn't do drugs, didn't party. She went to school and work, and that was it. I don't know who did this."

"It was random," Paige said. "That's the only answer."

I highly doubted that. Who murdered someone randomly with poison? Maybe in a mass scale attack. That had been done before. But to break into someone's home and poison them with cyanide?

No. Someone wanted Ella Kerns dead.

Figuring I wouldn't get any more out of Paige and Dave, I scooted forward on my seat, preparing to stand. "I'm sure Detective Fiore will figure it out. He's quite good at his job." Especially when he got a little help from me. Which was why I needed to go talk to Allie alone. I just hoped she was in the kitchen or living room when I went inside. I would do many things for answers, but exploring the Kerns's house uninvited wasn't one of them.

"He assured us he was doing everything he could." Paige shredded more of her tissue. Rolling her bottom lip in, she bit it, holding back sobs as more tears rolled down her face.

"That's good." I rose slowly to my feet. "I'm sure he'll figure it out."

Dave started to stand, but I waved him back down. "Please, don't get up. I can show myself out." A sympathetic smile graced my face. "I've imposed enough." Taking a step to the side, I rounded the chair grouping. "If my family or I can be of any assistance, please reach out. We'll do what we can."

"Thank you, Delaney. That's much appreciated." Dave tried to return my smile but failed.

"You're welcome." With a quick waggle of my fingers, I said goodbye and let myself inside.

The door snicked shut behind me.

My gaze roved over the kitchen.

No Allie in sight.

Not that I expected her to be hovering over the island and staring pensively out the window.

But she could be in the living room. I wasn't sure if she lived here. I'd seen a car in the driveway, but that didn't mean she was a visitor, just that there was no room in the garage for her car. I thought I remembered hearing at church, though, that she'd moved out not too long ago.

I could be wrong, though. It might have been someone else. The Kerns sisters weren't the only young people their age in the church.

She could also just be staying with her parents again temporarily because of what happened. I knew if I were in her shoes, I'd want to be as close to my family as possible in the early days. It would help me process the grief. If she was here, she could be upstairs in a bedroom.

Only one way to find out.

I crossed the kitchen and entered the hallway, walking swiftly over the hardwood floors to the living room.

To my disappointment, the room was empty.

A frown pulled at my mouth. *Rats!* I really wanted to ask her more about Ella's ex.

Stifling a sigh, I continued to the front door and let myself out. I'd have to ask around town about him. Or even ask Scarlett where Allie worked so I could bump into her accidentally on purpose.

I stepped through the door and into the sunshine. The birds no longer squawked in the rose bushes but instead chirped in the trees.

With my eyes on the birds, I didn't notice Allie near my

car until I reached the edge of the driveway. Arms crossed, she leaned against the front fender.

"Hi." I offered her a quick smile, happy she found me, even if I wasn't sure why.

Her frowning expression didn't change. "You have that detective's ear, don't you?"

The smile on my face died as curiosity took over. "I'm not sure about that, but I can certainly pass on a message. Have you not spoken to him?"

She chewed on the corner of her mouth and glanced away. "I did, but Mom told me not to mention Leo and Ella's relationship issues. That Leo couldn't be responsible for what happened. At the time, I was too shocked over my sister's—" She broke off and swallowed. Glancing at the ground, she kicked at a small twig on the driveway with the toe of her shoe before looking up again. "I didn't argue with her. He doesn't know about my reservation about Leo."

"What happened between them? Why do you think he murdered Ella?"

"Because I saw the pattern. He was trying to isolate her from us. Before she broke it off with him, she cancelled plans more and more. With Mom and Dad, with me. We were supposed to go boating with some friends on Labor Day. She called me that morning and said she couldn't make it because Leo insisted they go to his family's cookout." She clenched her teeth, making the muscles in her cheek shift.

"That was the last straw. I drove over to her apartment and laid out what I thought was happening. How he was manipulating her and trying to cut her off from her family and friends to make her fully dependent on him."

"I take it she believed you? Because earlier, you called him her ex-boyfriend."

"Yeah. She broke down, crying. She knew something was off but didn't know how to get herself out of it. I told her it was simple. She was going to let me answer the door when he arrived, and she was going to block his number from her phone and remove him from all her social media accounts. He didn't have a key to her apartment, so that was one thing we didn't have to worry about."

"How did he take it?"

"Not well. He tried to force his way in to talk to her, but I slammed his hand in the door, then screamed at him through it that I'd call the cops if he didn't leave."

"Whoa."

"Yeah. But he left. I made sure Ella blocked and deleted his number from her phone and blocked him on all her social media, then I bundled her into my car, and we went out on the boat with our friends." She shifted, unfolding her arms, propping her hands behind her on the car and leaning back.

"The next day, he accosted her outside her apartment on her way to work. Luckily, there were other people around, so he couldn't make too big of a scene. He tried to stop her from getting in her car, but she told him she'd scream if he didn't let go of the door. It was enough, and she was able to leave."

Allie pushed away from the car. "But you know what I don't understand?"

I stayed silent and waited for her to continue. She didn't really want me to answer.

"I don't even know why she was at her apartment yesterday."

My forehead wrinkled in confusion. "What do you mean? Why wouldn't she have been home? She was getting ready for work."

"She wasn't supposed to be there. After the incident with Leo outside her apartment, I convinced her to come stay with me. I live across town at that new complex that just went in, and I thought it would be safer for her. When I left for work the day she… she died, she was at home. I don't know why she went to her place."

"Clothes, maybe?"

"I thought about that, but she packed everything she wanted when she came to stay with me. And we'd just done laundry, so most of her stuff was clean."

I thought about the pile of towels on the couch. How long had those been there? And the dishes in the sink. Were they from the day she left to stay with her sister?

"You didn't tell Detective Fiore she was staying with you, either, did you?" I asked.

She flattened her lips and shook her head.

"Okay." Jack really needed to hear all of this. "We should go down to the police station. You need to tell him all of this."

Allie chewed on the inside of her cheek and glanced toward the house. I watched a war wage in her eyes before her expression hardened and she turned to me. "Okay. Let's do it. But will you drive? My keys are in the house, and I don't want to go back in there."

It was my turn to hesitate. "What about your parents? Won't they get worried if you just disappear?"

"I'll text my dad and tell him I went for a walk." She pulled her phone from her pocket.

"That works for me. Let's go." I gestured toward my car, then headed for the driver's side.

Seven

It took everything I had not to get up and pace around the police station lobby while I waited on Allie to talk to Jack. I wasn't sure he'd be here when we'd arrived—it was Sunday—but he'd been in his office working on Ella's case. Probably digging into her life.

He sure hadn't been happy to see me, though. When he walked into the lobby, the glower on his face could have withered the healthiest rose.

Good thing I wasn't a plant.

Some of his irritation faded once he realized why I was here and who I brought.

My phone dinged. Lifting it from my lap, I glanced at the screen.

It was a message from my sister, Darcy, asking if I'd learned anything. At lunch earlier today, I filled her and Daphne in on my plans for the afternoon. Daphne, ever cautious, had encouraged me to be careful. Darcy, though, had offered spying suggestions if I couldn't get inside to speak to the Kerns.

I clicked on the message and replied. *There are some interesting developments about Ella's ex. I'll fill you in later.*

Dots appeared on my screen, then, *Fine... I'll stop by this evening. We need to discuss Daphne's shower, anyway.*

Sounds good, I replied, then turned off the screen.

Blowing out a long breath, I leaned my head back against the wall. How much longer was this going to take? They'd been back there at least thirty minutes. Allie must have known more about Ella's life than she told me.

For a moment, I debated wandering down the hallway to listen at his door. The officer at the desk wasn't really paying attention to me. I could slip down there, and he'd be none the wiser. The bathroom was down that way. I could just say I needed to use the restroom if anyone asked why I wasn't in the lobby.

But it would be my luck Jack would open the door and catch me eavesdropping. I could always ask Allie what they talked about when I took her home. I'd probably get more out of her than I would by listening at the door. She could fill me in on what I'd already missed.

Crossing my legs, I wiggled a foot and let my mind wander. I needed to make a grocery list. My cupboards were getting a little bare.

That had been on my agenda today too. Grocery shopping.

I probably still had time. Though whether I could meal prep the way I wanted was another question.

The creak of hinges, then the sound of Jack's deep voice echoing down the hall and into the lobby brought me to my feet. A moment later, he and Allie appeared.

I smiled and stepped forward, but before I could say anything, he turned that glower on me again.

My smile faded to a confused frown. Why was he still angry at me?

I looked at Allie. "You ready to go?"

The woman's gaze cut to Jack.

"I'm having Officer Kauffman take her home. You can go have a seat in my office." He pointed back the way they came.

My frown deepened. "What?"

He just arched an eyebrow, silently telling me to go.

I huffed. "Fine." Aiming a glare of my own at him, I made sure he saw it before turning to Allie. My expression smoothed out. "Remember my offer and pass it along to your parents. If you need anything, please reach out."

She smiled kindly. "Thank you."

"You're welcome." Lifting a hand, I walked around Jack, refusing to look at him as I headed for his office.

Anger built with each step until I was seething by the time I stepped over the threshold. What was his problem? I brought him a lead. Why was he upset with me?

I stepped in front of the guest chair, intending to sit down, but the notepad on his desk caught my attention.

Had he really left his notes from their conversation out where I could see them? Had he learned nothing about me in the last few months?

Not one to look a gift horse in the mouth, I tilted my head and read his messy scrawl. A logging company name jumped out at me. It was the same one Morris Beach worked for.

Interesting.

Soft footfalls on the tile floor reached my ears. I backed up and sat down, folding my hands over my waist just as Jack entered the room.

He shut the door, then rounded the desk and sat down. Leaning forward, he steepled his fingers together and stared at me.

I stared back.

If he thought intimidating me would work, he really hadn't learned anything about me this summer.

Finally, he sighed. "Why?"

"Why, what?"

"Why were you at their house? And don't" —he raised a hand and pointed a finger at me—"say to pay your respects."

"Well, it was."

"That's what you said about why you went to visit Phil Brunswick's widow."

"And? It was true. It was this time too. I wanted to offer my condolences to Ella's family. They weren't at church—as I'm sure you noticed—so I took them some treats to hopefully cheer them up a little. I also wanted to offer to help in any way I could." And if that meant I learned things about Ella and her life, then so be it.

Jack hummed. "Sure."

"You should be happy I did. You wouldn't have known about Leo Stanhope, otherwise. What all did Allie tell you about him? Did she mention how controlling he was?"

"Yes. We had quite the conversation. None of which I plan to share with you."

I flattened my mouth and crossed my arms. "Maybe you should. I might be able to tell you some things."

"Such as?" He arched an eyebrow.

I lifted a shoulder. "I don't know. I need information to know where to start."

A sardonic smile tilted one side of his mouth. "Nice try."

Again, I shrugged. "Not trying anything. Just stating facts."

He groaned and leaned back, scrubbing his hands over his face. "You try my patience, Delaney."

I bit back a grin. Exasperating him was how I typically got him on my side. He'd tell me things just so I'd stop. "I don't even know why you're upset. I brought you a lead," I reminded him once more.

"You did. So, I will say thank you for that. But I'm also going to tell you to keep your nose out of this. Remember what happened the last time you didn't listen to me?"

I did, but I'd been hoping he wouldn't bring that up. "It all worked out, and I saved myself if you recall."

"No, James Brunswick saved you. Mandi would have reached her gun and shot you if he hadn't arrived when he did."

I'd been hoping he wouldn't bring that up, either.

"Promise me, Delaney. Promise you'll stay out of it."

I chewed the inside of my cheek as I thought frantically of how to promise what he wanted without actually promising anything. "I promise not to go looking for trouble." I never went looking for trouble. It just seemed to find me.

Probably because I went looking to ask questions.

He narrowed his eyes, and I could see the debate warring in them about my sincerity.

I struggled to keep a neutral expression on my face.

It must have been passable, because a moment later, he nodded. "Good." He waved a hand toward the door. "You can go home now. But I mean it. Stay out of this case. Someone went to great lengths to poison Ella Kerns. They'll go to the same lengths to keep from getting caught. I don't want you to end up as collateral damage."

Neither did I. But that just meant I'd have to be more conscious of the way I worded things when I asked my questions. "Thank you for your concern. I'll be fine."

Putting on my best sunny smile, I rose from my seat and headed for the door.

On my way out, I paused and looked over my shoulder. "Oh. If you want some skinny on Leo Stanhope, you should talk to Morris Beach."

Jack frowned. "Morris? Why?"

"He works for the same logging company." I pointed at the notepad on his desk.

Jack glanced down with a confused frown, which quickly disappeared when he realized I had read his notes. The glare returned in full force. "It's not nice to snoop, Delaney."

"I didn't."

He arched an eyebrow.

"Really. I saw it when I sat down. You're the one who left it out where it was visible. I mean, have you met me?"

An exasperated chuckle escaped his lips. "Go home."

"Geez, not even a thank you." I rolled my eyes, but a smile toyed with my mouth. "Enjoy the rest of your Sunday, Jack." Waggling my fingers, I whirled around and walked away, confident I'd won that interaction. Even if I—inadvertently, of course—found myself talking to someone I perhaps shouldn't, I doubted he'd be too angry.

At least, I hoped.

Eight

"Spill it, sister." Darcy stepped over the threshold, shoving a bottle of white wine into my hands.

I blinked, frowning at the bottle. "What?"

"The tea. I want to know what the developments were about Ella's ex that you mentioned earlier."

"Oh." I shut the front door, then headed for the kitchen. "For a moment, I thought you meant spill the wine."

"Heaven's no. That's the good stuff." She nodded to the bottle as she set her purse on the counter.

I could see that. It was from one of our favorite California wineries. Opening a drawer, I dug out the corkscrew. "Thanks for bringing this. I could use a little relaxation." I'd planned to sip a glass from the bottle I had in the fridge while I soaked in the tub before bed, but starting now wouldn't hurt. "Do you want some?"

"Just a little. I have to drive home." She opened a cabinet and grabbed two stemless wineglasses.

I poured a small amount in hers, then double that in mine. I didn't have to go anywhere tonight.

"So, spill the tea." Darcy picked up her glass and headed for the living room.

"I don't know much, honestly." I followed her with my glass and settled on the couch, tucking my legs up beneath me. "Ella was dating a guy named Leo Stanhope up until about a week ago. Her sister said he was rather controlling, but I guess he was pretty charming. Her parents never saw it. They liked him, from what I gathered, and didn't understand why Ella broke up with him."

"Controlling? How so?"

"Just trying to isolate Ella from her family and friends, from what Allie—Ella's sister—said. I really don't know much more than that. He works for the same logging company as Morris Beach. I told Jack to talk to him."

"Morris or Leo?"

"Morris, though he'll talk to both men, I'm sure."

Darcy took a sip of her wine, frowning as she stared off into space. "So, do you think Leo's the one who killed Ella?"

"I'm not sure. He had motive, but was it strong enough to kill over?" I lifted a shoulder. "Maybe."

"Who else would want to hurt her, though? I mean, I didn't know her well. I only talked to her when I stopped into Scarlett's store and she was working. But she seemed nice. Not like someone who would be on someone's hit list, you know?"

I nodded, knowing exactly what she meant. "I don't know who else would want to hurt her. I'm like you; I didn't really know her well."

"Did Scarlett have any ideas?"

"No. I'll ask her about Leo the next time I see her, though. Maybe her opinion will jive with Allie's."

"He had to give off some sort of creeper vibe. Men like that are charming, but there's usually something about them that sends off a weird signal."

"Yeah." I knew what she meant. They just rang... false. "So, did you get the last of the decorations for Daphne's shower?" I asked, changing the subject.

Darcy nodded. "We're all set. Do you need help with the food? You weren't sure last week."

"I should be fine." I shifted, sitting a little taller as excitement took hold over my news. "I hired Carol Prosser to be my assistant."

Darcy's mouth dropped open. "Shut up! You did not."

I smiled. "I did. She and Morris are getting married."

"What?" Darcy gasped. "When did you find all this out? And when did you hire her? Does her mother know?"

"I don't know if her mom knows about her working for me. All this happened at church today. She came up to me and told me her news, then asked if I could bake their wedding cake. Morris is footing the bill for the entire wedding because Lucile's not happy about how fast it's happening and is refusing to pay for anything."

"It's happening quickly? Is Carol pregnant?"

I laughed. "No. Nothing like that. The wedding won't be until next spring, but you know Lucile. She'd be perfectly happy if Carol and Morris dated for decades before marrying. Even then, I doubt that would be long enough for her."

Darcy chuckled. "True. Go on."

"Well, Carol asked if we could keep the cake simple since they were trying to keep costs down, but I could tell she wanted something more elaborate. Pretty, you know?"

Darcy nodded.

"So, I proposed she come work for me a few hours a week, and I'd bake the cake in lieu of paying her. Once she works off the cost of the supplies, I'll pay her a salary. I'm hoping it'll give her a little independence. She plans to use whatever she earns on the wedding, but afterward, I'm hoping I can convince her to stay on. Then she can save that money for herself, you know?"

"Yeah. It's always good for a woman to have an emergency fund, even in the happiest of marriages. Especially if her husband is the sole breadwinner. You never know what can happen."

"Exactly."

"So, when does she start?"

"Tuesday. For now, she's going to help out Tuesday and Thursday mornings. I might see if she'll help for some of the larger weddings I have coming up." I had one I knew I needed an assistant for. It was similar to the one Jack showed up to. I was making the cake, but the couple also had multiple food vendors coming in to set up.

"If she can't, let me know. I'm sure I can help you. Or maybe James will."

A slow smile spread over my face. Lifting my wineglass, I took a sip and watched her over the rim. "So, how's that going?" Darcy and James Brunswick had been dating for almost two months. I was pleasantly surprised to find he was nothing like his father.

Pink stole over Darcy's cheeks. "It's fine."

I arched an eyebrow. "Fine?" It was much more than that, judging by the starry-eyed look on her face.

"Maybe a little more than fine," Darcy hedged. She smiled. "He's amazing. I'm thoroughly enjoying getting to know him. He's nothing like I thought he would be. Which I'm happy about. I thought he'd be stuck up and a snob like his dad was. But he was raised by his mom. She didn't live the same luxurious life Phil did. James said she got enough child support to keep them comfortable, but they weren't rich. He's only got the money he does because his father put it into a trust when he was born. It's what paid for college and allowed him to start his business. He's very down-to-earth."

"That's good. You need to bring him to Sunday brunch. If you're that enamored with him, he needs to get to know the rest of us and vice versa."

"I know. It's just a matter of getting him to take time off

work. And when he's not working, he's trying to deal with untangling his father's legal mess. He wants to sell that property Phil bought with Skyler and Nile but can't until their trials end and they're sentenced. It's holding up a lot of things." She swirled the wine in her glass, staring at the pale-yellow liquid.

"Sometimes, I think he uses work as a method of not dealing with his feelings. If he stays busy, he doesn't have time to think."

"What about when he's with you? I hope he's not boxing up his feelings for you."

"No. He's affectionate and attentive when we're together. But he definitely doesn't want to talk about his dad or any of the things going on with his aunt." She wrinkled her nose and glanced away, then shrugged. "I don't know. Right now, everything is really new between us. I don't want to push stuff and jeopardize what we're building. It's a delicate balance. I really like him."

"I know you do." I didn't know what else to tell her. It had to work itself out. James had to deal with those emotions on his own. She couldn't do it for him. No one could. A therapist could help, but ultimately, it was up to him.

"Enough maudlin crap. I sold three paintings at Peabody's."

Immediately, my mood brightened. "What? Darcy! That's great! Is this in addition to the first couple that sold right away once Coral agreed to show your artwork?"

"Yep. They're new ones I dropped off a month ago. She said she has a buyer interested in a custom piece too. I'm supposed to meet them later this week." She wrinkled her nose. "I'm going to be run ragged by the time Daphne's shower is over. I have to go to Seattle Wednesday for the meeting."

"You couldn't move the meeting?"

"No. The buyer was only in town until Friday."

I scrunched my nose. "Well, boo. Okay. I'm glad you told me. And that I hired Carol."

"Me too." She tipped the last dribbles of wine into her mouth. "Anyway, that's about all I had in mind to talk about. Except for what time we're setting up Saturday. Do you have an idea about that?"

"Probably around nine. That'll give us time to change before the party, don't you think?" I had a list of all the setup that needed done. It wasn't that much. Tables set up, decorations, food. Mom and Dad would be around to help since the party was at the inn. I could probably rope Morgan into helping too. He and Dad were going golfing with some other friends while us ladies partied, but they weren't leaving until around lunchtime.

"Sounds good." Darcy stood. "I'm heading home before the wine hits. Not that the tiny bit I had will have much of an effect. But still better safe than sorry."

Smiling, I got up. "True. I'm going to top off my glass and take a bath. Let the crazy weekend melt away before I have to be up at four-thirty for work."

Darcy grimaced as she headed for the kitchen. "I don't know how you do it. That's too early."

"It's easy." I opened the fridge and took out a macaron from the stash I kept, offering it to her. "It's for these."

"Oh, yum." Darcy took the cookie and ate it in one bite. "I love pastries," she said after swallowing. "But not enough to get up that early and make them myself."

"That's okay. Few people do. Which is why they pay me to do it."

Darcy laughed. "I like your business sense." She headed for the door.

"It's in my business plan. 'Make things so others don't have to.'" We reached the front door, and I opened it.

"Well, it works. Keep it up," she tossed over her shoulder as she walked through.

"I plan to." And I did too. So long as people continued to buy, I'd keep baking. I had so many ideas to expand. One day, I would have a storefront. Slowly, I was getting there.

Nine

My headlights swept over the church's gravel parking lot as I rounded the bend just past the bridge. I wasn't surprised to see Carol's little nondescript, beige SUV already parked near the basement doors.

I pulled up beside her and parked.

The interior light in her vehicle lit up as she got out. I gathered my tote and coffee and joined her.

"Good morning." I sent her a sunny smile as we met in front of the vehicles.

"Good morning!" she echoed. A wide grin sat on her face, making her eyes sparkle.

I chuckled. "Are you always this perky at this hour?" My keys jingled as I quickly flipped through them, looking for the one to unlock the church.

Carol laughed. "No. I've had three cups of coffee already. I couldn't sleep." Her smile turned slightly shy. "About three-thirty, I decided to just get up."

"And you drank three cups of coffee in ninety minutes?"

"Well"—Carol tipped her head—"two-and-a-half." She lifted the travel mug she carried. "I still have a little left."

Finding the key, I slid it into the lock. "That's good. It'll tide you over until I can make a pot." With a quick turn of my wrist, I pushed the door open, then swept out an arm. "After you."

Carol ducked inside. I followed, flipping on the lights before shutting and locking the door behind us.

We made our way down the steps and rounded the corner into the kitchen. I flipped on more lights, then led her to the shelf where I kept my bag. "You can put your things here."

She set her purse next to my tote.

I opened another cabinet and withdrew two aprons, handing her one.

"So, where do we start?" she asked, tying the apron strings around her waist.

"Every morning, I have a list. Usually, it's a mental one, but on the days you're here, we can write it down." I picked up the small notepad on the counter and a pencil to scratch out what needed baked this morning.

Carol stood beside me, head cocked to the side as she watched me write. "That's not too bad. Though it's still more than I would expect you to bake in just a few hours."

I shrugged. "I have it down to a science."

She chuckled. "You'd have to. Okay, which one do you want to start with?"

"The cinnamon roll dough. It needs to rise." Reaching for my bag, I extracted my recipe book. I didn't need it, but she would until she memorized the recipes. "If you want to start on that, I'll get some coffee going for us."

"Sure." She took the book and opened it. "Oh, yum. There are so many good things in here." Carol looked up with a smile. "Thank you again so much for offering me a job. I—I think I really needed this."

I offered her a kind smile, knowing exactly what she meant. "You're welcome. I'm glad it worked out."

She let out a little snort as she flipped through the book. "Depends on what your definition of that is."

"Uh-oh." I paused, my hand on the coffee canister. "Is your mother not happy?"

"No. Morris has reservations, too, but he's easier to convince of things than she is. I've been under Mother's thumb my entire life. With him, I was able to start as the woman I wanted to be, you know?"

I nodded, encouraging her to continue, and opened the coffee can.

"I've been trying to be more independent since Morris and I started dating. Being with him and realizing I could have a life I wanted to lead—for myself—gave me the courage I'd been lacking. She hasn't liked the pushback, but I'm tired of being in her shadow. I don't want to go out and party every night or dress in revealing clothing—which she seems to think is what I'm working toward." She shot me a dry look as she reached for the sugar.

A soft chuckle escaped me at the image of Carol cutting it up. "That could be fun, though. I'm sure Darcy could help you with that if you want." My sister knew how to throw caution to the wind and how to dress her body to its best advantage.

Carol chuckled. "I'm sure, but no thank you. I really just want to be my own person. Mother's been so afraid for so long that I'll go off and leave her like my father did, that she's stifled any life I could have outside of her control." The smile on her face faded as a worried frown took hold.

"We had a conversation last night. Things really boiled over. She basically screamed at me that I wasn't allowed to work nor was I allowed to see Morris again."

A gasp left me. I glanced over, coffee scoop hovering over the filter basket. "What? What did you say?"

"I told her I was a grown woman, and she couldn't keep me prisoner. Then I zeroed in on what was really bothering her and told her if she didn't want to lose me completely, she needed to back off. I'm marrying Morris, and I want to work. At least until I have children." She paused, a small frown between her brows as she glanced around the kitchen. "Where's the yeast?"

"Oh. In the fridge." I pointed to the ancient refrigerator in the corner.

Carol walked over and opened it, grabbing the jar off the shelf. "Anyway, she asked me what Morris thought of that. I said he would be fine with whatever my decision was because he respects my opinion."

I let out a low whistle. "He's been good for you." I was surprised at just how good. It also surprised me he was being so understanding about Carol's desires. He'd been pretty certain he wanted a wife who would stay home.

A bright smile transformed Carol's face. "He has. And don't get me wrong. I know we'll probably butt heads some about me working after we start a family. But I don't want to lose the independence I've gained."

"I agree. And just so you know, you're welcome to bring any children you might have with you. Even if I move into my own building, we'll make some space where they can play and stay safe while you work." It's the plan I had for my own children, if I ever had any.

"Really?" Her face brightened.

I nodded, shutting the lid on the coffeemaker. "Yes." I pushed start. "I'd love to have you, even if you only want a few hours a week." I quite liked Carol and would be happy to foster her independence.

She beamed. "That would be great. I'll keep that in mind."

"Good." Turning away from the coffeepot, I walked to the fridge and took out butter, eggs, and buttermilk so I could get started on cupcakes.

"So how are your wedding plans coming?" I set every-thing down and lifted the bowl off the mixer.

"Pretty good. I decided to use silk flowers for my bouquet. They'll travel better than real ones. Plus, they're cheaper. I can repurpose them, too, as a memento." She moved to the sink and turned on the water, letting it run over her wrist until it reached the right temperature to proof the yeast.

"What about a dress? Have you found one?"

A blush stole over her cheeks. "I decided to make it." Picking up a measuring cup, she held it under the water stream.

My eyes rounded, and I blinked twice. "You're *making* your wedding dress?"

She nodded, shutting off the water. "I looked online for bridal gowns, and I saw some that I liked certain elements of, but none where I liked everything. So, I decided to put what I liked about each together and make my own." Her blush deepened and she bit her lip. "Do you want to see my sketch?"

"Yes! Do you have it with you?" I set down the butter I just unwrapped and wiped my hands on a towel.

"It's in my purse." Setting the measuring cup down, Carol moved to her bag and withdrew a folded piece of paper. "It's pretty rough, but you'll get the idea." She held it out.

The paper crinkled as I took it and unfolded it. What I saw was far from rough. "Oh my goodness. Carol, this is beautiful." She'd drawn a sleeved gown with lace flowers that started full at the wrist and waist and slowly faded as they rose until only a few dotted the tops of the shoulder and the collarbone area. From the waist, a full flowy skirt billowed and fanned out into a short train. More flowers cascaded down from the waist, fading away like they did on the top. "What are you making the skirt out of?"

"Organza. I wanted something flowing, but not poofy. The top is that thin, nude stuff. They call it an illusion neckline. I'm sewing on all the floral appliques and beading. I'm still debating if I want to put a beaded belt on it."

"Are you thinking pearls or sparkles?"

"Probably a mix of both."

"Well, it's just beautiful, and I'm sure the final product will be stunning."

That shy smile peeped out again on Carol's face, but now a bit of confidence shined alongside it. "I hope so. Thank you."

"If you need any help with it, let me know. I'm not the best seamstress, but I know the basics. I'm sure Darcy would help too. She makes a lot of her clothes." My sister loved her flowy skirts and peasant blouses and frequently made her own things. She said it kept her mind busy. I sort of knew what she meant. That was one of the reasons I baked.

"I'll do that." Carol took the sketch and folded it up. "I'm sure once I get further along, I'll need a little help. Especially when I get to the final fittings."

Returning to my cupcake batter, my thoughts shifted to the reason Carol was here. "So, do you have ideas for your wedding cake?"

"A few." Carol picked up the measuring cup and dumped the warm water into her yeast and sugar mix, then grabbed a whisk. "I think I want three tiers. Cream or white. I'm not sure about the decorations yet, though. We're doing earth tones, so something neutral to go with that."

Ideas swirled through my mind. "You said your wedding is in the forest, right?"

"Yes."

"What if we did something that looked like birch bark? And then put a few flowers on the bottom of the tiers?"

Carol's hand stilled as a contemplative frown crossed her face. "I think I know what you mean. That might work. Can we put birds on it, though? Morris loves birds."

I wrinkled my nose; not in distaste, but in uncertainty. "I can try. I'm not the best sculptor. There are some places online I could look to find premade birds, though."

"It's just a thought. We don't have to." Carol's smile dimmed a bit.

"It's fine. It's a great idea. Let me do some digging and see what I can come up with. I might be able to talk Darcy into helping too. She's done some clay sculpting. Modeling chocolate isn't all that different."

That brightened Carol's face. "Okay. That sounds good."

"You'll have to sit down with Morris and figure out what kind of birds you want."

"We can do that."

"The sooner the better too. It'll give me time to practice." I glanced at her with a grin.

Carol chuckled. "Noted."

We worked in silence for several minutes, and I let my thoughts wander. They landed on a subject I'd dwelled on much too frequently over the last few days. Ella Kerns.

I hadn't heard much about Jack's progress on the investigation. But I hadn't exactly been out and about, asking questions, either. When Monday rolled around, I threw myself into work. I hadn't even talked to Scarlett yet about what I learned from Allie.

"What's put that frown on your face? You're not worried about my cake idea, are you?"

"Huh?" I looked up from filling cupcake tins with a frown. "Oh. No. I was thinking about Ella Kerns."

Carol's eyebrows drew together, and she shook her head. "That's such a tragedy. She was so young."

"I know."

"Do the police have any leads? I haven't heard much, but then I don't socialize like you do."

"Jack doesn't have much. She was poisoned. Cyanide, but he doesn't know how or where it came from. At least, as far as I know he doesn't. And when it comes to suspects, he's low on those too. Her ex-boyfriend is the only one I know of." Scooping out the last of the batter, I set my mixing bowl down and tapped the pans on the table to release the trapped air bubbles.

"Don't tell my mother that. She'll get even more worried about me dating Morris."

A corner of my mouth lifted. She wasn't wrong. "Mum's the word. I do have a question for you, though."

"Oh? What's that?"

"Do you know Leo Stanhope?"

A small frown bit into Carol's forehead. She picked up a measuring cup and scooped flour out of the container, scattering it over the counter. "The name doesn't ring a bell. Why?"

"That's Ella's ex-boyfriend's name. Her sister, Allie, mentioned he worked for the same company Morris works for. I thought maybe you'd run into him."

"Oh." Carol blinked, then shook her head and turned the cinnamon roll dough out onto the floured countertop. "I don't know him, but I can ask Morris."

"You don't have to. I'm sure Jack has tracked Leo down by now."

Carol shrugged. "It won't hurt to ask him and get his impression of the guy if he does know him. It might be useful. You never know."

"That's true."

"We're supposed to have dinner tonight. I'll say something and let you know on Thursday what he says." She gave the dough a couple of turns. "Jack really doesn't know anything about who did it?"

I shook my head. "Not that he's sharing. I just can't imagine who would want to hurt her. She was a nice kid."

The silence returned, and we continued working our way through my list until it was time to load up for my morning route. I wouldn't park anywhere until lunchtime, but I had several deliveries to make this morning.

To my delight, I talked Carol into joining me on the

delivery route and into staying for the lunch event. Today, I was at a nursing home near the school. I liked that spot, because I got not only staff and patients from the nursing home, but also teachers from the school who snuck out on their lunch breaks for a sweet treat.

Once all the deliveries were made, we returned to the church and loaded up for the lunch rally, then set off. I hoped Tyson would be there today. I needed a burrito. Hunger gnawed at my stomach, and one of his burritos sounded delicious.

When I turned into the nursing home parking lot, I saw him right away and did a mental fist pump.

"Wow. There are more trucks here than I thought there would be." Carol peered through the windshield at the other food trucks assembled.

"It's a decent rally. The nursing home is a good size and can support the variety." I pulled up behind the burger truck and parked. "Let's get set up."

We didn't have much to do. It was just a matter of opening the window, setting out the napkin dispenser, and turning on the register. I opted not to bring anything cold, except macarons. They would keep in the truck's fridge without the generator running.

"That was easy," Carol said, ducking back inside after setting the napkin dispenser on the window ledge.

"Yep. No generator today, and no frosting to make. If we run out of cupcakes, we run out of cupcakes." The lunch rally here was only a couple of hours long. For longer events, I brought my mixer and all the ingredients for buttercream. I couldn't transport the number of frosted cupcakes I needed for longer events, so I brought boxes of unfrosted ones and added buttercream as needed.

It wasn't long before the first people drifted outside from the nursing home's front entrance. We had a few people come up, but I knew we'd get busier in about a half an hour. A lot of people stopped to get a cookie or a cupcake to go after they had lunch.

"Hey, is that your sister?"

I glanced over from where I bagged up cookies for the person at the window to see Carol pointing to the left. Shoving the last cookie into the bag, I stepped closer and peered outside. Darcy walked toward the truck from the school.

"It is. I wondered if I'd see her." As she got closer, she stopped, turning to wave at someone I couldn't see. A moment later, I saw James lope into view.

"Who is that?" Carol asked.

I passed the cookies through the window to the nurse waiting on them. With a smile, I thanked her, then glanced at Carol. "James Brunswick. He and Darcy are dating."

"Really?" Carol's expression brightened and she turned to watch them come closer.

"Yep. He's actually a pretty nice guy." I turned to the next person in line, greeting them.

Carol did the same on her side of the window.

Darcy and James got in line. With a smile, I waved. She waved back and looped an arm around James's elbow.

Luckily, we still weren't too busy, so when Darcy and James arrived at the window, we were able to chat.

"How good are you at sculpting birds?" I asked Darcy after she and James placed their orders.

Darcy frowned. "Birds?"

I nodded. "Carol wants birds on her wedding cake. I'm not the best sculptor, so I thought I'd ask you to teach me."

"Oh. I've never made a bird, but I've done other animals. We could definitely work on it." She smiled. "That would be fun. Maybe we can draft Daphne and Scarlett too. Make a girls' night out of it." She looked at Carol, her smile warm and welcoming. "You should come too."

A soft pink blush stole over Carol's cheeks. "Really? That sounds like fun."

"Yep. We'll pick a day sometime soon and get together. Maybe after Daphne's bridal shower. I think we'll all be ready for a break after that." She glanced at me. "I don't know about you, but I'm ready for her to be married already."

Chuckling, I ducked into the truck to grab the cupcake she ordered and James's macarons. "I know what you mean. I knew planning a wedding was stressful, but sheesh! And it's not even my wedding."

"Right?"

Cookie bag in one hand and a red velvet cupcake in the other, I leaned into the window again. "Here you go."

"Thank you." Darcy took her cupcake and immediately peeled back the paper liner. "The whole thing makes me want to elope if I'm lucky enough to ever get married." She cast a quick look at James, who seemed unbothered by the exchange.

"Geez, give a girl a confidence boost, why don't you?" Carol muttered.

When I looked at her, I could see the dismay written on her face, and I winced. "Sorry, Carol. We're not trying to scare you. It's just a lot of work."

"I know." She waved a hand. "It's fine. Daphne's wedding is probably much more elaborate than mine too. I doubt I'll even have a bridal shower. Our wedding and the reception won't have too many people, either. Maybe fifty or so."

I frowned. "Why wouldn't you have a bridal shower?"

The younger woman shrugged. "Who's going to throw it for me? My mom won't, I know that. She doesn't want me to marry Morris. And I don't have many friends. Certainly not a best friend who would jump on the chance."

A sliver of anger unfurled in my gut directed toward Carol's mother, Lucile. That woman had robbed her daughter of so much by sheltering her the way she did.

I glanced at Darcy and saw the sympathy in her eyes. Before I could stop them, words tumbled from my mouth. "My sisters and I would be happy to throw your shower."

Carol's eyes rounded. "You would?"

"Of course we would," Darcy chimed in.

I nodded. "Consider it done."

"Oh!" Tears welled in Carol's eyes. She fanned her face with a hand. "Thank you."

"You're welcome." Smiling, I laid a soft hand on her shoulder for a moment.

"None of that." Darcy fluttered her fingers at Carol. "I'm not about to cry, too, and go back to school looking like a squirrel clawed at my eyeballs. I came over here not just to get this delicious cupcake" —she held up the aforementioned item—"but to get the skinny on the latest in Ella's death."

James sighed. "Do we have to get involved in this? Remember what happened when you guys got involved in my dad's death?"

"Yes. You and I wouldn't have met."

He frowned but didn't contradict her. Instead, he looked at me and blew out a long breath. "Fine. Then you should know that I had an… unusual interaction with her."

My brows drew together. I glanced past him, glad there was no one in line currently, and willed all potential patrons to stay away a little longer. "What do you mean? When?"

"The day before she died. I was downtown to meet with Morgan for lunch so we could discuss my father's probate and go over the current state of the law firm. He was running a little late, so I decided to do a little shopping for Darcy's birthday." He glanced at her, and I saw my sister's cheeks flush. A soft smile lit her face. She practically glowed with happiness.

"I stopped in Scarlett's boutique to look around," James continued. "No one was up front, so I wandered for a bit. I found…" —he trailed off, casting a quick look at Darcy—

"something I wanted to buy, but no one had come out from the back yet, so I walked to the employee's only door and peeked through. Ella was in the back in a quiet, but heated argument with a man."

My mind instantly went to her ex-boyfriend. "What did he look like?"

James lifted a shoulder. "He was older. Maybe fifty. I heard him say something about stopping the nonsense, but then she saw me and quickly ended the conversation."

That was interesting. What nonsense? And who could it have been? Maybe her dad? He was the right age. "What did he look like?"

"Average height and build. Silvery blonde hair."

That sounded like Dave Kerns. "Was he really tan?"

James nodded.

Now I was even more intrigued about what this "nonsense" was. If it was her dad she'd been talking to, he didn't let on that anything was amiss with his daughter when I spoke to him.

"The odd part wasn't so much the man and the argument, but what she said to me when she came out front to ring up my purchase."

"Oh?" I lifted an eyebrow.

"She must have recognized me, because she asked me not to tell Scarlett about the man and leaving the front of the store unattended."

"Maybe she was worried Scarlett would reprimand her for not manning the register," Darcy said.

"Maybe," I said, my voice soft as I stared into the distance, lost in thought.

The shuffle of people at Carol's window pulled me out of my thoughts. Business was picking up.

"You need to talk to Jack." I aimed a look at James. "If nothing else, he can show you some pictures of a couple of people and see if you recognize any of them. He's grasping at straws, trying to find a suspect."

Again, James nodded. "I'll stop in the police station later today and talk to him. I've been debating it, anyway."

"Good." And in the meantime, I would talk to Scarlett and see if she could look at her security camera footage. If it wasn't Dave Kerns, maybe one of us would recognize the man.

Ten

Standing near the edge of the inn's private deck, lemonade in hand, I let the noise of Daphne's bridal shower wash over me. Nearly thirty women filled the space, spilling out from the deck and down the steps onto the lawn that sloped gently toward the dock and the lake beyond. Creamy tablecloths with their gauzy golden runners fluttered in the light breeze. Aqua-colored Ball jars filled with fresh, blush peonies and white roses dotted the tables.

Daphne called it perfect. I agreed.

The afternoon air carried just enough crispness to hint that summer was heading south for the winter. The trees had the faintest blush of orange touching their leaves. In another week or two, the whole hillside would look like it was on fire. I loved this time of year, but today I wasn't quite ready to let go of summer. The weather was glorious, and I planned to savor it.

"Those lemon bars are going fast." Darcy appeared at my elbow, refilling her glass from the pitcher on the nearby table. "You should snag one before they disappear."

"I had one earlier. I also might have made a little extra and left it in my refrigerator." A sly smile tilted one side of my mouth.

Darcy chuckled. "Remind me to raid your fridge the next time I'm over." Lifting her glass, she took a sip, turning to stare out over the lawn. "Everything looks beautiful, Laney. We did a good job."

"We did. Daphne looks happy." I nodded toward our sister, who stood with her best friend, laughing over a comment another of their friends made.

"She does," Darcy replied. "She's been so stressed. It's nice to see her relax."

It was. I was sure the worry about all the last-minute details would return soon enough as the wedding crept closer, but for today, she was enjoying herself.

We stood companionably for a moment, watching the scene. Mom floated through the crowd, making sure everyone had enough to eat, doing what she always did and making sure everyone had the best experience possible. It was one of the reasons the inn was so successful. No detail went unnoticed.

Movement at the far corner of the deck caught my eye. Scarlett leaned against the railing, smiling at something a woman beside her said. To anyone who didn't know her, she looked perfectly fine.

But I knew Scarlett, and I could see the slight distance in her eyes, and the way her smile wasn't quite as full as normal. Something still bothered her. Whether it was Ella's death or the issues with her dad, I didn't know. I wished she would talk to me more about it; she'd feel better. I made a mental note to check in with her and remind her she could bend my ear whenever she needed.

Darcy nudged me with her shoulder. "Mom's waving us over."

I looked toward the lawn, where Mom stood at the top of

the dock steps, beckoning. A small cluster of women had gathered near her, drifting toward the water. If it were warmer, I was certain several would be in the lake, swimming. I would be, too, but it was too chilly now for that.

We made our way down, the sound of small waves lapping against the pilings mingling with the happy conversations happening around us.

"Isn't this just gorgeous?" Mom swept a hand toward the water. The late afternoon sun had shifted, and it now glimmered on the water, casting a honeyed glow over everything it touched. "I never get tired of it. Not once in all the years we've been here have I looked out and thought, 'I wish I saw something different today.'"

I knew how she felt. If I'd been able to afford it, I'd have bought a house nearby, so I could continue to watch the water whenever I wanted. But a baker's salary didn't really lend itself to buying a million-dollar home. Maybe one day I'd go viral and make the big bucks. Until then, I just drove here whenever I needed a lake fix.

"That young woman who worked for Scarlett who died—the one you asked me about and whether it was all right if she photographed the lake from the deck"—Mom nodded at me—"she framed a copy of one of the prints and gave it to us."

I tipped my head, thinking about the art on the walls inside the inn. "Is that the one hanging in the guest hallway now?"

Mom nodded. "Isn't it beautiful? She captured this so well." She swept a hand out toward the water. "I don't know how she did it, but this glow is front and center. I've taken pictures of the lake for years and could never get it to translate onto film."

"You should have said something, Mom," Darcy said. "I know how to do that."

Mom waved a hand. "You're busy. It wasn't a big deal. But

I was still very happy to have that picture." Her expression fell. "I was sorry to hear about what happened to that girl too. Not just because of her talent, either. She was such a lovely person."

A shout from the lawn drew our attention.

Daphne stood at the edge of the water, motioning to us. "I'm ready to open gifts."

Looping her arms through mine and Darcy's, Mom grinned. "Come on, girls. Let's not keep the bride waiting."

The rest of the afternoon flew by in a happy blur. By the time the last guest hugged Daphne goodbye and the patio lights had come on over the deck in the early dusk, I was pleasantly tired and not entirely ready to leave.

Mom had gone inside to start on the dishes, waving away all offers of help. Darcy and Dad were hauling left-over food up from the lawn tables. I was about to head down, when Daphne came up the steps and flopped down in one of the loungers, kicking off her sandals with a tired sigh.

I sat down next to her. "Good day?"

She nodded, smiling. "Really good day." Turning her head, she looked out at the water, now a rippling shade of pewter in the fading light. "I keep thinking I should be worried about something, though. There's always something to worry about."

"Not today." I patted her knee. "Today was about relaxing and enjoying this time in your life."

"It was, and that's how I felt." She turned her attention back to me. "Thank you. You and Darcy and Mom. This was exactly what I needed."

"Good. That was the intent. Make Daphne forget about all that's left to do and to just let loose."

She chuckled. "And now I'm thinking about it again."

I rolled my eyes. "Well, stop. Put it away until tomorrow and just enjoy the entirety of this day."

With a sigh, she looked at the water again. "One more month. Then I can put it all away forever."

"Exactly. It's temporary. And for today, it's tucked away in a box."

Daphne mimed holding a key and locking something. "All put away."

Chuckling, I settled back in the chair. "Good."

We sat quietly for a moment, watching a group of ducks take flight as a boat buzzed a little too close to their resting spot on the water. Quacking up a storm, the rose fifty feet off the surface before landing again about a hundred yards away, shaking their wings as they settled into place on the water once more.

I really needed to find a way to make more money, so I could live out this way again.

"There you are. Slacking off, I see."

Pulled out of my reverie by Darcy's voice, I looked toward the stairs to see her and Dad heading toward us with an armload of serving dishes.

"I'm not slacking," I said, getting up to take a few things off her stack. "Daphne and I were just talking."

Darcy hummed. "Sure you were. That's why you were sitting there, silent."

I laughed. "Okay. Maybe I was slacking off a little." I reached for the top couple of trays she carried.

Deftly, she sidestepped me. "There's plenty more where this came from. Go get your own."

"Please?" Dad added, giving Darcy an admonishing look.

She rolled her eyes. "Please?" she parroted.

"Already going." I turned toward the stairs but paused before heading down to the lawn. "For the record"—I raised a finger—"I was the one who made a good chunk of this food. I think I've earned a five-minute sit-down. So has Dad, for that matter, since he made the rest."

"Pfft. You two can sit when you're dead," Darcy tossed

over her shoulder, making her way toward the sliding door that led inside.

Dad just shook his head. "She's a taskmaster."

"That she is." Laughing, I skipped down the steps to gather up a pile of dishes before Darcy came outside again and yelled at me for not being fast enough.

Eleven

If I have to hold this smile for another second, it might break off my face.

Blinking, I nodded once more at the pastor's wife, Crystal, as she continued to extol me on the benefits of her wildflower garden for the bees. It wasn't that I minded hearing about saving the bees, but it was hard to follow the conversation and serve breakfast to the congregation when she expected me to pay attention.

My forced smile turned more genuine, though, when Carol walked up with Morris in tow.

Crystal, ever eager to include more people on her mission, turned to include them in the conversation.

"Morris, you should agree with me."

I held back a chuckle at the look of boyish confusion on his face.

"About what, Mrs. Glendale?"

"That wildflowers are important for the bees."

"Oh. Yes, I do agree. It's one of the things that flourishes, actually, after we log an area. More sunlight reaches the forest floor, and the wildflowers explode."

With Crystal distracted, I turned to Carol, offering her a

cheery smile. "Good morning."

She smiled back with a soft, tinkling laugh. "Good morning. I see you've been… entertained."

I rolled me eyes. "Quite. What can I get for you?" I motioned to the array of pastries on platters in front of me.

"I'll have one of the cranberry-orange muffins, please." She pointed to the plate of giant muffins.

I lifted one onto a napkin and handed it to her. "There you go." My eyes traveled to her fiancé. "What do you think he'd like?"

"One of your cinnamon rolls, of course."

I grinned. "Of course." Morris was a creature of habit. He'd chosen a cinnamon roll every Sunday morning since I started offering breakfast at church. I doubted he would change his mind today.

Someone called Crystal's name as I set a gooey roll onto a small paper plate. She excused herself and wandered away.

Morris let out a huff as he turned back to Carol and me. "That woman should have become a politician. She'd be great at the filibuster. Is this for me?" He pointed to the cinnamon roll as Carol and I laughed.

"Yes," I said.

He picked it up, along with a plastic fork, and took a bite.

"So, I didn't get a chance to ask yesterday," Carol said. "Have you learned anything new about Ella's death?"

My mouth twisted into a frown. "No. I've been too busy to talk to Jack about what James told him. Same with Scarlett. I know she gave him the security footage, but that's all. This past week was a whirlwind with Daphne's bridal shower."

"Well, that's done now, so hopefully you can catch a breather until closer to her wedding."

"Yeah. We've got a little over a month."

"I bet it's got your biological clock ticking," Morris said.

I cast him a quick look. "Why would it?"

He lifted a shoulder. "You and Daphne aren't that far

apart in age. She's getting married and will presumably start a family soon. I would think it would make you want the same. You know, we have a new guy on the team. He's about your age and single. You should let me introduce you."

I clenched my back teeth to stop the rude retort. Instead, I pasted a sickly-sweet smile on my face. "No, thank you. I don't need any help finding a boyfriend."

Just then, Jack walked into the lobby, drawing my eye.

Carol let out a soft chuckle. "No. No, you don't."

I speared her with a fierce look. "Stop. There's nothing there."

"Sure, there isn't." She grinned.

Jack didn't help any when he walked straight over to the breakfast bar, a wide, kind smile on his face and his gaze locked on me.

A soft blush stole over my skin.

That wasn't helping, either.

"Good morning, Delaney." His low tones washed over me, sending tingles down my spine. I did love his voice.

He glanced at Carol and Morris, nodding to them. "Morning."

The two of them echoed his greeting.

Jack's gaze dropped to the plate Morris held, then he looked at me. "You have any of those left?" He tipped a finger toward the cinnamon roll.

"I do." Flipping back the foil, I picked up the tongs and wrestled one out of the pan.

"Thanks." He took the plate I offered and grabbed a fork. "Hey, I, um…" He stopped and cleared his throat. "I wanted to say thank you for bringing me the lead with James and the man at Scarlett's shop."

My expression brightened as curiosity took hold. "Oh? Well, you're welcome. I take it, it's panned out?"

"Too soon to tell. I'm still working it, but it's more than I had before."

"Do you know who the man is?"

"Not yet. But I was able to track him on surveillance footage from other businesses, and he got into a gray sedan."

Interesting. That meant it wasn't Dave Kerns. Jack certainly would have showed James a picture of him.

"Did you get a license plate?" Carol asked.

Jack glanced her way. "We did, but it was fuzzy. Forensics is working on enhancing it. We'll see what happens."

I smiled and reached for the muffin I'd been picking at in between churchgoers. "Good. What about Leo? Did you and Morris talk?" I gestured to him.

Morris looked up at his name, a forkful of frosting pausing in mid-air. "What? Sorry. I was enjoying my roll." He offered me a sheepish smile.

A quick laugh rolled past my lips. "I'm flattered, Morris. I asked if you and Jack had talked about Leo Stanhope."

"Oh." His fork resumed its journey to his mouth, and he nodded as he ate the icing. "We did. I couldn't offer much, unfortunately."

"Yeah, they don't work together," Jack added. "Leo's in the field all the time. Morris is mostly in the office."

I pressed my lips together and wrinkled my nose. "That's a bummer."

"I did talk to Leo, though," Jack said. "He swears he was nowhere near Ella the day she died. I haven't been able to verify that, however."

If you'd asked me last weekend whether I thought Leo did it, my answer would have been a resounding "Yes!" But with the argument James witnessed between Ella and the mystery man, I wasn't so sure now. I couldn't help but wonder who he was and why he'd been in the back of Scarlett's shop. What could Ella possibly have to argue about with a man twice her age? A man who wasn't her father.

"At least you still have a suspect and an angle to keep working," Morris said. "That's a place to start."

Jack nodded but stayed silent.

Done with his roll, Morris dropped his plate and fork into the trash near the breakfast bar. Carol had finished her muffin while we chatted and already tossed her wrapper and napkin.

"Let's go find your mother, dear, shall we?" Morris held out a hand to Carol.

Carol sent a quick look of dismay toward me but took his hand. "Sure."

I tried to put as much sympathy and encouragement into my smile as I could. "I'll see you Tuesday."

She waggled her fingers and nodded as Morris led her away.

Suddenly, I was alone with Jack.

Which seemed implausible, since we were in a room full of people, but that's how it felt—like we were the only ones around.

It didn't help that he was staring at me with those deep, dark, fathomless eyes.

"So, are you going to your parents' after church for lunch?" he asked.

Needing to keep my hands busy so my emotions stayed under control, I recovered the trays of pastries while I answered him. "Yes."

"What about afterward? Do you have any plans?"

"Oh, probably more baking. There's always something to do." Which was no lie. My business kept me on my toes, but I liked it that way. Every cookie and cake I sold got me one step closer to my own storefront.

"Do you think you could take a bit of a break? Maybe go on a—" He stopped abruptly as a hush fell over the church members gathered in the lobby.

I glanced out at the crowd and followed their gazes toward the door.

Dave and Paige Kerns stood just inside the doors. The pinch to Dave's face and the nervous twitch to Paige's hands around the handles on her bag said they were not comfortable with the sudden attention.

A pang of sympathy clutched my heart. I glanced at the clock, a plan forming. We only had a few minutes until the organist would start playing, signaling that the service was about to begin.

"Last call for breakfast!" I raised a set of the metal tongs into the air and clacked them together.

Every eye in the lobby turned toward me.

Success!

Grinning, I waved the tongs. "Come get it, so I don't have to take it back downstairs."

Jack shifted to the side as several people approached. "That was a good thing you just did."

I sent him a coy look through my lashes. "I have no idea what you mean."

A slow smile spread over his face. He tapped the counter. "I'll see you in the sanctuary."

"Save me a seat?"

With a nod, he backed away and left me to serve the last few stragglers.

I watched him go, wondering what it was he'd wanted to ask me before the Kerns arrived.

"Good morning, Delaney."

The soft female voice drew my attention away from Jack's retreating form. I turned and smiled at Paige Kerns. "Good morning, Mrs. Kerns. It's nice to see you here. I'm glad you two could make it. I know it probably wasn't easy to come today." If I were in their shoes, I'd probably stay locked up where I wouldn't have to deal with anyone's prying eyes or questions.

"Yes," Dave said, "but we missed our church family and friends."

Paige nodded. "Frankly, we needed the support."

"Well, we're always here for that. Can I get you some breakfast and coffee before you step into the sanctuary?"

Paige rolled her lips in, eyeing the baked goods with interest. "I suppose a muffin might be nice."

I reached for a napkin. "Blueberry or cranberry-orange?"

"Blueberry, please."

Placing one on the napkin, I handed it to her. "Mr. Kerns, would you like anything?"

He waved a hand and shook his head.

"Where's Allie?" I glanced past them, searching what was left of the crowd for the young woman.

Paige's hand stilled on the paper wrapper as she peeled it away from the muffin. Her gaze darted toward her husband, who now frowned fiercely.

"She decided to stay home," he said.

A low level of anger simmered in his tone. I decided not to push by asking more questions. I doubted he'd offer more, anyway. "Well, tell her we're all thinking about her and praying. Not just for her, but your entire family."

Dave's face softened. "Thank you, Delaney."

I offered him a soft smile, not having to fake the sympathy in my expression. What they were going through was nothing short of horrendous. "You're welcome. And again, if there's anything my family or I can do, please don't hesitate to reach out."

Music swelled from the sanctuary, signaling the start of the service. The three of us glanced toward the sound, then Dave turned to me, nodding. "We will, thank you." He looked at his wife. "Come, dear. Let's go find our seats."

With a strained smile, Paige lifted a hand in a quick farewell, then followed her husband toward the sanctuary.

I watched them go as I covered up the remaining pastries, wondering what the issue was between them and Allie. My guess was it had something to do with her talking to the police about her suspicions regarding Leo. Why, I didn't understand. If my daughter were murdered, I would want the police to look at everyone, even the most unlikely. Leo Stanhope was far from unlikely if even a portion of what happened between him and Ella was true.

And while that seemed like the most plausible reason for the strife within the Kerns family, I had trouble believing it. The Kerns loved their daughter, and she loved them. That had been obvious during my visit.

But if Allie going to the police about Leo wasn't the reason something was amiss, then what was?

Twelve

Elbow-deep in flour and jamming out to my favorite playlist, the knock on the church door didn't register until the person outside banged so hard, the entire thing rattled in its frame.

Startled, I paused staring at the wall that hid the staircase from view. Did Carol forget something?

I cast a quick glance around the kitchen, but nothing looked out of place.

The door rattled in the frame again.

Who on earth could it be? More importantly, what was so urgent they were ready to break down the door?

Dusting off my hands with a towel, I hurried out of the kitchen and up the stairs. With a quick flick of my wrist, I unlocked the door and opened it.

I frowned at the young woman standing on the other side. "Allie?"

"Hi. I'm sorry to bother you. Do you have a minute?"

"Of course." Stepping back, I motioned her inside and closed the door. Curiosity sped through my veins. "We missed you at church Sunday. Your parents said you opted not to come."

Her eyebrows slammed together. "We had an argument. They want to include Leo in Ella's memorial service tomorrow. I told them he probably murdered her, and I wouldn't be attending if they insisted on including him in the service. I can't stop him from coming, but pigs will fly before he gets up and gives a speech at it."

I understood her point. If I suspected my sister's boyfriend of killing her, I wouldn't want him giving speeches at her funeral, either. "Let's go downstairs. You can have a cinnamon roll and tell me more about why you're here."

The younger woman let out a long sigh and nodded.

I led her down to the basement and pointed at one of the tables set up in the meeting space. "Have a seat. Would you like some coffee too? Or milk?"

"No. You don't have to feed me at all. I'm fine."

"Nonsense. Sweets make everything better. Endorphins and all that." I waved a hand and smiled as I rounded the counter.

Allie chuckled. "How about just a cookie, then? I don't think I can eat a whole roll."

"Sure." Changing course, I opened a plastic container filled to the brim with giant chocolate chunk cookies and took two out, one for each of us.

Returning to the table, I perched on a chair across from Allie and passed her a cookie on a napkin. "All right. Tell me why you're here. Is it just to vent? Because that's fine. I'll listen. But I think there's more, isn't there?" As good of a listener as I was, I doubted she was here just to talk. Before Ella's death, we'd only met briefly a few times. Most people ranted to close friends or family, not strangers they barely knew.

Allie picked at the cookie, breaking off a small piece and eating it before answering. "Did you mean what you said about helping in any way you could?"

"Of course," I responded without hesitation. "What can I do?"

She bit her lip, looking down at her cookie for several seconds before lifting her head. "Can you go with me to talk to that detective again? I—" She stopped and swallowed, eating another bite before continuing. "He's a bit scary, and I haven't been entirely truthful with him."

I tipped my head, more curious than ever now. "Oh? How so?"

Allie ate more cookie, then met my gaze. "You know how I told you Ella was staying with me while she worked on extracting Leo from her life?"

"Yes."

"Well, Detective Fiore asked me if she'd left anything at my apartment that might be useful to the investigation. I told him all I had were some of her clothes and toiletries."

"But there's more, isn't there?" It wasn't hard to figure out where she was going with this.

Allie nodded but held up a hand. "At the time, I didn't lie. I didn't know about the other stuff. But he did ask me to call him if I had any more information." Her mouth twisted, and she glanced away again. "I wanted to look at it first and do a little digging on my own."

A frown marred my face. "What did you find?"

"Some papers. It looked like work orders for Leo's logging company."

My frown intensified. "To cut down trees?"

"No. For chemicals. One of them was cyanide."

My eyes went wide. "Ella had paperwork for an order of cyanide from the logging company?"

Allie nodded.

"And you haven't already turned it over to Detective Fiore?"

She shook her head. "I know. I should have. But I wanted

to know if Leo was involved in ordering it. His name isn't on the invoice."

"What did you do? Did you ask him?"

"Of course not." Her brows dipped as she gave me an indignant look. "He would never admit to it. I followed him. Then I asked another friend who works in the logging industry if they use cyanide for anything."

"Do they?"

"Yes. As a fumigant against pests."

I stuffed the last of my cookie in my mouth and dusted off my hands, removing my apron as I chewed. The rest of my baking could wait. Jack needed to know this.

While Allie finished her cookie, I covered up my mixing bowls and gathered my tote. Ushering the younger woman up the steps, I turned off the lights as we exited.

"Let's take my car." I stepped toward my blue SUV. "Unless you'd rather follow me?" I added.

"I'll just follow you. I don't want to tie you up at the police station."

I nodded but didn't tell her I probably wouldn't leave until after she talked to Jack, anyway. "Okay. I'll see you there."

Retreating to our cars, we were soon on the road with me in the lead.

I kept an eye on her vehicle as I drove, more uncertain now than ever about who killed Ella. Leo had begun to look less likely, but with this new information, I wasn't so sure. I didn't envy Jack his job, that was for certain. Better him than me who had to figure out who was at fault.

The police station came into view, and I turned into the parking lot and pulled into a visitor's space. Allie parked next to me. Without a word, we walked inside together.

At the window, I asked for Jack. Luckily, he was in.

Although, once he walked out into the lobby to meet us, that dark scowl in place on his handsome face, I sort of wished he wasn't. Being greeted with suspicion most of the time was growing increasingly tiresome.

"Delaney." Jack nodded to me, still frowning. "What can I do for you?"

I tipped my head toward Allie. "I'm just here for emotional support. Allie has information for you."

"Oh?" He raised an eyebrow and looked at the younger woman.

Lips pressed tight, Allie took her handbag off her shoulder and opened it, withdrawing a sheaf of folded papers. She held them out to him. "I found these with some of Ella's things."

Jack took the papers and unfolded them, quickly skimming through the pages. His frown intensified as he read. "She had these in her possession?"

Allie nodded. "They were tucked into her suitcase, under some clothes."

"And she never mentioned them to you, or how she got them?"

"No."

He was silent for a moment as he studied her. "Have you been through all of her things now?"

"Of what was at my apartment, yes. I haven't been to her place. You've had that closed off."

"What about stuff she might have at your parents' house?" Jack asked, ignoring her comment.

"I haven't looked. I don't want to upset my mom and dad. I'm not sure how much she has there, though. She hasn't lived at home in a few years."

Jack tapped the papers against his hand. "Okay. Thank you for this information. I'll look into it."

A polite, but strained, smile tipped Allie's lips. "You're welcome. I hope it helps."

"Yes, ma'am." Jack turned to me. "Can you hang back a minute?"

I fought the urge to let my shoulders sink and to groan. Of course he would want to talk to me. Probably to give me another lecture about how I was sticking my nose where it didn't belong. "Sure," I said, my tone clipped.

I turned to Allie. "I guess it's a good thing we drove separately."

Her smile turned more genuine. "I guess so. Thank you for coming with me."

"You're welcome." Reaching out, I squeezed her forearm. "If you need anything, you know how to find me."

"Yes, thank you." Lifting a hand in farewell, she waved to Jack, then left.

When I turned back to him after watching her leave, he had crossed his arms, that scowl back in place.

I rolled my eyes. "Don't look at me like that. I wasn't trying to get involved. She came to me of her own free will."

He snorted softly. "Of course she did. You're a danger magnet."

"I fail to see how delivering a few invoices to you constitutes putting myself in danger, but okay. Sure." I mirrored his posture, refusing to let him intimidate me.

Jack blew out a breath and let his arms fall. "You're involved. That's enough. Did you do anything else with this information?" He raised the papers.

"No. She brought them to me right before we came here. All she wanted was some moral support when she brought them to you." I didn't tell him Allie found him intimidating. I wasn't entirely sure he wouldn't grin and say, "Good," in that low, sexy voice.

"Did she tell you anything else about them?"

"Only that she followed Leo around a bit after she found the papers. She said she never confronted him to ask what he knew about them, but she asked someone else she knows in the logging industry what they use cyanide for. I guess it's a fumigant for pests."

"And that's all you know?"

"Yes."

"Do you know who this is listed on the invoice?" He pointed to the name on the papers.

"No. Ask Morris. He might."

"I plan to."

"Good. Did you find out anything more about the man James saw with Ella?"

Jack tipped a finger at me, shaking it. "There you go, asking questions that are none of your business."

I huffed. "I'm only trying to help. Maybe I know the person." I met a lot of people in my job, and I was active in the community. It was highly probable I'd seen the man around town somewhere.

"I'm sure you do, but I can find out what I need to know without putting you in danger."

"Telling you details about a person is hardly going to put me in danger. Anyone could tell you the same thing."

Jack sighed and pinched the bridge of his nose. "Delaney…"

I couldn't help but chuckle at his exasperation. Goading him made up for the scowls he directed my way. "Fine. I'll stay out of it."

"Thank you." He dropped his hand.

"For now."

"Delaney."

The warning note in Jack's voice sent shivers down my spine. Not the bad kind. No, these were the, growl-at-me-like-that-while-you-say-naughty-things-to-me, kind of shivers.

Grinning, I backed away and waggled my fingers. "Bye, Jack."

Even though I could feel the daggers he glared at my back as I walked away, it couldn't stop the satisfaction that poured through my veins. I'd managed to get under the handsome detective's skin.

Thirteen

"**Y**ou have to save me, Delaney."

Daphne breezed into my house the moment I opened the door, clutching her wedding binder. Her fiancé, Morgan, followed her inside, carrying several reusable shopping bags.

I met his gaze. Exasperated amusement shone in his dark eyes.

Eyebrows twitching with a curious frown, I turned to my sister as I shut the door. "Save you from what?"

"Mom." She plunked her binder down on my kitchen island.

"Mom?" Even more curious now, I glanced at Morgan again. He just shrugged.

"What did she do?" I asked Daphne.

"You know how I've been trying to figure out the final menu for the wedding?" She flipped open the binder.

"Yes. I thought you had it figured out, though."

"I did. Then our cousins down in Nevada RSVP'd. Stella called Mom and asked if there would be a gluten-free option for dinner. Mom decided rather than adding a dish to the menu, she would just have Dad alter *all* his recipes to make them gluten-free." Her nose wrinkled. "That is not going to happen." Plastic slid against itself as she flipped through the sleeved pages.

"Okay. So, how am I supposed to save you from her? Dad's the one doing the cooking."

"We're going to put our collective heads together this evening and figure that out. I don't mind a gluten-free dish on the menu, but I refuse to eat gluten-free pasta at my wedding."

I chuckled. That I understood. Dad made the best home-made pasta. I was sure whatever gluten-free option he came up with would be great, but it would never be on the same level as his regular pasta. "Okay, well then, let's figure this out. Do you have any idea of a plan yet?"

Before Daphne could answer, a quick knock sounded on the front door a second before it opened again. Darcy breezed in, holding James's hand.

"All right. What's the emergency?" Darcy asked.

"Gluten," Morgan answered.

Daphne smacked his shoulder. "This is serious." Despite her words, a small smile toyed with her mouth. "Do you want gummy pasta at our wedding?" She waggled a finger at him. "Because you know that's what will happen if Dad has to make a lot of it. It'll sit in the pans and just absorb sauce and condensation, turning it into a gelatinous mess." She shuddered.

Darcy sidled up to the island. "You called an emergency family meeting because of gluten-free pasta?"

"Yes. Now sit down and help me find the best—but easiest —gluten-free meal for Dad to make for just Stella and her family."

"How are we supposed to do that?" James asked. "None of us eat gluten-free."

Daphne turned the binder around, then pointed to the

shopping bags Morgan held. "I have a bunch of recipes for us to try, and I brought the ingredients."

I heaved a sigh. Apparently, we were cooking. "Warn a girl next time, would you? I was looking forward to my date with my book boyfriend."

Darcy snickered. "Real men are more fun."

I grinned. "Oh, I don't know about that. This guy is pretty, um, adventurous."

Morgan groaned and held up a hand. "You can spare us the details."

"You just don't think you can measure up," Darcy quipped.

"Hey." Daphne pierced Darcy with a look. "He measures up just fine." She waggled her eyebrows.

Darcy's nose wrinkled as we all laughed.

"Okay, let's get down to business, shall we?" I nodded to the binder. "What's the first recipe you want to try?"

Daphne pointed at a recipe for soup, and the five of us got to work.

"Delaney, you should call Jack and invite him over to help us."

Heat crawled up my neck. I shot a glare at Darcy, who stared back with a smirk. "I'm good, thanks."

She shrugged. "I'm just saying… I bet he's better than your book boyfriend."

Daphne snorted, choking on suppressed laughter.

"Speaking of Jack, how's the investigation into Ella's death going?" James asked.

Happily, I pounced on the change of subject. "I'm not totally sure. I know he's working a few leads, but where those will take him, or if any of them will pan out, I'm not sure." I shot a curious frown at James. "Didn't you say you saw Ella arguing with someone on the street?"

"I did. No clue who the man was. Just some older guy. Not her dad. Jack showed me a picture of him."

"Could you hear what they were talking about?" Morgan asked.

"No. They were too far away. The weird thing, though, is she looked like she knew him, but not well."

"You never mentioned that." Darcy frowned up at her boyfriend. "What do you mean?"

James shifted and shrugged one shoulder. "You know how if you run into someone you know, but only as an acquaintance, it's a bit awkward and your posture can reflect that?"

She nodded, as did the rest of us.

"That's what it felt like. She was just... standoffish. But not in a stranger danger sort of way." He shrugged. "I don't know. Like I said, it was weird."

"So, what suspects does Jack have?" Daphne looked over her shoulder as she washed potatoes at the sink.

I donned my apron and opened the gluten-free flour Daphne bought, measuring out several tablespoons to make a roux. "As far as I know it's just Leo, Ella's ex-boyfriend, and the guy James saw."

"He hasn't found any other enemies or skeletons in her closet?" Morgan measured out some oil into my stockpot.

"If he has, he isn't sharing." Which drove me crazy. I provided him with information. He could have the decency to do the same. Logically, I knew his job probably prevented it, but it was still irksome.

"So, what do we know about Ella's life?" Darcy asked as we settled into a rhythm, cooking.

I glanced up. "Not that much. She has a younger sister, she worked for Scarlett, and she was a college student."

"What was her major?" Morgan dumped a pile of vegetables into a pot.

"Photography," I answered, still stirring my roux.

That brought a thoughtful frown to his face. "Has anyone looked at her image files? Maybe she photographed something she shouldn't have."

I paused, considering that. "I don't know." Leave it to the lawyer to think of something like that.

"You should call Jack," Daphne said.

"He's probably already looked into it." He was already annoyed with me over my involvement. Calling him to check on how thoroughly he's investigating would only make that worse.

But what if he hasn't, my conscience whispered. My lips tightened and my eyes narrowed. That nagging little voice would just linger unless I did what Daphne suggested. I glanced down at the pot on the stove. The roux was ready. Reaching for the vegetable broth, I poured an entire carton into the pan, gave it a good stir, then turned up the heat so it would boil. "Darcy, can you add the pasta to that when it boils?" I pointed to the pan as I backed away to get my phone. My sister nodded and dug into one of the grocery bags for the gluten-free pasta Daphne brought.

"Tell him to come over," Daphne said, aiming a knowing smile at me. "We have plenty of food."

The words to tell her to forget it were on the tip of my tongue when it occurred to me that feeding him might soften him up and make him less defensive.

Giving my sister the side-eye, I unlocked my phone and found Jack's number.

It rang just twice before he picked up. "Fiore."

The bit of low grumble in his slightly distracted voice sent a delightful shiver down my spine. He had such a nice voice.

I cleared my throat. "Hi Jack. It's Delaney."

A short pause met my greeting.

"Hi." The distracted note was gone, replaced with a healthy dose of caution. "What's up? You didn't find another body, did you?"

I huffed. One day, he'd stop assuming that. "No. I was calling to invite you over for dinner. My sisters are here, and we're trying out some recipes for Daphne's wedding. We got on the subject of Ella's death, which got us talking about you, and we just thought you might appreciate a nice meal." I crossed my fingers and silently asked for forgiveness for the blatant white lie.

James snorted, and I shot him a glare, daring him to say something.

"Oh. Actually, um, that sounds nice. Are you sure?" Jack asked.

My heart rate kicked up. Was he saying yes? "Of course I'm sure. We're at my house. Do you know the address?"

"Not off the top of my head. What is it?"

I rattled it off.

"You want me to come now?"

"If you can, sure. We're still cooking, but you're welcome to join us. Morgan and James are here too."

"Okay. I'll be over in a few minutes, then. Thank you, Delaney."

Guilt threatened to overwhelm me, but I clamped down on the urge to rat myself out. "You're welcome. We'll see you soon." We said goodbye and hung up.

I tossed the phone on to the island and aimed a fierce look at my siblings and their significant others. "This will not be an interrogation, understand?" I waited for each of them to nod in turn before continuing. "We'll just let the conversation flow naturally. I don't want to alienate him by making him think we only invited him over to pick his brain." I raised a finger. "Which we didn't. That's only part of the reason."

Morgan chuckled. "I'm sure he has his suspicions, Delaney. He's not a stupid man."

No, he certainly was far from dumb.

And I was also rather predictable. He knew I couldn't keep my nose out of a good mystery.

Fourteen

T he doorbell pealed through the house, setting off a quick tattoo in my chest.

Jack was here.

Calling myself all sorts of silly for being nervous, I wiped my hands on my apron and stepped away from the stove. Crossing to the door, I unlocked it and pulled it open.

A friendly but cautious smile flitted over Jack's face. "Hi."

My cheeks heated, and I quickly stepped back to let him in, hoping to disguise my reaction. "Hi." Tamping down the flutters erupting in my belly at that innocent but handsome smile, I shut the door behind him.

"It smells good in here."

I chuckled. "Hopefully, the food tastes as good as it smells. It's all gluten-free."

A small frown twitched between Jack's eyebrows. "Why wouldn't it taste good?"

"I'm just joking. It'll be fine. Well, except for maybe the pasta." I wrinkled my nose. I still wasn't too keen on that. Daphne was right. If you didn't cook it correctly, the texture was terrible.

"I will not overcook the pasta." Daphne, from her spot in front of the stove, held a wooden spoon in the air over a pot.

Jack chuckled. "Good to know." He turned to me. "Thanks again for the invitation. I was debating what to do for dinner when you called. I much prefer home cooking to take-out." He glanced toward the stove. "Even gluten-free home cooking."

Turning, I headed back to the kitchen. Jack followed, sidling up to the island beside James.

"What do you all want me to do?"

"Tell us what you've been up to," Darcy said.

Jack's expression closed slightly.

I glared at my sister. "Ignore her. You can set the table, if you want. Plates and bowls are up there." I pointed to the cabinet to the right of the sink. "Silverware is in the drawer below."

With a bit of wariness still marring his handsome features, he wandered over to the cupboard. "I'm under no illusion I'm only here for dinner. You might as well ask your questions and get it all out of the way."

The guilt eating at me tore deeper into my gut. Shame swiftly chased. "I'm sorry, Jack. You're right that we had an ulterior motive for inviting you here, and that's wrong. We won't ask anything of you, because despite evidence to the contrary, we would all like to get to know you better." I looked at the others. "Right?"

A chorus of affirmatives sounded.

Jack let out a quick snort and opened the cabinet. "I appreciate your honesty and contrition, Delaney, but let's not put off the questions." He took down a stack of plates, then glanced at me, a small smile tipping one side of his mouth. "Besides, I have to admit, you've been useful."

I blinked, my mind refusing to register his words for the compliment they were.

Who was this man?

Apparently, the way to get Jack to loosen up about my involvement in his case was to invite him to dinner.

"Okay, fine," I conceded. "It's not so much a question for you, but an observation." I walked over and picked up the plates, taking them to the table.

Jack followed with a handful of silverware. "What sort of observation?"

"Ella was a college student." I sent him a pointed look as I laid out the plates. "Studying photography."

His brows twitched. "Okay?"

"Have you looked through her photographs? Maybe she took pictures of something someone doesn't want to get out."

The twitch turned into a deep vee. I could see he hadn't considered that.

"We didn't find any cameras in her apartment."

"None?" Morgan asked. "That seems unusual for a photography major. Was there any other photography equipment?"

"A few lights and backgrounds. Her computer had photo editing software installed. And before you ask" —he held up a hand—"we looked at all the images she had saved. Nothing stuck out."

"So far." James tipped a finger. "As you learn more, something might make more sense."

"Where else would she keep her equipment?" Darcy asked. "Her parents' house?"

"Maybe." I went back to the kitchen for bowls. "They could be at school. Can you store that sort of thing at a photography lab?" I looked at Jack.

"I don't know," he answered. "But I'll find out."

"I'll talk to Scarlett tomorrow and see if she might know where Ella kept her stuff. You could ask Allie too," I added absently, thinking out loud.

Jack's slow chuckle filled the room, bringing me out of my thoughts.

I frowned. "What? Why are you laughing?"

He grinned and shook his head. "Is this what you all do when you get together? Speculate?"

"Hey, he's learning." Darcy waved a hand at him and laughed. The rest of us chuckled.

"Many heads are better than one," Daphne said.

I nodded, sending a pointed look at Jack. "It's true."

"I hardly work in a vacuum."

"No, but the Fernwood police force isn't that large. And we offer a different and unique perspective." I gestured to my sisters, Morgan, and James.

Jack arched an eyebrow and went back to putting silverware at each place setting. "Possibly. In any case, I agree that it's good to have a different set of eyes on things sometimes."

I set the last bowl down, then propped my hands on my hips. "All right, where's the scowling cop who keeps telling me to keep my nose out of things?" This was twice now he'd indicated he wasn't upset at our interference. What was going on?

Jack waved a hand. "He's off duty."

I could only stare.

He chuckled. "I'm allowed to relax, Delaney. Now, can we talk about something else? I don't have any more information that I can give you about Ella, so unless you have something else you wish to impart, let's change the subject."

I narrowed my eyes at his choice of words. "No other information that you can give? Does that mean you have other information, but you just can't share it?"

He sighed and glanced heavenward. "Of course it does. There's always information in a murder investigation that's kept in-house. I need something to help me determine I have the right person."

"Maybe you should share it with us. You know none of us did it. Maybe we can help you figure out the information's significance."

A slow, amused smile formed on his face. "You just don't quit, do you?"

I couldn't help but smile back. "No."

His grin widened. "I admire your tenacity." Holding my gaze for another moment, he looked past me. "So, is anyone a Mariners fan?"

Darcy snorted a laugh. "Subtle."

With an amused glance at his girlfriend, James raised a hand. "I like baseball."

From there, the conversation devolved into the stats for the Mariners' star players, and their chances in the post-season. As we sat down to eat, I couldn't stop sneaking glances at the handsome detective. He fit into our group so effortlessly. This would no doubt fuel Daphne and Darcy's attempts to get me to date Jack.

I had no problem with that. But before tonight, I had my doubts about whether he was interested.

I spared him another glance as I ladled soup into my bowl.

Was he interested now?

Did I want him to be? Because fantasizing about a relationship with a handsome, intense man was one thing. Living it was another.

Jack looked up and caught me staring. Those deep, dark, fathomless eyes arrested my breath. Electric tension arced between us, making my blood race.

Breathe! my mind screamed.

I blinked, breaking the trance.

Whoa.

That was intense. Whether I wanted a relationship with him or not, I might not be able to resist him. It seemed like biology might take over and make the decision for us.

I cast another look at him through my lashes. A soft frown turned down the corners of his mouth and wrinkled the space between his eyebrows as he twirled a bit of pasta onto his fork.

Maybe I wasn't the only one grappling with my feelings.

Fifteen

Warm sunshine kissed my skin as I walked down the sidewalk toward Scarlett's shop. I had a half hour to kill before I needed to pack up my dessert truck for a street festival in a neighboring town this evening. It had been a few days since I talked to my friend, and I wanted to see how she was doing, both in coping with Ella's death and with her dad. I also wanted to check with her about Ella's photography equipment.

The bell over the door chimed as I entered. My gaze went to the counter as I crossed the threshold, but no one was at the register.

"Oh, hey."

I turned at the sound of Scarlett's voice. She peered out from behind a rack of fall sweaters, smiling at me.

I returned her smile. "Hey. How's it going?"

"Oh, fine. Just putting out some new inventory while it's quiet." She hung up the last sweater. "What's up?"

"Nothing much. I just came to see how you were holding up."

Some of the joviality left Scarlett's face. Wrinkles appeared in her forehead. "I'm doing okay. I miss her, but it's not soul-crushing. She and I weren't friends like you and I are. If you died, I would be a blubbering mess, and the store would not be open right now. I would be on my couch in my pajamas and my fluffy bear slippers while I stuff my face with ice-cream and mac and cheese."

I let out a quick snicker. "Good to know I'll be missed."

She chuckled. "Very much so."

"Have you advertised for her replacement yet?"

"No." Scarlett fingered one of the sweaters she just put out. "We might not have been terribly close, but it feels too soon to fill her position. I don't mind working her hours for a few weeks. I can rearrange other aspects of my life for a bit."

I hummed a non-committal sound, then after a brief pause, continued. "Jack was at my house last night."

Scarlett's melancholic expression shifted instantly. Her eyebrows shot up with surprise and curiosity. "Really? Why?" A sly smile overtook her face. "What did you do?"

I laughed. "Nothing. Daphne and Darcy came over with Morgan and James. We were trying to come up with a gluten-free food option for Daphne and Morgan's wedding." I waved a hand. "Anyway, we got to talking about Ella, and my sisters, being who they are, convinced me to invite him over."

"To help with the food or to discuss the case?"

"Both." I tilted my head to the side, briefly. "Though it was probably mostly to discuss the case." I held up a finger. "They're both working hard to convince us to date, though."

Scarlett chuckled. "With good reason. I've seen the way you two look at each other."

My face heated. I cleared my throat. "That's beside the point. As part of our discussion about Ella, we pointed out she was a photography major."

"What does that have to do with anything?" Scarlett frowned.

"We surmised that maybe she took pictures of something she shouldn't have."

"Ohhh." Scarlett's eyes widened. "That would make a lot of sense. She was always walking around with her camera, taking pictures. She used to do it here when business was slow. She'd find an interesting print on a piece of clothing and photograph it in different ways. She even did most of the mannequin shots I used on social media."

"But you know what Jack didn't find when he searched her apartment?" I arched an eyebrow. "Her cameras."

A quick frown slashed Scarlett's forehead. "What? Why wouldn't there be any cameras at her apartment? Did he find other photography stuff there?"

I nodded. "Some of her lights and backdrops. He said there were some images stored on her computer, but nothing stood out to him. Do you know where she might store her cameras? Would they be at school?"

"Maybe? I'm not too sure. She never said anything about where she kept them. She always just showed up to work with one in tow."

"How many did she have, do you know?"

"Oh, gosh." Scarlett looked heavenward, thinking. "At least three. She had the fancy one with the interchangeable lenses, a digital camera—that one she used a lot in here—and a Polaroid. She liked that one for collages."

"Did she ever mention taking pictures of something that felt… I don't know… sketchy?"

Scarlett's mouth flattened, and she shook her head. "Not that I remember."

I let out a long breath, discouraged that Scarlett didn't know more. I shouldn't be, though. I hadn't expected her to know much.

"I'm sorry I couldn't be of more help. I want her murder solved as much as anyone."

I waved a hand. "I know. It just feels like the camera thing is important, you know? Like it might be the missing piece of the puzzle. I was just hoping you could shed some light on where they might be."

"I wish I could too. But at least now you can tell Jack they're not—" She stopped, her eyes growing round. "Wait."

I frowned. "What?"

She dipped around a clothing rack and headed for the back of the store.

Perplexed, I blinked twice. "Where are you going?" I hurried after her.

She didn't answer as she pushed through the swinging door to the back, just held up a finger as she rounded the corner to go down the basement stairs.

Our footsteps scuffed over the concrete steps as we descended. Scarlett flipped the light switch and several bare bulbs flickered to life. She breezed past the first set of shelving, then stopped about halfway back.

"So, Ella asked if she could commandeer this section of shelving for some of her photography stuff. There were a lot of days where she would come directly from school, then work the next morning before she had a class in the afternoon, and it was just easier for her to leave some things here instead of hauling them home. I completely forgot, because there was never much down here."

I glanced at the shelf. My heart rate kicked up. A small digital camera and a little blue case sat squarely on the shelf.

Sixteen

"You know, when we talked about Ella and all her photography equipment last night, I never actually thought you'd find any of it." Jack sent me a quick but quietly exasperated look.

I shrugged as a small smile tugged at the corners of my mouth. "What can I say? I guess I'm just lucky."

He gave a short scoff. "You're something, but I don't think I'd call it lucky." Sweeping a hand out, he nodded toward the back of the store. "Show me what you found."

Scarlett, who'd been standing nearby, spun on her heel and led the way to the basement. The three of us stopped in front of the shelf. Scarlett pointed at the camera and small case.

Jack's lips flattened. "Did either of you touch it?"

"No," I said. "As soon as Scarlett showed it to me, I called you."

"Okay." He reached into his pants pocket and withdrew a set of black nitrile gloves. Snapping them on, he took a small kit from another pocket on his cargo pants and unzipped it. Withdrawing a foldable ruler, he opened it and set it beside the items on the shelf. From yet another pocket, he took a digital camera.

After photographing both the camera and the small case, he turned on the camera, checking for stored images.

Scarlett and I crowded in as he pulled up the image files. Jack aimed a quick frown at us but didn't stop us from looking at the pictures with him.

"Most of these look like they're of the store." The camera beeped softly as Jack pushed the button to flip through the pictures.

"Yeah," Scarlett said. "They're photos for social media. She would stage mannequins and post the pictures."

Picture after picture of clothing racks and staged mannequins scrolled over the screen before it shifted to images of students in a classroom, then to quick shots of pictures clipped to a drying line.

I squinted at those, trying to make out what was in the images, but the tiny digital screen made it hard to tell.

"I need to blow these up," Jack muttered, echoing my thoughts. "Do either of you recognize anything from these beside the store?"

"It just looks like a college classroom to me," Scarlett said. "She probably took them at school."

"What about the people?" he asked. "Is anyone familiar?"

I shared a glance with Scarlett. "I don't recognize anyone. Do you?"

She shook her head. "No."

He reached the end of the camera roll and shut it off. "Is there anything of Ella's anywhere else in the store?" His dark eyes studied Scarlett's face.

"I don't think so." She glanced around the basement, a small frown between her eyebrows. "You're welcome to look. I think most everything down here is inventory or stuff for displays. She asked to use this shelf, specifically, so her things wouldn't get lost in the shuffle. There was never much on it. Her purse or backpack. Sometimes a camera. I don't know if she ever put anything elsewhere. There aren't any cameras down here."

The bell from the front door dinged, the sound muffled through the floor. All three of us looked up, then Jack nodded once.

"I'll have a look around."

Scarlett turned toward the steps. "Let me know if you need anything else."

"I will."

She hurried away, her feet making quick scuffling sounds on the steps.

"There is a lot of crap down here." Jack sighed.

I glanced up at his handsome face, noting the perturbed expression turning down his eyebrows and mouth. "I can help you look."

For a moment, he hesitated, his gaze still roaming the dingy basement, before he turned those dark eyes on me.

My heart fluttered. Why, I didn't know. It wasn't a particularly flirtatious or heated look. Just a normal glance.

"Are you sure? It might take a while."

Mentally, I ran through the things I needed to do before my event later. I always gave myself a cushion when packing up, just in case. I decided to cut the time to the bare bones. "I can spare about twenty minutes. I have an event in Longfellow tonight I need to get ready for soon."

"Okay. I'll take it." He looked around again. "Because there is a lot here."

My gaze followed his. "I think it's less than you think. A lot of it is sealed inventory."

"I hope so. Let's get to work."

We split up, each taking a side. I headed for the darker, more chaotic end of the basement. Scarlett stored a lot of her seasonal display stuff at this end. I knew mostly what should be there. If something didn't belong, I would likely recognize it. Plus, letting Jack have the other end where most of the inventory was might make him feel like he was getting through more.

"Thank you again for dinner last night."

My head popped up from the box I was rooting through. "Oh. You're welcome. I'm sorry we had ulterior motives, but I'm glad you came regardless." I offered him a soft smile.

A lopsided grin formed on his face as he shifted one box to look at another. "Like I said, I expected some degree of inquisition. I still appreciated the meal, though."

"We'll have to do it again. No strings attached."

His smile shifted to something softer. "I'd like that. Maybe we could try just the two of us."

Every fiber in my being froze right down to the breath in my lungs.

Did he just ask me out?

I blinked, forcing my body back into action. "Oh. That would—"

"Get out!"

Jumping at Scarlett's shout, I turned my face toward the ceiling. A muffled male voice carried through the floorboards.

The scuff of shoes on the dusty concrete floor drew my attention away from above. I turned to see Jack hurrying toward the stairs.

I ran after him.

As I crested the top of the stairs, the voices grew louder, and I could make out what was being said.

"I don't care! I told you I don't want to talk to you ever again. Why won't you listen?"

Even from this distance, I could hear the anger seething in Scarlett's tight voice.

"Scarlett—your mother—"

I walked through the swinging doors to see Scarlett raise a

hand to point an angry finger at a man. Angled away from me, I couldn't see his face.

"Don't you dare mention her! You're not fit to utter her name."

"Hey." Jack moved swiftly through the clothing racks toward the checkout counter. "What's the problem here?"

The man turned and I got my first good look at his face. It was one I'd seen just a handful of times in pictures: Scarlett's father, Don.

Oh boy.

"This is none of your business." Don raised his nose, looking down it at Jack. "Go back to shopping. We'll be done in a minute."

Scarlett's mouth dropped open in an O of surprise. My eyes widened at his audacity.

Before either of us could say anything, a self-satisfied smirk appeared on Jack's face.

He reached into his pocket. "Really? Because you're disturbing the peace, and this"—he held up his detective's shield—"let's me intervene to restore the peace."

I wrapped an arm around my middle and propped the other on it, hiding my sudden smile with my hand.

Don's face paled, but to his credit, the confidence in his expression remained. "I'm sorry we raised our voices. My daughter is spirited, and we were having a disagreement."

Scarlett snorted and rolled her eyes.

My grin widened behind my hand. Don needed to stop talking. He had no idea who Jack and I were or our relationship to Scarlett.

"I heard." Jack put his badge away. "Regardless, this is Scarlett's store, and I clearly heard her tell you to leave. Now, are you going to comply, or would you rather leave in handcuffs?"

Some of the confidence bled from Don's face. His gaze

darted to Scarlett, who now stood with her arms crossed, glaring at him.

"Whether he leaves voluntarily or not, will you trespass him, please?" Scarlett asked.

A quick grin slashed across Jack's face. "Happily."

"There's no need for that." Don held up a hand. "I'll leave—"

"Where's your paperwork for that?" I stepped forward, eyes locked on Jack as I cut off Don's protest. "Is it in your cruiser?"

"It is." Jack removed a set of keys from his pocket. "Would you care to get it for me?"

"I was just about to offer." I took the keys when he held them out.

"The car's out front. Forms are in the trunk in a file box. Everything is labeled. I need the one marked 'trespass form.'"

"Really, this isn't necessary." Don huffed, now clearly annoyed.

"Oh, but it is," I said, walking toward the door. "I'll be right back."

Exiting the store, I glanced around, spotting Jack's department SUV parked a few spaces down to the left. I hurried over to it and pressed the unlock button. Trespassing Don was hardly all he deserved after the things he said to Scarlett, but it would have to do. Maybe he'd put up a struggle while I was gone, and Jack would have him flat on his belly by the time I returned. The man needed to spend some time in jail.

Opening the back hatch, I quickly located the file box and the form Jack wanted. After locking the vehicle up again, I went back inside. Unfortunately, Don was still on his feet and unencumbered by handcuffs.

"Here you go." I held out the form to Jack.

"Thank you." Taking it, he set it on the counter and pulled the pen off his collar. "May I see your ID, sir?"

Hesitation flitted over Don's face briefly before he produced his driver's license with a scowl.

I bit back another grin and moved closer to Scarlett, watching Jack fill out the paperwork and inform Don of what would happen if he violated the trespass order.

Finally, Don stomped out the door as unsatisfied as a fox who got chased out of the chicken coop by the farm's guard dog.

As the last notes from the bell over the door faded after his departure, Scarlett blew out a breath, ruffling the few wisps of hair around her face. "I'd like to say I could have handled him fine, but I'm glad you were here. Thank you, Jack."

"You're welcome. And might I suggest you file a restraining order first thing Monday morning? He can still contact you without any legal ramifications until you do."

Her mouth flattened. "Yeah. I should probably do that."

I reached out, running a hand over her arm. "I'm sorry, Scarlett. Parents shouldn't be jerks to their children." Fate could be cruel. Scarlett didn't deserve to have a crappy dad. No one did, really.

"No, they shouldn't. But now I know he's not worth my time. All he wanted was money." She looked at Jack.

He nodded once, sympathy shining in his eyes. "I'm going to head back downstairs."

"Are you going to be okay down there alone?" I asked. "I need to get going." Lifting my arm, I gestured to the watch on my wrist.

"It won't be the first chaotic basement I've searched alone. Go ahead and get ready for your event. I'll talk to you later."

Was it just me, or was there more to that statement? It was hard to tell with Jack. Not only did he have all that police training on keeping his cool, those dark eyes of his hid all his thoughts. But I swear there was a bit of... *something* in his gaze.

In the next instant, though, his cool mask slipped back

into place with a blink, leaving me wondering if I was imagining things.

Tamping down my curiosity about what that fleeting look meant, I pasted a friendly smile on my face. "All right, then. I guess I'll leave you to it." I turned to Scarlett. "If you want to get away this evening, come hang out with me in Longfellow. I'll drown your troubles in chocolate chip cookies."

She laughed. "I might do that."

Seventeen

"Come on, come on, turn, lady," I muttered, frowning at the car in front of me. All I wanted was to turn right into the grocery store just up ahead, but a little old lady in her ancient Buick wanted to turn left into the local doctor's clinic. When I packed up for tonight's event, I realized I was short on butter to make extra buttercream if I needed to. I was already running behind because of the drama at The Whispering Fern, but if I ran out of buttercream for my cupcakes, it would be a disaster. My truck didn't have enough storage—cold or otherwise—to carry the amount of extra frosting or iced cupcakes I would need for an event like today's.

Finally, the lady made her turn. I gave the food truck some gas and sped past, braking a moment later to swing into the grocery store lot. Parking where there were several open spots, I killed the engine and hopped out, snagging my purse as I slid from the seat. Quickly jogging across the parking lot, I breezed through the sliding doors as they swished open for me.

Passing the shopping baskets, I snatched one from the stand without stopping and hurried toward the butter at the back of the store.

I didn't even bother with the single boxes, instead filling the basket with the bulk packs. In seconds, I had what I needed.

Planting my heel, I spun. In my haste to get my butter and get out, though, I didn't notice the young man coming out of the back, pushing a cart full of inventory.

A soft squeal left me as I pulled up, trying not to crash into the stacks of boxes. Windmilling my free arm, I somehow managed to stay upright and only bump the top box at the end of the cart.

"Oh, sorry."

Somehow, the young man managed to sound both ticked and bored.

I glanced up, deciding to ignore the former. It was my fault I nearly crashed into him. That didn't excuse the slight note of censure in those two words he uttered, but it wasn't worth making it out to be something. "No worries. I should have watched where I was going."

He tipped his chin. "Yeah."

My mouth flattened. I glanced at his name tag, then frowned when I read it.

Leo.

What were the odds this was Ella's Leo?

Probably low, I argued with myself. He worked for the lumber industry, not for the local grocer.

My gaze returned to his face. He was the right age, though.

Never one to shy away from difficult questions, I let my curiosity get the best of me. "Are you Leo Stanhope?"

The young man paused, the bored expression on his face darkening as a deep frown took over his features. "Who wants to know?"

"Oh, I'm no one. Just a friend of your girlfriend's boss."

His already deep frown grew darker. "Then didn't you hear? She dumped me and she's dead."

My eyebrows shot up. *Whoa.* Someone was a bit bitter. I cleared my throat. "I did hear that. I'm sorry."

"Don't be." He gave the cart a shove, nearly hitting me with it. "I'm not. Excuse me. I have work to do."

Well, that was interesting...

Stepping back, I let him go without another word. There was a lot to unpack in that short interaction, but it would have to wait until later when I had time to think about it. Right now, I had butter to buy and an event to get to.

Checking out only took me a minute, thanks to self-checkout. I knew some people hated it, but I wasn't one of them. The faster I could get in and out of the grocery store, the better.

Back in my truck, I tossed the sack full of butter onto the passenger seat and headed out. A quick glance at the clock told me I was cutting it close, but I should still be up and running with a few minutes to spare, so long as nothing else slowed me down.

Reaching for the radio, I flipped it on and hummed along as I made the twenty-minute drive to Longfellow. Trees whizzed by, the colors just starting to emerge now that we were into late September.

I loved this time of year. Not just for the changes in the landscape. Fall festivals abounded. One of my favorite things about owning a food truck was going to them all and getting to meet all the people who came out for a few hours of family fun.

Turning off the highway, I meandered down a couple side streets before finally arriving at the address where I was supposed to set up. The town closed off the main street and a few side streets and had all the vendors set up on the roads.

Angling between two other food trucks, I set the parking brake and shut off the engine.

"All right," I muttered to myself, unbuckling my seat belt. "Let's get busy."

Set up went quickly. After so many events, I had it down to a science. Even running behind, I had a few minutes to spare by the time I finished. I definitely didn't like cutting it so close, but it was nice to know I didn't need as much time as I thought I did.

The warm evening drew quite a crowd as people soaked up the last days of summer-like weather. The queue to my truck window quickly grew, and I suddenly wished I'd asked someone to come work this event with me. I didn't think I would need help, though. It was just a weekend street festival. Nothing too special. But this weather… it was bringing everyone out.

Tightening my apron strings, I pulled my resolve around me like a cloak. I could do this. My truck was set up for efficiency. I was a well-oiled machine.

Thirty minutes later, my well-oiled machine was overheating and starting to wheeze a bit.

I wiped a bead of sweat from my brow and sucked down a gulp of water from my giant tumbler to quench my dry throat. Silly me had forgotten to bring a fan.

Correction: I hadn't forgotten it. I decided not to lug it into the truck. It was an evening event at the beginning of fall. I hadn't thought I'd need it.

Boy was I wrong.

I took another draw on my water. Before long, I would need to find a way to get a refill.

Putting the cup down with a metallic clunk, I leaned down to peer through the window at the next customer. "What can I—hey!" A wide smile turned up my mouth at the sight of Jack's handsome face. "I didn't expect to see you here."

He lifted a shoulder and offered me a cockeyed smile. "Decided to go for a drive and explore a little."

"Yeah? So, what do you think of Longfellow?"

He turned his head, glancing around. "I think it's busy."

I laughed. "You should be on this side of the window."

A small frown marred his forehead as he peered inside the truck. "Are you by yourself?"

"Yep."

"Why? Couldn't anyone come with you?"

"I didn't ask. I honestly didn't think it would be this busy." I nodded to the line behind him.

He glanced back, then at me with a contemplative look in his eyes. After a moment's hesitation, he spoke. "You want some help?"

My mouth dropped open. Just as quickly, I snapped it shut, lest I look like a guppy. "You want to help me?"

Jack shrugged. "Why not? I'm here. I've already walked around some, but I'm not ready to go home." That cockeyed smile returned, bringing a spark of daredevil to his eyes. "What do you say? You want an apprentice?"

A slow, answering grin spread over my face. Oh, I could have some fun with this. "An apprentice, huh?"

He nodded.

"Do you solemnly swear to listen to me and do whatever I say?"

He chuckled. "So help me God?"

I laughed. "Something like that."

"Sure. Just pay me in one of those fruit tarts, and I'll do whatever you want."

Heat licked my stomach at the thought. "That can be arranged. Come around back." I gestured behind me.

When he disappeared from view, I swiped my suddenly damp palms on my jeans.

Down, girl. He's here for food treats, not any other kind.

I knew my inner voice was right, but it didn't stop me from wishing for more. Maybe one day.

The back door opened, and Jack stepped inside, immediately filling the small space. The truck was tight, but his mere presence made it even tighter. This was probably a bad idea.

"All right, put me to work." He clapped his hands and rubbed them together, giving me another tipsy smile.

A laugh bubbled free and some of my tension eased. "Grab an apron." I pointed behind him, where a couple extras hung from a hook on the wall.

While he turned around to find one, I went back to the window. "Thanks for your patience, folks. We're going to open a second window, if you give us just another minute."

Turning around again, I was happy to see Jack tying apron strings around his middle. "I hope you're a fast learner, because it's time for a crash course."

"Yep. Hit me."

"I have cookies, cupcakes, and cheesecake today. Nothing's labeled, because, well, I made it all, so I know what everything is. Cookies are in there"—I pointed to the tall cabinet to my left—"cupcakes are there and there"—my finger moved to indicate another tall cabinet and a countertop one as well—"and cheesecake is in the fridge. If you have any questions about what's what, ask."

I turned around and woke up the second tablet, typing in my password. With a couple more clicks, I had the payment app open. "This is pretty self-explanatory. All the items are individually listed. Just tap the ones you want, and it'll give you a total. Hit 'Charge' and the payment screen will come up. If they use a card, you don't have to do anything else. The reader is there." I gestured to the card reader by the window. "If they give you cash, tap 'Cash' on the screen and it'll do the math for you. The cash box is under the counter by the window."

"Sound easy enough. Let's get to work." He motioned me back to the window.

"It's definitely not solving murders, but it'll keep you hopping." I reached for the second window and slid it open. Leaning down to smile at the line of customers, I spoke to the first one in line. "Sorry about your wait. Seems I've found myself a volunteer helper. What can I get you?"

It took us over thirty minutes to catch up. True to his word, Jack quickly learned what everything looked like, and after the first few transactions, didn't have to ask for help.

When a lull in people finally appeared, I sagged against the counter and picked up my water, draining the last ounces from the cup until it slurped.

Jack chuckled. "Do you want me to find you another drink?"

I held out the oversized tumbler. "Yes, please."

He took it. "What do you want?"

Opening the cash box, I took a twenty off the stack of bills. "Lemonade from the lemonade truck. Tell Trudy to fill it up."

He waved away the cash. "I've got it."

A small frown drew my eyebrows down. "No. You're helping me out. If anything, I should buy you a drink."

"Nope. My treat." He backed toward the door. "I'll be right back."

"Jack—"

"You have another customer." He pointed at the window, then stepped out of the truck.

I spun around. A smiling woman with two young girls in tow had stopped to read the menu board.

"Hi." I smiled. "What can I get you?"

The woman ordered cookies for each of her kids and a cupcake for herself. I waited on two more families before Jack returned.

"One fresh lemonade." He held out my tumbler as he stepped inside and shut the door.

"Mmm, thank you." I took a healthy sip. Soury-sweet goodness filled my mouth. I set the cup down. "Thank you for staying to help me. It's been a lot busier than I thought it would be. I might sell out tonight."

"I hope you do. Baking more inventory will keep you out

of trouble." A teasing smile lit his face as he took a sip from the cup of lemonade he got for himself.

I let out an inelegant snort. "Have you met me? I don't have to go looking for trouble."

"That's the truth."

"Case in point, guess who I ran into at the grocery store on my way here?"

Jack groaned and set his lemonade down, crossing his arms over his chest. "Who?"

My gaze stuck on the tanned, sinewy forearms now on full display.

He asked you a question, Delaney.

I blinked. Right. Grocery store encounter.

My gaze snapped to his face. "Leo Stanhope."

"Please tell me you didn't play twenty questions with the man?"

"No. I tried not to knock all the things off his stock cart."

"Stock cart? Wait. Is he working there?"

I nodded. "Odd right?" It didn't really strike me at the time, but it did now. The lumber company paid well, so why did he need to work at the grocery store too? "Is he having money troubles?" My eyebrows went up as I had a thought. "Maybe he's been gambling. Could be Ella didn't like it and wanted him to quit. Or she didn't know and found out and confronted him. Or"—I raised a finger—"maybe he secretly used her money, she found out, and he killed her to keep her silent."

Jack stared at me for several moments. "You have a very wild imagination."

He may not have meant it as one, but I took that as a compliment. "Thanks."

He huffed a soft laugh. "I'm sure there's a perfectly rational reason for Leo to have a second job. Maybe he wanted to buy a house and was saving up for a downpayment. Or he wanted a new car."

My nose wrinkled. "Those are a lot more boring reasons."

"Yes, but they're also more likely."

I sighed. He had a point. "True."

"In any case, I'll have to talk to him about that. I want to ask him about those invoices Ella found too. Haven't had a chance to do that yet." He raised an eyebrow. "Did you talk to anyone else involved in my case in the"—he paused, lifting one arm to glance at his watch—"seven hours since I saw you last?"

"No." I propped my hands on my hips and frowned, pretending to be affronted by the question, but couldn't hold the expression. A wry smirk formed on my face. "I was too busy baking."

Jack laughed. "I knew I had the right idea." He glanced around the truck. "I might have to buy out whatever you don't sell. Keep you in the kitchen and away from my suspects."

"You don't like sweets that much, remember?" I still found that appalling. I'd never met someone without a raging sweet tooth.

"But my colleagues do."

I hummed. "Good point. So, what other quirks do you have besides not liking sweets?"

He let his arms fall to his sides and leaned against the counter. "I have an irrational fear of automatic car washes."

I sputtered a laugh. "What?"

"Automatic car washes. Have you ever been in one? They're terrifying."

"No, they're not. It's just a giant tunnel with brushes."

"Yeah. Brushes that spin at seventy rpm, which is fifteen to twenty-five miles per hour, depending on the size of the brush. If a car hits you at that speed, it hurts. Bones break and deep bruises form."

"Those bristles aren't going to break your bones."

"No, but they'll still hurt. And that's not even the biggest problem with automatic car washes."

"No?" I raised an eyebrow, still in disbelief.

He shook his head once, his expression dead serious. "No. That motorized belt is what nightmares are made of. Your wheels sit in those tracks and are held there, like something out of one of those dystopian novels where people line up willingly for slaughter. What happens if the conveyor belt breaks and stops halfway and you're surrounded by those spinning brushes? You're trapped, that's what. If you don't have a sunroof, you can't get out. Even then, you risk drowning in that nasty, soapy water." A disgusted wrinkle of his nose broke the hard planes of his face.

An amused smile toyed with my lips. "Let me get this straight. You, who has no problem chasing down an armed suspect or busting down a door into a known drug house, are afraid of some soap and water?"

"And large, rapidly spinning brushes that can leave you with an awful case of road-rash, yes. I will choose to spend an hour or more washing my car in my driveway every time over the death trap that is an automatic car wash."

I couldn't stop the bubble of laughter that spilled free.

"Laugh all you want, but if you ever get stuck in one, well, I told you so."

I only laughed harder.

After a moment, he joined in with a chuckle. "I am aware of how crazy it is." He shrugged. "But I still won't use one."

Wiping moisture from my face, my laughter slowly subsided. "Oh, thank you, Jack. I needed to laugh like that."

That lopsided smile returned. "You're welcome. But if you ever take me through a car wash, I will find *some fault* with your driving and make sure you get every ticket I can legally give you."

Another laugh bubbled out. I clamped my lips together. "Duly noted."

Eighteen

The fragrant, rich scent of dark-roast Italian coffee wafted to my nose as I lifted my mug to take a sip. Flavors exploded over my tongue, and I let out a soft hum of appreciation. "This is delicious. Thank you for bringing a bag in for us to drink." I smiled at Carol, who had just poured her own cup.

She returned my smile. "You can thank Morris, actually. He's the one who introduced me to it."

"Well, no matter how you found it, I'm glad you did. It's really good." I took another sip, then set the coffee to the side. "Are you ready to get started?" Being Tuesday, Carol was here with me at the church to bake.

"Yep. What are we doing today?" She set her mug down and reached for an apron.

"Today, I need you to bake about a million cupcakes and a three-tier birthday cake. While you do that, I'm going to work on decorating the cakes we made last Thursday." I had several birthday cakes to crank out before the weekend, as well as the finishing touches for a wedding cake. "First, though, I need to make some tart dough." I promised Jack a fruit tart for helping, and I intended to keep my word.

"Sounds good. I'll start with the cake batter for the three-tier cake. What kind?"

"An eight-inch vanilla, a ten-inch vanilla, and a twelve-inch chocolate. Oh, and a six-inch vanilla for a smash cake. It's for a one-year-old's birthday party." The decorations for those cakes would be a lot of fun. I loved doing little kids' birthday cakes. "But make a lot of batter for those flavors. We need a lot of cupcakes."

Carol's head bobbed. "Got it."

We split up, each grabbing the ingredients we needed, and got to work.

"So, what's the tart dough for? Are you putting that on your dessert truck?" Carol glanced up from cracking eggs into a mixer.

"No. I don't really have the cold storage to store tarts for food truck events. This is a special order. I promised Jack a fruit tart."

Carol's brows twitched into a small frown before she raised an eyebrow. "Jack? Do you mean Detective Fiore?"

My eyes darted up, then back to unwrapping butter and chunking it up into a bowl. "Yes. He helped me at the Longfellow street festival on Saturday. The man doesn't like regular sweets that much, but he likes fruit, so I said I'd make him a tart."

Silence filled the kitchen for several seconds. I looked up to see Carol blinking at me, a smile slowly tipping up her mouth.

"No." I shook my head, cutting her off before she could start. I knew where she was going with that look. "It's not like that. He helped out because I was slammed and just happened to be there. We're friends."

Carol rolled her lips inward, her eyes sparkling with mirth. "Mmm-hmm. Sure, you are. Just like the way he hangs out at the breakfast bar and sits with you at church means you two are just friends."

I let out a soft huff. "That's really all it is."

She chuckled. "You just keep telling yourself that."

My mouth flattened as I kept my lips shut tight to hold in a reply. There was no point in arguing. She, like many others in my life, would just shoot down anything I said.

He did ask you to have dinner alone, my inner voice reminded me.

Shut up, I shot back. We'd been alone together for several hours Saturday, and he hadn't asked again.

Carol chuckled again as she shut the egg carton and reached for a bag of sugar. "So, what did the two of you talk about while you were hip-to-hip in the truck? As friends, I mean."

I sent a quick glare her way, but it had little effect. She just grinned. Rolling my eyes, I let it go. People could think whatever they wanted. I wouldn't let it ruin my mood or get under my skin. "Nothing important. Just chit-chat." Jack's story about his fear of automatic car washes came to mind, and I couldn't completely stop the smile that emerged. "Mostly, we worked, but we had fun."

"That's nice. Did he impart anything else about Ella's death? I spoke to her mother Sunday at church. She's a tough lady. I don't know if I could be out in public yet after something like that."

My smile faded. "Yeah. I'd probably still be tucked under a blanket hoping the world would swallow me up. But no, we didn't talk much about it. The only thing, really, was I mentioned an encounter I had with Leo Stanhope at the grocery store. He's working there, which I found a little odd. I know he's not high up on the totem pole at the lumber company, but those jobs still pay well, don't they?"

"As far as I know, yes. Morris doesn't really talk about pay scales. But you know"—she tipped her head—"when we were talking about the case again the other day, he mentioned that even if Leo didn't kill Ella, he wasn't too impressed with him."

"Oh?" I paused, measuring cup of flour in hand, and frowned over at her. She told me a week or so ago that Morris knew Leo, but not well. That's all the further the conversation went. "How so?"

Carol shrugged and dumped a cup of sugar into the mixer. "Basically, he just thought Leo was immature. I guess he asked for overtime a couple weeks ago, because he needed the money, then didn't show up for work. It left a crew short-handed."

"Did he call in?"

"I don't think so. I think he just didn't show up."

That was interesting, but it also fit with what I'd learned about Leo from Ella's sister, Allie. He seemed a little self-absorbed. "Did Morris say anything else about Leo?"

"Just that the crews didn't care for him much. I guess when he was at work, he slacked off."

I shook my head and went back to adding ingredients to my mixing bowl. "What did Ella see in him?"

"I don't know. He must have had some redeeming quali-ties. She was a nice kid." Carol put down the measuring cup and secured the bowl to the mixer stand. "Even if he was lazy and immature, I can't see her dating someone who could be a killer."

I couldn't either, but I also was coming up blank on other suspects, and I knew Jack was too. I could only hope he found the rest of Ella's cameras. I had a feeling the answer was on one of them.

Nineteen

E lbow deep in buttercream flowers, I glanced over as my phone trilled from its spot on the opposite counter, barely audible over the music blaring from my Bluetooth speaker. I was alone today, so I'd turned it up.

Tipping the piping tip toward the ceiling so frosting wouldn't spill out, I walked over to look at the screen. My sister Darcy's name scrolled by.

With a knuckle, I paused the music, then answered. "Hey. What's up?"

"So, I might have both a business opportunity and an investigative opportunity for you."

An amused smile flirted with my lips. "What are you talking about?"

"I got a call from the chair of the photography department at the local college. He wants me to be a guest lecturer for his students on Monday. I guess the person they had fell through, and someone somewhere mentioned my name. Anyway, when I talked to him, I asked if I could bring a guest or two. He said yes. Then I mentioned I would like to bring my sister who bakes and asked if they needed any refreshments for the evening."

I groaned. "You didn't offer my services for free, did you?" I could afford to bring samples, but cater an entire event for free? No.

"I'm not an idiot. Of course I didn't. He said they had soda and some store-bought cookies but that it would be nice to have something a little fancier to go with the talk. I guess they've got some bigwigs in town, which is why they didn't cancel the lecture when the presenter canceled."

"What's the budget?" My mind cycled through my "fancy" desserts that were quick to make and how much it would cost me to make them. I could bring my profit margin down a little, if I needed to, but I didn't want to bring it down too much.

"I'm not sure. I told him you'd give him a ring if you were free."

"Do you at least know how many people they're expecting?" That would give me a better idea of what items could be on the menu for him to choose from.

"Yes. There are fifty students from the department who are required to attend, five faculty, another three to five from administration, half a dozen of the important people he wants to impress, and then they opened it to the public with another fifty tickets. I don't know how many of those have been claimed. It's a free event."

That wasn't too bad. A few cheesecakes, some macarons—that was doable. "Okay, text me his number. I'll call him once I finish the flowers I'm working on. That's a bit short notice for you too. What are you going to talk about?"

"The importance of persistence."

I laughed. "Will this include our escapade to Coral Peabody's art gallery in Seattle?" I still wasn't sure how we didn't get thrown out when we snuck into the employees-only area of her gallery this past summer. Luck, I guess, and the fact that Darcy had an actual appointment.

Darcy chuckled. "Quite possibly."

"Well, whatever you talk about, I'm sure it'll be riveting." My phone dinged softly, and a banner appeared at the top of the screen with a text. "Your text just came through."

"Awesome. While you have him on the phone, you should ask for an extra ticket and bring Jack."

What was it with people lately and trying to throw us together? "I'm sure he's busy."

"Stop denying the chemistry, Delaney, because you can't. I've seen it with my own eyeballs."

I knew inviting him to dinner that night would come back to haunt me.

"And I have it on good authority you two were together, *alone*, on Saturday."

My mouth dropped open. How did she know that? We were in a different town, and I hadn't told anyone except Carol that he helped me at the festival. "Who told you that?"

"Oh, I have my sources," Darcy hedged. I could hear the smug smile in her voice a moment before she chuckled. "One of my friends was at the Longfellow festival and saw him in your dessert truck. You really need to stop denying the connection between you two. What man would volunteer to help you like that if he didn't like you?"

"One who is a *friend*."

Darcy hummed a non-answer. "So, when do you plan to see him again?"

I let out a frustrated growl and clamped my lips together, refusing to tell her I planned to deliver his tart to him this evening. The only reason I didn't yesterday was because my schedule had been jampacked. It still was, but I could spare a few minutes to stop at the police station to drop it off. "I'm sure we'll run into each other at some point. Can we change the subject, please?"

"You're no fun."

"I'm just getting tired of being bullied about my non-relationship. Jack is a friend, and that's all." If and when anything ever happened, it would be on our terms and not because someone pushed us together.

Darcy was silent a moment. "I'm sorry if it feels like I'm badgering you. I just want you to find the same sort of happiness Daphne and I have with Morgan and James."

So did I, but it had to happen in its own time. "It'll happen one day. Is there anything else you need? My buttercream is melting." I could feel it settling around my hand, getting softer from the warmth of my skin.

"No. I'll let you go. Let me know what you decide about Monday."

"I will. Even if I don't bring treats, I'll go with you. I think I'd like to hear your speech." In addition to being pushy, Darcy was also funny and quite intelligent. The lecture promised to be entertaining. Plus, it gave me an excuse to ask about Ella's camera equipment. Jack had probably already talked to people at the college, but he hadn't shared that information, and I didn't like being kept in the dark.

"Sounds good. Talk to you later."

"Yep. Love ya."

"You too. Bye." The phone clicked, and the screen went dark as she hung up.

I blew out a breath, ruffling the hair around my face. Hopefully, she'd pass along the message to Daphne to leave me alone about Jack. I doubted my reprieve would last long, though. I'd put money on Darcy finding out I made Jack an entire fruit tart for helping me. I should have known she'd know someone at the street festival who would report back on what they saw.

Rolling my eyes, I got back to work. While it bothered me that my sisters—and others, like Carol—harped on me about my relationship with Jack, it also didn't, because it meant they cared. It was nice to know I was loved enough for people to want me to be happy.

Happier.

I was already happy.

Twenty

Tart in hand, I closed the back driver's side door of my vehicle and headed for the front door at the police station. Hopefully, I wasn't too late. After I talked to Darcy and finished the set of flowers I'd been working on when she called, I gave Roland Garner, the photography department chair, a call. He'd given me a very reasonable budget for some higher-end desserts, so I'd started on the cheesecakes. Those froze well and getting them out of the way early would free me up to make macarons. He also wanted some madeleines. Apparently, they had some tea drinkers who liked to dunk them.

But, as a result of our conversation, and my inability to manage time when I got deep in the flow of things, it was after seven pm.

He probably wasn't here.

And if he wasn't, fine. I'd take it home and try again tomorrow.

Walking into the lobby, I headed for the reception desk. The officer behind the glass was one I recognized. He'd been here several times when I stopped in.

"Hey, Delaney." His tinny voice came through the speaker

in the glass. "If you're here to see Detective Fiore, he went home."

My shoulders slumped. I knew it. "Okay. I just wanted to drop this off. I'll try again tomorrow." I shifted, turning to leave.

"I can give you his address."

I paused. "You can? Won't he mind?"

"Honestly, I'm surprised you don't have it already. If he does mind, then I've misread the situation, and I'll apologize."

Again with people assuming we were a couple… But in this instance, I wouldn't argue. It would save me time tomorrow and give Jack more time to eat his tart before the fruit went bad. "I've just never had the opportunity to go over there. I've always come here, or he's come to my house." Mentally, I crossed my fingers at the lie. But really, was it a lie? It was more of an implication.

The officer picked up a pad of sticky notes and scrawled a couple lines on it. Pulling the yellow note off, he passed it through the small slot at the bottom of the window. "There you go."

I took the note. "Thank you."

"You're welcome. You have a good night."

Nodding, I left.

Back at my car, I stowed the tart box on the backseat again, then got in the driver's seat and looked at the address on the sticky note. I was surprised to see it wasn't that far from my house.

Starting the engine, I buckled up and pointed my car in that direction.

When I pulled up to Jack's, a warm glow burned in the front window. It looked like he was home.

Nerves fluttered in my belly.

What would he think about me just showing up here? I hoped he'd be happy, but there was always the possibility he would be upset the desk sergeant gave out his address, even if it was to me.

"Only one way to find out." I yanked on the door handle, exiting the car. After grabbing the tart off the backseat, I headed up the driveway to the short path that led to the front porch.

His single-story house was neat and tidy, much like I would expect from a man like Jack. The tan paint on the cement board siding looked fresh. So did the white trim. Neatly landscaped hedges lined the front of the house, and the grass was freshly mowed, no more than a day or two.

I walked up the two concrete steps to the porch and rang the doorbell before I could change my mind.

A moment later, the front door opened, and my carefully prepared speech about dropping off the tart as a thank you completely left my brain.

Jack was shirtless.

And glistening.

My mouth went dry, then abruptly flipped direction to the point I had to snap my jaw shut, lest I drool all over the porch.

"Delaney? Hey. What are you doing here?" A small frown marred his sweaty face.

"Um…" I cleared my throat and forced my eyes off his impressively muscular chest. "I brought you this." I gestured with the tart box in my hands.

His dark eyes dropped to it. "What is it?"

"A fruit tart, as promised."

The frown on his face disappeared, softening his features. "You didn't have to do that. I wasn't serious. I was happy to help."

I shrugged. "Well, I'm still thankful, so here." I held out the box.

Taking it, he lifted the lid far enough to peer inside. "Oh, wow, it's a big one."

"Yep. I wanted it to last."

With a smile, he looked up, shutting the lid. "Thanks. It can be dessert tonight to start. Do you want to come in?" He shifted, motioning to the house's interior.

"Oh, um, sure." I hadn't expected an invitation to come inside, and really probably should just go home, but the words of acceptance were out of my mouth and my feet were moving before my conscious brain could formulate an objection.

Jack stepped back as I entered, then shut the door. I glanced around the open-concept space, taking in the gleaming, dark laminate flooring, leather furniture, and beige walls. Gray granite countertops shone over white cabinets in the kitchen.

Heading for the fridge, he opened it and put the tart inside, then grabbed a wadded up black t-shirt from a barstool at the island. After swiping sweat off his face, he shrugged into it.

"Sorry. I know I'm all sweaty. I was out back putting together the Blackstone I just bought. It didn't want to cooperate, and it's not exactly light."

"Well, once you get it up and running, I'm sure you'll love it. I have one. It's great."

"Yeah?" He arched an eyebrow. "You'll have to give me some of your favorite recipes for it."

"Meat." I chuckled.

Jack laughed. "Just meat?"

I nodded. "Pretty much. Add some seasonings to it—you'll never want to cook meat on the stove again. I like pancakes and eggs on it too. And potatoes."

His other eyebrow rose, and I couldn't hold back another chuckle.

"I use it a lot if you can't tell."

He grinned. "You don't say?" Turning his head, he glanced toward the sliding glass doors, leading to the backyard. "Do you want to stay and help me test it out? I have plenty of food. Burgers. And some chicken."

Dinner? He was asking me to stay for dinner?

His comment from the other day in the basement of Scarlett's shop about repeating dinner together, alone, echoed through my mind. Was this what that was?

Before I could read any more into it, I went with my gut. "Sure. That sounds great." Just because I protested when people assumed Jack and I were a couple didn't mean I didn't want it to happen. But I wanted it to take a natural course and not be forced because people thought we should be together.

"Okay." He straightened, looking toward the fridge, then me, then outside. "I'm almost finished setting it up. Do you want to look through my spices and find whatever you think will work? I was just going to throw some salt and pepper on the burgers. I bought barbeque sauce for the chicken."

My nose wrinkled. "Salt and pepper? That's it?" Even when I made burgers on the stove I added more than just that.

A sheepish smile tilted his mouth. "Pretty much. If I want something tasty, I order it from a restaurant. At home, it's the basics."

"Do you even have many spices?" I moved toward the cabinets, raising a hand to point between them, silently asking him to tell me where he kept things.

He gestured to one near the stove. "I have some. My sister bought some stuff when she was here helping me move in."

I filed that little tidbit about him away and opened the cabinet. There were a couple of all-purpose seasonings on the shelf as well as some more basic things, like onion powder and garlic powder.

"I think I can work with this." He definitely needed to up his spice game, but for now, I could give the food a little bit of flavor beyond salty.

"Great. The meat is in the fridge. Come out when you're ready."

Looking over my shoulder, I saw him backing toward the sliding door. "Okay. Do you have enough butter to season the cooktop?"

"That's in the fridge too."

I gave him a thumbs up. "I'll bring it out."

With a nod, Jack went outside.

Turning back to the spice cabinet, I took several of them out, then opened the fridge to get the meat and butter. Determined not to make two trips, I opened several cupboards until I found a large bowl, then put the butter and spices in it. Stacking the plates of plastic-wrapped meat, I put them on top of the bowl and headed for the door.

"Perfect timing." Jack smiled at me as I walked out. "I just got the last screw tightened." He raised the lid on the cooktop.

I set my load down on the patio table. "Glad I could be here for the hard work."

He chuckled. "I wish you had been. It might have gone faster and resulted in a lot less swearing."

But then I wouldn't have been treated to the wonderful view of his sweaty chest.

Feeling a blush come over my cheeks, I turned away, moving the meat off the bowl to get to the butter and to give myself a moment to regain my composure. That image would stay with me for a long time. I imagined it would even haunt some pleasant dreams tonight.

Darn…

"All right." Spinning around, hands full of butter, I walked closer. "Fire it up."

Jack pressed in on the starter and I heard a click, then a whoosh as the gas lit. Together, we unwrapped butter and coated the cooktop. It would take several times of coating and letting it cook down before it would be ready for food.

"So, what all did you find to season our food with?"

"Oh, a little of this, a little of that." I smiled. "Your sister left a decent assortment. I'll give you a list of the ones I use, though, so you can beef up your repertoire."

"Nothing complicated. Remember, I was about to just use salt."

Laughing, I nodded. "We can even label them more specifically, so you know what to use them for."

While we waited for the top to heat and the butter to brown, I told him about some of my favorites, and we chatted about different things to cook on the Blackstone.

"I need to write this stuff down." Jack tore another handful of paper towels off the roll to wipe up the last of the butter. The top was finally ready to cook on.

"We can make a list later."

"Good. I've noticed when I do something that's sort of mindless, but requires concentration, it helps me relax after a hard day. I've conquered pasta—I'm Italian, after all—but I'd like to make more than a good bolognese, you know?" He raised an eyebrow.

I nodded. "I bake to relieve stress."

"I might have you show me a few things. If you don't mind, I mean?" He reached for the package of chicken.

A slow warmth spread in my chest. He wanted lessons? "I don't mind at all. But you don't like sweets, so what do you want to learn?"

"I like some sweets. Like that tart you brought." He tipped his head toward the house as he used a set of grill tongs to put the meat on the cooktop. "And those little filled cookies you made for Grant's wedding."

I searched my memory banks for what he mentioned liking that day. "Macarons?"

"That sounds right. A little crunchy, but filled with frosting or something?"

"Yep. Those aren't easy. They take time, and you have to

be precise in your measurements or they don't rise correctly or they crack."

He waved a hand. "I don't care how they look, just that they taste good."

I chuckled. "Well, you're in luck. As it happens, I need to make a bunch of them for an event on Monday. If you have some free time this weekend, you're welcome to come learn." The words were out before I could stop them.

But I didn't regret them. This, right here, spending time together as we prepared food, was nice. I wouldn't mind doing it again.

"Really? You're sure you don't mind?" He set the empty chicken package down, then picked up the plate of hamburgers.

"Of course not. How does Saturday morning sound? Around nine?"

"I can do that, so long as nothing comes up at work. Where?"

"The church. I work out of the basement."

"Oh, that's right. Okay." He nodded once. "Saturday at nine. It's a date."

Immediately, my face flamed.

Date?

Oh boy.

Twenty-One

"You're going to end up with hard pancakes for macaron shells if you keep stirring like that."

Jack paused, mouth set in a tight line, as he glanced at me. "I'm doing what you said. Folding the ingredients together until it's like lava."

"Thick lava, Jack. That's not folding. That's whipping." He'd been smacking his spatula back and forth against the sides of his bowl through the macaron batter, not scooping and turning in a proper fold. "Do this." I tilted my bowl and neatly folded my batter, demonstrating the proper technique once more.

"That's what I did. Just faster."

I chuckled. "It's not a race. Not with macarons."

Heaving a sigh, he resumed stirring, but a slower, more methodical pace. "Better?"

"Yes." I had my doubts whether his macarons would rise because of all the whipping, but at least now they stood a chance.

Checking my own batter, I did a few more turns, then checked again. It flowed off my spatula in a smooth, thick ribbon. Perfect.

I looked over at Jack to see him do the same. It ran off his spatula in a ribbon, but it was a glossy, runny one.

Yeah. Those were going to be like hockey pucks.

Keeping that to myself, I grabbed a couple piping bags I prepared with tips earlier and stuffed them down into some tall cups to make them easier to fill.

"Here." I handed one to Jack. "Spoon some of your batter into that. Don't fill it higher than the rim of the cup."

With a nod, he took it.

I put the other near my bowl and quickly filled it. Lifting the edges of the bag, I tugged it from the cup. "When you're done, raise the ends of the bag and twist it, like this." Quickly, I showed him.

I couldn't hold back the small smile at the look of boyish concentration on his face. Those dark eyebrows knitted tightly together over his rich, brown eyes, and he had his tongue tucked into the corner of his mouth as he copied my movements.

"Crap." He tipped the end of the bag up as a rivulet of batter ran out of the tip. "Why is it doing that? Yours isn't running out."

I sputtered a laugh. "You overmixed it a little." Setting my piping bag back in the cup, I grabbed a couple of parchment-lined sheet pans and brought them over. "Do your best to pipe some circles on these about this big." I made a two-inch circle with one hand. "Space them about an inch or two apart."

He let the bag hover over the baking tray. Batter ran down to pool in a smooshed circle. "Like that?"

"A little less batter, but yes."

While he tried again, I fetched the other baking sheets and set about forming my own macaron shells.

"This is a disaster," Jack said, a chuckle in his voice.

I glanced over at his trays. Misshapen circles were scattered over the parchment, some with thin strings of batter connecting them to another. I couldn't hold back a quick laugh. "I told you they weren't easy."

"They better at least taste good."

"They will." Of that, I would have no doubt. Even flat, the flavor would be there.

"Don't ever tell anyone I work with about this. I'll never hear the end of it." He pitched his voice higher and continued. "Are you sure you know what a clue looks like? You can't even bake a simple cookie."

I laughed harder. "Macarons are far from a simple cookie."

"They won't know that." He waved a hand but smiled. "Uncultured, the lot of them."

"Says the man who didn't know the name of it before Wednesday."

"Shh." Offering up a sly smile, he put a finger to his lips.

Shaking my head with a chuckle, I picked up a tray and slammed it on the counter to pop the air bubbles in the cookies.

"What on earth are you doing?"

I slammed the tray down again. "Popping air bubbles. You need to do the same." Though I doubted there was much air left in his to tap out.

Loud thwacks filled the kitchen for several moments.

"Okay. Macarons have been beaten. What's next?"

"Now they sit for a little bit to dry."

"Why?"

"It helps them rise and get their little feet."

Jack blinked several times and frowned. "Macarons have feet?"

I nodded. "At the bottom. That textured part." Crossing to the fridge, I opened it to take out the ones I made yesterday and show him what I meant. "Like this." I removed one from the box on the shelf and held it up, pointing to the bottom edge.

Tipping his head, he studied it. "Oh, okay. I didn't know it had a name."

"Yep." I put the cookie away.

"So, what are these for, anyway? You didn't say."

I took an extra couple of seconds closing the fridge, debating how to answer. Truthfully, I'd been hoping we could avoid this subject, which is why I hadn't said anything previously. Telling him would likely ruin the camaraderie we had going.

But he'd asked outright. I couldn't lie.

I mean, I could, but it wasn't wise. One, I couldn't lie to this man to save my soul; he could spot it on my face in an instant. Two, if I somehow managed to slip a lie past him, it would just sow distrust when he eventually found out.

And I had no doubt he would uncover the truth eventually. Fernwood was a small town, and people talked. Plus, Jack was a police detective—a good one. Finding out the truth was what he did.

Pushing the door closed, I turned. "The photography department at the community college."

Instantly, his eyebrows turned down.

I held up a hand before he could say anything. "I'm not snooping." Yet. "Darcy was asked to be a guest lecturer Monday evening. In asking questions about the event, she learned their refreshments were subpar and asked if they would like to hire me to make better ones. The department chair said yes."

His frown smoothed out, but the skepticism remained in his expression. "So, asking around about Ella's photography equipment didn't play into her decision to recommend your business at all? I'm assuming you told your sisters about her missing cameras, because that feels like something you'd share."

I feigned an affronted air. "Haven't you heard that

assuming makes an ass out of you and me? I don't particularly feel like being labeled that."

He arched an eyebrow and crossed his arms. "Tell me I'm wrong."

My mouth flattened into a thin line. Of course he'd call me on that. "I can't."

Jack inhaled a breath, then huffed it out through his nose. "Delaney…"

"It's not like I'm going to walk up to everyone there and say, 'Hey, Ella's cameras are missing. Did you take them?'" I rolled my eyes. "Give me some credit. I know how to be subtle."

"You don't need to be anything. It's none of your business."

"Maybe not, but I'm still going, and if someone brings her up, I'm going to listen and engage in conversation." I crossed my arms, mirroring his posture. "It's not like I plan to go off alone with anyone. We'll be in a lecture hall at a public event."

"Just because it's public, that doesn't mean someone won't come after you in private later. Look at what happened with the Brunswick murders." He uncrossed his arms to hold one out, then let them both fall to his side.

"I'm aware, Jack. You won't let me forget."

"And I don't plan to, either." Sucking in a deep breath, he looked away. A muscle in his jaw ticked, and he turned back to me. "This isn't about you interfering in an investigation. I told you last week, you and your sisters have been helpful. But that doesn't mean I want you to go out of your way to play detective. It's dangerous."

I opened my mouth to protest, but he held up a hand.

"Even if the person you talk to is completely innocent, someone could overhear, or that person could mention the interaction to someone else. Someone who isn't so innocent.

So, please, don't get involved any more than you already are."

My lips pursed. He might have a bit of a point. Wasn't I just thinking about how word could get around in this town?

Still, though, I wasn't sure I could promise what he was asking. Sometimes, people just talked to me. And sometimes, the questions slipped out before I could stop them.

However, I could promise to try. "I will do my best." I raised a finger. "I'm still going to the event Monday. This is a big deal for Darcy, and I'm going to support her."

That full mouth of his pursed as he chewed on the corner of his mouth and stared at me for a long moment. "I can't stop you." A slow smile took over his face. "But I can tag along."

I rolled my eyes. "I do not need a babysitter."

"I'm not babysitting. I'm supporting your sister."

Fixing him with a hard stare, I shook my head. "Sure you are."

His smile grew. "I am. Plus, you have one thing right. It's a great opportunity to hear what people have to say about Ella."

My stare morphed into a confused frown. "Have you not talked to them yet?"

"I have. But that was in an official capacity." He held out his arms. "I'll be there as just a regular person."

I snorted. "Yeah, totally." Jack would never be just a "regular person."

"You can vouch for me."

A soft groan escaped. I was beginning to regret this friendship.

Twenty Two

"Hold the door, please!" With a reusable shopping bag full of plastic forks hanging off my arm and slapping against my side, I hurried forward with my armload of cheesecake boxes, hoping the young woman entering the building heard me and realized I was talking to her.

Thankfully, she glanced back and stopped.

"Thank you." I offered her a smile as I breezed inside, then waited for Jack, who had insisted on picking me and my boxes of desserts up and bringing us to the lecture. I'd only protested slightly. While I knew he'd likely stick to me like glue, so I couldn't get in trouble, I didn't mind the company or the help.

He murmured a thanks to the woman as well, then followed me deeper into the building. Darcy had given me some basic directions on where to go once inside, and we were soon in front of the doors to the lecture hall.

It wasn't quite time for most people to arrive yet, so the door was only cracked open. When I spoke to Professor Garner, he said to just come in, that he would be there.

Wedging my toe in the crack, I gave the door a nudge. It

swung open. Jack stepped up and put a shoulder into it, so I could pass through, then followed me inside.

The lecture hall was stadium-style, and we were at the top. Ten rows of seats rose from a central, semi-circle pit area where a podium sat in the middle. Behind it, the wall stretched the width of the room, covered by large whiteboards. Several eight-foot tables were tucked against the wall in the corner by the stairs. An industrial, thermal coffee dispenser and two cold-drink dispensers took up one. The middle one contained platters of assorted cookies. The third was empty.

A short, balding man with wire-framed glasses popped up from behind the podium. With a cautiously welcoming smile, he came around front. "Ms. Fowler?"

"Yep. Hello." I gave him a friendly smile.

His gaze darted to Jack and his expression turned curious. "Detective Fiore? I didn't expect to see you this evening. Did you have more questions?"

"No. I'm here with Delaney and to listen to Darcy's talk."

"He's a friend," I added, motioning to Jack with a quick flick of my head.

"Oh." Professor Garner's smile returned. "Well, then, welcome."

"Thank you," Jack said.

"Where would you like us to put these?" I nodded to the boxes I carried.

"You can arrange them on the empty table however you like." Professor Garner gestured to the tables in the corner.

"Okay, thanks." Descending the stairs and making our way over to the dessert setup, we deposited our boxes onto the table.

"Is there enough room?" Jack asked.

I eyed the length of the table. "There should be." Opening the first box of cheesecake, I lifted it out. "The cheesecakes all come out of the boxes. For the macarons, just take off the lids." I'd deliberately packaged things to make it easy to set up. I figured there wouldn't be much space at something like this.

We set to work, quickly unloading.

The door at the top of the stairs squealed on its hinges as it opened. I glanced up to see Darcy and James walk through.

"Hey." I greeted her with a sunny smile.

She smiled back and descended toward us. "Hey yourself." Her gaze moved to Jack. "Well, hello."

Raising a hand, he tapped his temple with two fingers and tipped them toward her. "Darcy." He glanced past her. "James."

James nodded a greeting. "Hey."

I whipped the lid off the last box of macarons and pushed them toward the front of the table.

"Oh, yum. Macarons," James said, stopping just feet away.

"Those look really good, Delaney." Darcy peered into the boxes. "I can't wait to try one."

"They have feet." Jack pointed into the box closest to him.

"What?" Darcy sent him a quizzical look.

A short chuckle escaped as I looked at him and rolled my eyes. "Ignore him. Are you ready for this?"

Darcy held up her laptop and nodded. "I think so. I worked all weekend on my presentation."

"It's true," James said. "I kept her supplied with tea and snacks."

Smiling up at her boyfriend, Darcy wrapped an arm around his waist and squeezed. "He's the best, isn't he?"

James hugged her back and kissed the top of her head.

"Ah, Darcy. Hello." Professor Garner walked up, a smile on his face. He held out a hand.

Darcy untangled herself from James's hold to shake it. "Hello, professor."

"Thank you again for agreeing to this last minute. You've

really saved us. These people coming are important, and we really want to make a good impression."

"Well, I'm flattered you asked me. I've, hopefully, prepared a presentation that will keep everyone interested and not bored to tears." She tapped her laptop with her nails.

"Great. If you'd like to follow me, I'll help you get hooked up to the media system."

"Sounds good." Darcy excused herself and followed Professor Garner to the podium.

"Do you guys need any help?" James asked.

I looked over the table. Everything was where it should be. "Maybe just taking the boxes out to Jack's car. There's no place to store them here." Normally, I tucked them under the tables, but the tablecloths were too short to hide them. Professor Garner wanted to make a good impression, so that wouldn't work.

"I can do that." He picked up a couple of the empty cheesecake boxes.

With James's help, the three of us made quick work of taking the boxes out. When we returned to the lecture hall, the first guests were arriving.

"Let's find some seats," Jack suggested.

We headed down the steps, stopping about three rows from the front.

"Kids these days have it easy," Jack said, settling into a plush desk chair. "None of my classrooms had chairs like these. I don't even have this nice of a chair at the station."

"It's all those tuition dollars at work," James said.

"I think I'd rather have crappy chairs and lower tuition," Jack replied.

So would I.

Over the next twenty minutes, more people filed in, filling the lecture hall until most of the seats were taken. As Professor Garner stepped up to the podium, I caught Darcy's eye and gave her a quick thumbs up and a bright smile. She'd do great. She spent her days standing in front of a room of elementary-age kids, trying to keep their attention when all they wanted to do was glue their fingers together. This would be a piece of cake.

"Hello, and thank you for coming to our monthly lecture series. I'm Professor Roland Garner, chair of the photography department. Some of you were likely expecting to hear from esteemed photographer, Michael Dotson. Obviously, this is not him." With a small smile, he glanced at Darcy who stood just behind him and to his left. "Mr. Dotson had a personal emergency and had to cancel. But we've secured a new guest speaker, who I'm sure will wow you all with her talk on the importance of persistence. Please give a warm welcome to local art educator and artist, Darcy Fowler."

A round of applause went through the room as Darcy stepped forward. She thanked the crowd and opened her laptop, bringing up her presentation slides on the projector screen Professor Garner lowered from the ceiling in front of the whiteboard.

"She looks really relaxed," I whispered to Jack. "She's going to crush this."

He hummed a non-answer. The distracted note in his voice drew my attention away from my sister to look at him.

He wasn't even looking at the lectern. Instead, his gaze roamed the room.

"What are you doing?" As soon as the words left my mouth it hit me why he was really here. "Are you... are you *working*?" I hissed.

"Of course I am," he murmured. "I told you I wanted to take this opportunity to observe people without them thinking of me as a cop. Most of the people in this room knew Ella Kerns. I want to see how they all interact with each other and how they handle you and your sister being here."

Indignation straightened my spine.

Oh, really?

He hadn't mentioned that last part the other day.

I guess I couldn't say much about being used, though. We'd done the same to him when we invited him to dinner. It still stung, though.

"See anything interesting?" Crossing my arms and my legs, I couldn't keep all the annoyance from shining through in my voice.

"Can you two knock it off? You're distracting." James leaned, keeping his voice low.

I let out a huff and did my best to refocus my attention on Darcy. James was right. We were here to support her. I needed to let it go.

It wasn't until Jack sat up and turned toward the aisle ten minutes later that I looked away from the projector screen.

Frown forming between my eyebrows, I followed his line of sight. Across the room, a young man tugged a hat down lower over his face, glancing Jack's way every few seconds until finally, he got up and left through a side door.

"I'll be back." Jack pushed out of his chair.

"What? Jack!" I said in a harsh whisper.

He didn't turn to look back. Long, powerful legs carried him up the wide stairs.

I let out a low, frustrated growl, watching him hurry around the back row, then down the steps on the other side of the room to go out the same door.

"Where's he going?" James murmured.

"I have no idea."

Indecision warred in my mind. Maybe I should go after him. I doubted he would need help, but he didn't know the building, and I would bet my dessert truck that kid he followed did; he looked like a student. What if the young man was dangerous?

Worrying my bottom lip between my teeth, I glanced at Darcy. She caught my eye with a small frown, her gaze flicking toward the door Jack exited through, but kept talking.

I could tell by just that small change in her demeanor that she, too, wondered what was going on.

I blew out a quick breath through my nose and rolled my eyes at myself, knowing I was about to follow him. My concentration was shot. Staying would just make the curiosity, and therefore my ability to focus on Darcy, worse.

Turning, I leaned toward James. "Don't wait for us. If we're not back by the time you two are ready to go, tell Darcy I'll call her."

"Oh, come on, Delaney," he whispered. "You don't need to get involved."

"I know, but I'm going to anyway." Staying low, I slid out of my seat and ran up the stairs, following the same path Jack took.

This was a dumb idea, but I couldn't shake the feeling that Jack might need my help.

The sound of Darcy's voice quieted to a low mumble as the door swung shut behind me. I peered down the empty hallway, listening for footsteps.

Silence.

My mouth twisted. How did they get so far ahead of me already? It had been less than a minute since Jack left the lecture hall.

At least I didn't have to guess which way they went. We were at the end of the hallway.

Taking off at a slow lope, I paused briefly as I passed rooms, checking to see if they'd ducked into any of them. They were all locked, so I kept going. When I reached a junction, I stopped to listen again.

More silence.

I huffed. Where the heck did they go?

Maybe I should go back to the lecture hall. Jack probably didn't need—

A dull thud down the hall to my left stopped my thoughts

in their tracks. My feet were moving in that direction before I could consciously decide to investigate.

This was such a bad idea. Why did I do stuff like this?

But I kept moving, peering in classroom windows as I went. They were all dark and locked. Which, honestly, I found a little weird. Didn't colleges have evening classes? Granted, it was after seven, but some of them ran late, didn't they? This was a community college. I would assume they had a lot of students who were pursuing a new career and had to take night classes while they worked. So, where was everyone?

Nearing another junction, a four-way, I slowed, listening. The noise had definitely come from this direction, but I didn't think it was this far down. Had I passed it? There were still a few rooms to check.

As I turned to check the rooms I missed, something rustled behind me. Before I could do more than turn my head a fraction, a hand clamped over my mouth and an arm went around my waist.

Twenty~Three

"Shh. Stop wiggling."

I froze at the sound of Jack's voice, then went limp from relief. Oh, thank goodness. I thought I was in a real pickle there for a moment.

"What are you doing out here?" Not letting me go, Jack tugged me into a dark classroom.

Reaching up, I peeled his hand off my mouth. "I thought you might need help."

He let out a soft snort. "What were you going to do? Chuck a macaron at someone?"

I huffed, turning my head to glare at him in the dark. "I could at least call for help if you were unconscious somewhere. Look at how easy it was for you to sneak up on me. That could have been you."

It was too dark to see his face, but I could feel the skepticism bleeding through the beat of silence that passed. I chose to ignore it and moved on. "What happened to the guy you were following?"

"He ducked into one of these rooms. I turned the corner and he was gone, and I know he didn't sprint down to the next hallway and turn. I'd have heard him."

"Well, this one was open, and it's the only one. I know; I tried all the doors."

"That doesn't mean there wasn't another one open, and he locked it behind him. I was hiding in here, waiting to see if he came out of one. Instead, I caught you snooping." His warm breath puffed against my face. He'd let me go but hadn't stepped away.

"Well excuse me for being concerned about your safety," I hissed.

"Delaney, I'm a cop. I know how to follow someone without getting hurt. You, on the other hand, would probably walk right into a drug deal and never be the wiser." He maneuvered around me to peer out the window in the door.

I glared at his back. Just because I was a little oblivious to my surroundings sometimes didn't mean I wouldn't realize something was amiss. I wasn't an airhead.

Crossing my arms, I cocked a hip out. "So, how long do you think we'll have to wait here?"

"However long it takes. I want to talk to that kid."

"What if he snuck out and you didn't see him? He probably goes to school here and knows all the ins and outs of the building. What if there's a back—"

The quiet tinkle of glass breaking behind me and to the right cut off the rest of my sentence. Jack straightened, and I spun around.

"What was that?" I whispered.

In the far corner, a soft glow flickered from under what I could now tell was a door. In the darkness, I hadn't realized there was another way in and out of the room.

Unless that was a closet? Did college classrooms have closets?

Jack moved past me, weaving around the tables. I trailed behind, wanting to know what was going on, but also wanting to stay out of his way.

He held up a hand that was barely more than a shadow in

the light coming in from the hallway, motioning for me to stay put.

When I complied, he bent down, messing with the bottom of his pant leg. Before I could ask what he was doing, I heard the click of the safety being removed from a pistol.

"You're armed?" My whisper came out low, but urgent. I shouldn't be surprised, but I was.

He didn't answer me, instead creeping forward.

Two feet from the door, a low hiss, like air escaping a container, erupted behind the wooden panel.

Noise at the front of the room, outside the door, had me whipping my head around.

"Hey!" I caught a brief glimpse of a man's silhouette. Something banged into the door, then I heard footsteps hurrying away.

Jack cursed, turning to sprint toward the door.

As he drew even with me, the hissing stopped. A split second later, a sound, like the air reversing itself, filled the room. Then it went silent for an instant before an explosion knocked me off my feet.

Letting out a scream, I rolled, covering my head as the remnants of the door rained down, pelting me. Smoke billowed from the hole in the wall.

"Delaney!"

Through the ringing in my ears, I heard Jack's muffled shout.

Raising up to my knees, I pressed a hand to a spot throbbing on the side of my head. Wet warmth filled my palm. I hadn't been entirely successful in protecting myself from the debris.

A strong arm wrapped over the back of my shoulders and under my arm.

"We need to get out of here."

I knew he was yelling, but it still sounded like he was at the end of a long tunnel.

"Come on." He gripped my arm, helping me to my feet.

Standing up put us directly into the smoke plume. My eyes watered as the acrid cloud attacked them like a swath of stinging nettle taken straight to the face. I blinked relentlessly, hoping to clear my eyes as we stumbled toward the door. My head throbbed, the pain a mixture of the assault from the smoke and my head wound.

Holding tight to my hand, Jack pulled me toward the exit.

I banged my hip into the corner of a table and sucked in a sharp breath as pain sliced through my flesh, but I didn't stop moving. The bruise wouldn't kill me, but the smoke would if we didn't get out of here. I didn't even want to think about what could be in it. I had a feeling we were in a lab of some sort. Something had made the hissing sound, then exploded. It could be anything from an oxygen tank to something toxic.

Reaching the door, Jack grabbed the handle.

When the door didn't open, I squinted at him through watery, scratchy eyes. "What are you doing? Open the door."

"I can't." He tugged. The door jiggled slightly in the frame but stayed shut.

"What?" A hard, hacking cough rattled my body.

"I mean, it won't open." Jack had started to cough as well.

The man!

Had that guy wedged something into the frame when he banged on it?

Jack rattled the door handle again, but the door still didn't budge. Fire alarms now blared just outside the door, adding to the cacophony, making my head pound.

Fear tried to take hold and paralyze me with its icy grip. I swallowed it down and forced myself to stay calm. Getting worked up wouldn't help us get out.

Turning, I scanned the room through blurry eyes. The fire had spread from its origin and now licked the cabinets lining the wall.

My heart thundered at the thought of what could be in those cupboards.

But it also thundered at what I didn't see: fire *in* the doorway.

"Jack." I slapped his shoulder.

He didn't turn; just kept rattling the door.

"Jack." I hit him again.

When he still didn't turn, I grabbed a fistful of his shirt-sleeve and tugged. "Jack!"

"What?" He glanced back.

I pointed at the far side of the room. "Look—" A cough interrupted my words. Once I could inhale again without hacking, I continued. "There's no fire in the doorway. Can we go through there? It has to connect to another room, doesn't it? How else did he get out to shut us in?"

In the glow from the hallway, I watched him glance back at the door, then toward the flames several times.

"Let's go." Pulling on his sleeve again, I urged him away from the door.

After one more glance at the hall through the window in the door, he followed me.

Making sure not to ram my body into a table again, I waded deeper into the smoky room. Heat from the flames now consuming the cabinets washed over me as we closed in on the ruined doorway. It prickled my skin with an itch I knew I couldn't scratch away.

Doing my best to ignore it—which wasn't hard with the tears streaming down my cheeks or the coughs shaking my chest—I moved as fast as I dared toward the doorway. Skirting the flames, I crossed the threshold.

Five feet into the space, the smell changed. Now a pungent chemical scent lingered in the smoke. It tickled my nose and lungs, increasing the coughs that were already growing worse.

"Go." Jack gave my shoulder a soft shove. "Go, go, go. We need to get out of here."

Not about to argue, I hurried forward but almost immediately ran into a shelf.

I let out a soft curse. "I can't see." The smoke was thicker in here, and there wasn't as much light.

A moment later, light flared behind me. I looked back to see Jack holding up his phone, using the flashlight on it to light our way.

Why didn't I think of that?

Reaching into my pocket, I took out my own phone and turned on the flashlight. The beam didn't penetrate far into the smoke-filled darkness, but it was enough we wouldn't crash into any more furniture.

As we wove our way through the room, I realized we were in a storage area of some sort. It looked like a closet, but it was too large to be one.

Clearing the last line of shelving, a wall loomed in front of us.

A moment of panic set in. Had I been wrong? Was it really just an extremely large closet?

The line of the wall changed as we moved along it, split by a piece of white trim.

A doorway!

"There!" Practically tripping over my feet, I scrambled the last few feet toward it. As we got closer, I could see it was partially open.

Jack and I pushed through, entering another classroom. This one was smoky, too, but not like the storage area we just left.

"That way." Jack nudged me toward the hallway side of the room.

Using our phones, we lit our way through the tables to the door.

"Please be open," I breathed, watching Jack reach for the handle.

He turned the lever.

Nothing happened.

I groaned, then dissolved into a hacking cough. Despair filled me. We'd just wasted so much time. Maybe we should just call for help. But could it arrive before we passed out?

"Wait." Jack fiddled with the handle, then tried again.

The door swung outward, taking Jack with it. He reached back, grabbing my hand, pulling me through.

Out here, the fire alarms were much louder, making my muffled hearing pulse with each grating buzzer-like blare.

Still holding my hand, Jack led me toward the closest exit. By the time we stumbled outside, my head not only pounded, but spun like a tilt-a-whirl from the combination of injury, smoke, adrenaline, and noise.

I collapsed onto the sidewalk.

"Delaney."

Jack's voice sounded even more distant than before. The ringing in my ears had intensified to the point it nearly drowned out everything else.

Warm hands framed my face.

"Hey. Delaney? Look at me."

My vision sparkled, turning dark at the edges, but I managed to look up.

His handsome face swam in front of me.

The darkness grew and the amount of sparkles dancing in my vision increased. My scalp prickled as a wave of warmth flushed my body.

"Delaney?" Jack tapped my face.

I watched his mouth move as he said something else, but the ringing had completely taken over my hearing.

A second later, the ever-increasing sparkles melded into a bright light, then the darkness swallowed it whole.

Twenty-Four

Who stuffed the cotton ball in my mouth?

Something sharp pricked my arm.

Moaning, I tried to force my eyelids open, but they just fluttered.

Through the ringing in my ears, I heard a voice I didn't recognize. "She's waking up."

Waking up? When did I go to bed?

Another, more alarming thought rushed in. If I was waking up, who was in my bedroom?

Summoning every ounce of strength I had, I contracted my limbs, pulling them in and hopefully away from whoever was nearby. My eyes cracked open, and I winced against the bright light.

"Whoa, there. It's okay, Delaney. You're in an ambulance."

Ambulance?

I turned toward the even-toned female voice and tried opening my eyes again.

It was easier this time, but I still squinted against the brightness. "Wh—" My tongue stuck to my teeth. Swallowing, I tried again. "Why?"

"Why are you in an ambulance?"

My head hurt too much to move, so I just grunted what I hoped was an affirmative.

"You fainted, according to Detective Fiore."

Fainted? What?

I forced my racing thoughts to slow, pulling out pieces of information to figure out why I had a splitting headache and was currently laid out on a stretcher.

Explosion. Fire.

Bleeding headwound.

Oh, yeah. That was why.

Leaning back, I closed my eyes again.

"We're going to take good care of you and get you to the hospital. That's a nasty gash you have on your head. I'm Bobbi, by the way."

"Nice to meet you," I mumbled.

The woman chuckled. "I'm sure."

That brought a sardonic tilt to my mouth. Under other circumstances, it would be nice, I was certain. But yeah… in the back of an ambulance? Not so much.

"Oh my God, Delaney!"

My sister's worried voice rose over the ringing in my ears, clear as a bell. I forced my eyes open again to see her standing in the doorway of the ambulance, James at her side.

"Jack found us and told us what happened. Are you all right?"

"My head hurts, and my chest feels a little tight from the smoke, but I'm okay." My voice was hoarse, too, even with my muffled hearing. I looked past her, hoping for a sign of Jack. "Where is Jack?"

"Off hunting the guy who tried to blow you two up," James said.

Bobbi snorted softly. "He refused medical attention. Just handed you off, said he was fine, and ran away."

Geez. He could have at least waited for me to wake up.

But maybe he had a lead on the man who did this, my conscience argued.

My mouth flattened. I hated it when she was logical. Sometimes, a girl just wanted to feel important to the man she fancied.

"Did anyone see anything?" I asked, shoving away the feeling of abandonment. "All I saw was a male figure outside the door a few moments before the storage room blew up."

"I think Jack was going to look at security footage," Darcy said. "Other than that, I don't think anyone saw anything. Everyone was in the lecture hall when the explosion happened." Closing her eyes briefly, her jaw tense, Darcy leaned in the ambulance to put a hand on my leg. "I'm so glad you're okay," she whispered, fighting back tears.

My scratchy eyes watered. "Me too."

Bobbi's partner appeared behind Darcy and James. "We've been cleared by the police to leave. There are no more casualties," he said.

"Okay, then." Bobbi reached for her seatbelt and looked at Darcy. "Would you like to ride along?"

"No. James and I will follow." She looked at me. "I'll grab your purse and bring it to the hospital."

"Thank you." I hadn't given any thought to my bag or to the tableful of desserts that now would likely not get eaten.

"You rode with Jack, right?"

"Yes."

"Good. We won't need to worry about your car, then."

"It's parked at the church. He picked me up from there, since I had to get the desserts ready to go."

"Okay." Darcy nodded once. "We'll get it back to your house."

"You're the best." Tears welled in my eyes again. I didn't know what I would do without my sisters.

Once more, Darcy patted my leg. "We'll see you in a little while. Behave for the medical staff."

I chuckled, then dissolved into a coughing fit. Waving at her, I nodded but couldn't speak.

Darcy waved back, then stepped away so the other paramedic could close the door.

Bobbi unbuckled, then stood up as the doors closed, leaning over me to get into a compartment. She straightened with a clear mask and some tubing in her hand.

"I'm going to hook you up to some oxygen. See if we can't clear some of that crap out of your lungs."

"Yes, please," I said, finally managing to calm the coughing. Oh, I hoped this didn't get any worse and that it went away quickly. I had too much to do in the next couple of weeks to be laid up. Daphne's wedding was just around the corner.

A low groan slid free.

I really should have stayed in my seat.

Twenty~Five

"Are you sure you want to work today?"

I glanced up from sorting through my keys at Carol. Shadows shrouded her face, half lit by the pole light illuminating the parking lot.

"I'm sure. I don't have time to be idle. Daphne's wedding is in ten days." My head injury and the toxic smoke I inhaled three days ago set me back. I'd wanted to go in Tuesday morning, but I didn't get home from the hospital until well after midnight. Darcy—bless her—called Carol and asked her to take on what she could by herself. But she also hid my car keys so I couldn't go anywhere. I would have in the afternoon if I'd been able to find them. She didn't give them back until after dinner Tuesday evening, and that was after I threatened to show James Darcy's middle school talent show tape, where she read an interpretive poem, complete with hand puppets. And I happened to know where Mom kept the puppets.

Begrudgingly, she'd given my keys back. Wednesday, I went back to work but kept it light. Carol had done a lot, for which I was grateful.

Today, though, I really had to dive into Daphne's cake. All the flowers wouldn't make themselves.

Finding the right key, I unlocked the door and let us in.

"So, where do you want me to start?" Carol set her bag down on the counter once we flipped on all the lights.

"Can you do the heavy lifting on all the baking? You did great Tuesday by yourself in checking the orders and baking what needed baked." All I had to do on Wednesday was frost things and deliver.

"Sure. Do you have the list printed, or do I need to log into the system?" On one of our other baking days, I'd shown Carol how to check the ordering system for orders, so on the days I had a brain fart in the mornings and didn't print my list for her, she could just keep rolling when she finished one task and needed another. She was truly becoming the best assistant I could have asked for.

I opened my tote and pulled out the list I printed before I left. "Here you go." I was proud of myself for remembering to print it off this morning.

"I'll get started." Smiling, she took the papers and set to work.

After putting on some music and washing my hands, I got out what I needed to make gum paste flowers. There weren't a ton of them, but there were enough. We'd decided to do a mix of gum paste and buttercream floral designs on a rich crimson background. It would be stunning once I finished.

"So, have you heard any more about the explosion at the college? Does Jack have a suspect?"

Looking up from coloring the gum paste, I frowned. "Not that I know of. I haven't talked to him." The man hadn't even called to check on me. I thought we'd turned a corner in our relationship and become actual friends. Maybe even on the road to something more. Now I wasn't so sure. Friends didn't not check on friends after something like that. Especially when they were present for said traumatic event.

Carol's eyebrows rose. "He hasn't called?"

"Nope." I squished gum paste and food coloring through my fingers. "Not a word."

"Hmm. Maybe he's just busy chasing leads."

I scoffed. "Yeah. I'm sure that's it." More likely he just decided I was too much of a problem for him.

And I wouldn't fault him for thinking that. I really should have stayed in my seat.

"You should take him some macarons. I know you still have some in the freezer." A coy smile lit her face.

She wasn't wrong there. I kept a personal stash on hand at all times. Jack wasn't the only one who loved them.

But that didn't mean I wanted to give up some of my favorite cookies to a man who couldn't be bothered to pick up the phone to check on me.

Conversation dwindled between us as we each dove into our tasks. By the time lunch rolled around, I felt like we made decent headway on both Daphne's cake and on the regular orders.

"I wish I could stay longer today and help you, but I have an appointment." Carol untied her apron and lifted it over her head.

"You're fine. I appreciate all the time you spent here on Tuesday to keep us caught up." I pulled off my disposable gloves and moved to the sink to wash my hands.

"Oh, it was no trouble. I was happy to help." She picked up her purse. "I'll see you at church on Sunday."

Smiling, I lifted a hand, dripping water on the counter as I waved. "Yep. Have a good weekend."

"You too." On her way out, she paused in the doorway and glanced back. "And Delaney?"

"Hmm?"

"Take some macarons to Jack." With a quick smile and a flutter of her fingers, she scampered away.

Take some... I rolled my eyes, pressing my lips together,

then huffed a breath through my nose. The man didn't deserve my macarons.

But I deserved an explanation. And if buttering him up with his favorite cookie got me that, then it would be worth it.

Drying my hands, I opened the freezer and took out the container holding my stash. After grabbing a small favor box, I selected a few and stowed them inside, then put the rest back in the freezer. Grabbing my keys and the small wallet that held my ID and my bank card, I left the church.

I wasn't entirely sure where to find him, but I figured the police station was the logical place to start. If he wasn't there, maybe the same officer who'd been working the last time would be there and could tell me where he was.

In just minutes, I breezed through the station's front doors. The officer at the window was a different one, but one I'd dealt with before. He recognized me and smiled.

"Here to see Detective Fiore?"

"Yep." Pasting a bright smile on my face, I raised the small box. "I came bearing treats."

The door to my left buzzed.

"He's in his office, I think. Go on back."

"Thank you." Reaching for the door, I stepped through and headed down the hall.

I paused outside his door, my heart suddenly working overtime. Why was I nervous? If anything, I should be angry. I wasn't the one who hadn't called.

Maybe I should just turn around and leave. I could eat the macarons in the car on the way back to the church and wallow in self-pity over a non-starter of a relationship.

The door opened, and suddenly I was face-to-Adam's-apple with Jack.

"Whoa." Jack's voice was little more than a low rumble.

I tipped my gaze up to meet his eyes.

"Delaney? What are you doing here?"

Just the fact he had to ask that question rebooted my brain

and my anger. I thrust the little box at him. "I came to let you explain why you haven't called."

Way to be subtle, Laney. What happened to buttering him up?

I shushed my inner voice and continued to stare at him.

His eyes darted to the side. "I've been a little busy."

"A phone call doesn't take long. You can even do it from the car on your way to check out a lead. They invented this great thing called Bluetooth. Have you heard of it?"

He sighed and pinched the bridge of his nose. "I really don't have time for this right now. I'm on my way to—"

"Oh, my bad. I thought we were friends. I guess I should have taken the hint when you didn't call to see how I was doing after you *dumped me in the ambulance.*" I propped a fist on my hip.

"Just because I haven't called you doesn't mean I haven't checked up on you."

I frowned. "What?"

"I talked to your dad. He said you were being stubborn and already back at work when you should be resting still." His gaze traveled to the butterfly strips over the stitches near my hairline. "That looks good."

Ignoring his last comment, I focused on the first. "Why would you call my dad and not me?"

"Because I knew if I called you, I would want to come see you, and I really don't have time for distractions right now. This case is finally breaking open."

My mind fractured, one part wanting to follow-up on how I was a distraction and what that meant, while the other wanted to know more about what he meant by the case breaking open.

Ultimately, I went with the safer option. "Breaking open how?"

His expression took on the hard cop stare, and he chewed on the corner of his mouth for a moment. I could tell he was weighing something in his mind as he stared at me.

"Come here." Stepping out of his office, he snagged my hand and led me down the hallway.

"Where are we going?"

"Someplace I probably shouldn't take you, but seeing as you're involved, I don't feel that guilty about letting you in on what's happening."

What did that mean? "I'm so confused."

He stopped in front of a door marked "Observation 2" and turned the handle, ushering me inside.

I paused, surprised to see someone else in the room.

An older gentleman in uniform turned away from the window set into the wall. It was Sheriff Driemeyer. He frowned when he saw me.

"Jack, why is she here?"

"Because she's proven useful, and she might pick up on something we won't."

My gaze swung to Jack. "What is going on? Who is that?" I pointed at the window and the young man seated at a table on the other side.

"That is Theodore Alcorn. He's the one who tried to turn us to ash."

A quick zing of adrenaline went through me. "Really? You're sure?"

"Pretty sure. He's who I followed out of Darcy's lecture. A camera caught him exiting the lecture hall just before me. Another caught him running out of the building just before the tank in the storage room blew."

For a moment, I studied the young man on the other side of the glass. He didn't look like the type to trap two people in a burning room. "He hardly seems the type."

"Scared people do dumb things," Sheriff Driemeyer said.

True. I glanced at Jack. "So, what do you want me to do?"

"Stay in here with Sheriff Driemeyer and observe." Jack took a step toward the door. "I'll be back." He let himself out.

"Have a seat, Ms. Fowler."

Warily, I eyed the sheriff. I'd met him briefly several times at local events and once more formally after Mandi Davis and Nile Flaherty tried to kill James and me a few months ago. I wasn't too sure what to make of him or even whether to trust him after the comment Mandi made about him suddenly growing a spine. It made me wonder how many shady deals he'd had his hands in over the years.

At the moment, though, it seemed like I didn't have much choice but to do as he asked.

Sinking into a folding chair in front of the window, I watched as the door on the other side opened and Jack stepped in. Sheriff Driemeyer positioned another chair next to me and balanced a notepad on his knee. I clutched the little macaron box and kept my eyes glued to the kid, watching his body language stiffen as Jack pulled up a chair and sat down across from him, setting a folder and a notepad on the table.

"Hi, Theodore. I'm Detective Fiore. Thank you for coming in to speak to me."

The kid rolled his eyes. "That officer who brought me here didn't really give me a choice. Said it would 'behoove me' to cooperate." He air-quoted, then crossed his arms.

"Well, he wasn't wrong. It's always best to cooperate with the police. Makes things go much more smoothly and gets you on your way much quicker."

"Yeah, whatever. What do you want? All the cop said was you had some questions about Ella's death. I don't know nothing. I barely knew her."

"First, let me read you your rights, okay?" Before he said anything else, Jack pulled a small card from his pocket and read the Miranda rights to him, then asked if he understood.

"Yeah, I know what they are."

"So, do you want to speak to me, then?" Jack spun a pen between his fingers.

"I ain't got nothing to hide." Theodore shifted his arms and cast a quick glance away.

I narrowed my eyes. He was lying.

"I never said you did. I just want you to tell me about your relationship with her."

"There wasn't one. I told you I barely knew her. We had, like, two classes together, and we usually sat on opposite sides of the room."

"Okay. You were just acquaintances, then? Classmates?"

"Yep. Can I go now?"

"Not yet. Let's talk about Monday evening."

That shifty-eyed look came back. "What about it?"

"Why did you leave Ms. Fowler's lecture? I assume you were there because your professor said it was part of your grade."

Theodore nodded.

"So, why leave? Wouldn't that affect your grade?"

"I had to use the restroom. Figured I'd be back before he noticed I was gone."

Jack hummed. "So, if you just went to the restroom, why did you run out of the building around the same time someone set a fire in one of the storage rooms that caused an explosion?" He flipped open the folder and pulled out a photograph.

I leaned forward but couldn't see what it was. "What's the picture of?" I asked the sheriff.

"Theodore leaving the building."

That answer made the lack of color in the young man's face make more sense.

"Why did you run, Theodore? Was it because you set the fire?"

"No."

"Was it because you knew it would ignite those pressurized tanks and make them explode?" Jack continued like he hadn't spoken.

"No." Theodore's voice rose slightly.

"Was it because you knew you might have just killed two people with your actions?"

"No!"

Jack slammed a fist down on the table, making it rattle and causing Theodore—and me—to jump. "Then what was it?"

"I saw you there, and I…" Theodore's voice trailed off. He swallowed hard, looking away.

"And you what?"

"Look, I smoked some weed before I came, okay? I didn't want to get caught."

"Theodore, marijuana is legal in Washington." Jack leaned closer. "I wouldn't have cared if you were just high." His eyes narrowed. "Did you have some on you?"

Once again, Theodore looked away but stayed silent.

Jack hummed softly. "Under a certain amount, you're allowed to possess it in public, you just can't use it. I doubt you're dumb enough to break it out in the middle of the lecture and use it, so were you carrying more than the legal amount? Is that why you ran?"

Theodore cast a quick look at Jack, then went back to staring at a point on the wall.

"Because I did some digging on you, Theodore. You have a past conviction for possession. I also heard a rumor you supply your classmates with weed. *That* is definitely illegal."

"That kid definitely had more pot on him than he should have," I muttered. He'd turned an even paler shade of white.

"Seems like," the sheriff replied.

Jack sat back in his seat, still twirling his pen. "In fact, I would bet I could search you right now and find enough on you to charge you."

Theodore shifted in his seat. A muscle in his jaw ticked. "You can't touch me without a reason. I know my rights. Your lackey patted me down for weapons before he shut me in here. That's all you're allowed to do. I'm here voluntarily."

"Oh, I know." Abruptly, Jack sat up, slapping his folder closed. "I guess that puts us at an impasse, then."

A bit of color returned to Theodore's face. "So, I can go now?"

I could hear the skepticism in his voice. He wasn't the only one unsure of the play here. What was Jack doing? He'd barely asked him anything.

Sheriff Driemeyer unclipped his radio mic from his shoulder. "Go ahead, Hauser."

My eyebrows drew together, and I glanced at the sheriff. A moment later, a soft, "Copy," came over the radio, then I heard footsteps outside the room. What was going on?

Jack's chair scraped across the tiled floor. "I guess so. Unless you have something to add about Ella?"

Theodore leapt out of his chair. "Nope. Didn't really know her."

Before he could take more than one step toward the door, it opened. Alex Hauser, an old friend of mine, and the department's K-9 deputy, filled the doorway. His dog darted past.

"Oh, crap," Alex said. "Sorry, man. I didn't know you were in here."

Theodore backed up against the wall, eyes so round I thought they'd pop out of his head.

"You didn't have the vacant sign flipped to occupied," Alex continued.

"Get control of your dog, man." Theodore flattened his palms on the wall, trying to become one with the paint. The fawn-colored German Shepherd advanced, like a laser-guided missile fixed on its target.

"Sorry." Alex stepped into the room, calling to the dog in German.

But rather than return to his handler, the dog sat in front of Theodore, then glanced back at Alex and whined.

"Yes," the sheriff said quietly.

I cast a quick glance at him, then back at the action in the other room. I was still so confused.

Alex's eyebrow went up. He turned to Jack. "Did you search him?"

"Just a pat down for weapons."

"Really?" Alex's gaze traveled back to Theodore. "Turn around and put your hands against the wall."

Theodore's eyes bulged again. "What? No, man. You can't touch me. I'm here voluntarily, and he told me I could leave." He pointed at Jack, then quickly snatched his hand back when the K-9 stood up and barked a warning.

"Atlas, *platz*," Alex said to the dog.

Atlas's butt hit the floor again.

Alex advanced toward Theodore. "That was before my dog alerted to the presence of drugs."

"I smoke weed, man. He probably smells that."

"He's not trained to scent marijuana. Turn around." Alex rested a hand on the butt of his gun.

"Oh, crap," I muttered, leaning closer. This was like watching a live-action thriller movie.

Theodore looked at Jack, then the door, then Alex before looking at the door again.

"He's going to run," I said.

"Yep." Sheriff Driemeyer stood, setting his notebook down on his vacant chair, getting ready to assist if needed.

"Don't do it, Theodore," Jack said, taking a step to the side, cutting off the kid's route around the table.

"My dog *will* bite you if you run," Alex warned.

"Don't be dumb," I muttered. I did not want to see the kid get bitten.

Desperation was in every line of Theodore's body. He glanced around the room again, before finally looking at the dog.

His shoulders slumped in defeat.

Jack and Alex shared a look, then slowly advanced

together. Alex took control of Atlas while Jack pulled a pair of handcuffs off his duty belt and slid one onto Theodore's wrist as he turned him around to face the wall.

"You're just being detained for now. If there's nothing on you, we'll let you go." Jack snapped the other cuff on.

Theodore rested his head on the wall. Even from here and with his hair partially obscuring his face, I could see the fear and defeat in his expression. I would bet my dessert truck he had drugs in his pocket.

A moment later, he confirmed my suspicion.

"In my jacket. Inside pocket. I have some pills."

Jack put some gloves on, then searched Theodore's pocket. He pulled out a small baggie with several white pills inside.

"Theodore, I have some bad news. You don't get to leave now. You're under arrest for possession of narcotics."

A soft thump echoed when the kid banged his head on the wall. "This is stupid."

"Well, you shouldn't have tried to kill me and my friend on Monday. I wouldn't have come looking for you."

"I never said I did that!" Theodore straightened and struggled against his cuffs.

Jack put an arm against his shoulder blades and pushed him into the wall. "Don't make this worse."

"I'm not, man. Look, what if—" Theodore stopped, running his tongue over his lips. He took a breath and let it out, then tried again. "What if I told you Ella had issues with one of our professors?"

Jack stilled and looked back at Alex.

I propped my elbow on my knee and put my chin in my hand. If I had some popcorn and a tall fountain soda, I'd be all set.

"Go on," Jack said.

"Uh-uh. I know how this works. I want immunity."

Alex scoffed. "You've got a trafficking amount of oxy in your pocket. No."

"We'll talk to the D.A. and see about getting you a lesser charge. *If* you can provide information that leads us to Ella's killer." Jack raised an eyebrow, silently asking if Theodore agreed to those terms.

With a huff, Theodore turned slightly. "Can I sit down, at least, while we talk?"

"Sure." Jack led him back to the table. "Here. I'll even cuff you to the table. How does that sound?"

"Peachy." Theodore rolled his eyes but didn't argue.

Taking a handcuff key from one of his pockets, Jack unlocked one of Theodore's cuffs, then secured it to a ring on the table.

"I'm gonna head out now unless you need me still." Alex hooked a thumb toward the door.

"No, I'm good, thanks."

"Any time." With a smile and quick two-finger salute, Alex called Atlas, and they left.

Something about the way Alex phrased his goodbye made me suspicious, especially when coupled with the sheriff's earlier cryptic "go" message over the radio.

I turned to Sheriff Driemeyer. "You guys planned that, didn't you?"

He grinned but stayed silent.

Sneaky, sneaky… but effective.

"Now that you're under arrest, I'll remind you again of your Miranda rights," Jack said, settling across from Theodore. "Do you still wish to speak to me?"

"I said I did. Ask your damn questions."

Jack arched an eyebrow at the kid's attitude. "Okay. Elaborate on what you meant by 'issues' with a professor."

Theodore licked his lips again, eyes darting around, before he set his hands on the table and leaned in to speak. "A few weeks ago, I came in to work on a project in between classes. Ella was there, but so was Professor Snyder. They were arguing."

"About?" Jack rolled a hand.

"Don't know. I was in the hallway and just heard raised voices in the lab. They stopped when I walked in. The only words I heard were from Ella. She said he needed to take her seriously."

Sheriff Driemeyer grunted. I looked over to see a contemplative expression pulling his eyebrows together.

"But you don't know what the professor needed to take seriously?" Jack asked.

"Nope." Theodore leaned back and attempted to cross his arms, but the one cuffed to the table kept him from doing that. He dropped them awkwardly to the table.

Jack asked several more questions, often the same thing just reworded, before eventually pushing away from the table to stand. "Thank you for your cooperation, Theodore. Someone will be in shortly to take you back for processing."

Theodore stayed quiet, staring at a point on the wall to his right.

Gathering his folder and notepad, Jack left the room. A moment later, he stepped into the observation room.

"Great plan, Jack," the sheriff said. "Worked like a charm."

"Well, it wasn't guaranteed, but I figured with his record, it was worth a shot." He crossed his arms and studied Theodore through the window for several moments. "Whether any of that info is useful, we'll see." He turned to me. "What do think, Delaney? Do you have anything to add or questions I should go ask before he's taken for booking?"

Tipping my head, I thought about the interview. Only one thing really stood out: Theodore's claims about his relationship with Ella. "You know, for someone who claims to not have known Ella, he sure does seem familiar with her."

"What do you mean?" Jack frowned.

"Well, for one he says they only had a couple classes together and that she sat on the opposite side of the room. But he immediately knew who you were talking about. And two, why would he remember one argument between a girl he 'barely knew'"—she air-quoted—"and their professor when all he really heard was loud voices? Why would her telling the professor to take her seriously stick in his mind?"

Jack's mouth flattened into a hard line as he studied me.

"And," I continued, "if what Theodore heard was true, what was it she wanted to be taken seriously about? I doubt it was her grade. It might have been about something else, like harassment or something. Maybe she told Professor Snyder someone was bothering her, but he dismissed her concerns."

The look Jack gave me intensified before he lifted his gaze to Sheriff Driemeyer. Some silent communication passed between the two men.

"Go talk to this professor," the sheriff said. "See if you can get some insight into any problems the girl was having on campus. Take her with you." He pointed at me.

"Me?" My gaze snapped between him and Jack.

Sheriff Driemeyer nodded. "That was good insight. Let's see what sort of read you can get on this Professor Snyder."

Jack sighed. "I'm not sure that's a good idea. Showing that she's publicly involved in the investigation makes her a target."

I scoffed. "I'm already a target. Or have you forgotten about what happened Monday?"

Something dark and angry entered his eyes, turning him from the stern-faced cop into someone whose bad side I would not want to get on. I was glad that energy wasn't directed at me.

"I remember. Fine. You can go, but you will let me do the talking. You're there to observe."

I held up my hands. "Okay." I crossed my toes, knowing that if a relevant question popped into my head during the interview, I would not hesitate to ask it.

But he didn't need to know that. In this instance, it was better to ask forgiveness than permission.

Twenty-Six

Our footsteps echoed on the painted cinder-block walls of the college's photography building as we made our way down the hall to Professor Snyder's office a few hours later. I'd had time to go back to the church kitchen and work for a little while before the professor's office hours started. Jack thought we'd get more and better information if we didn't pull him out of class. I agreed. I knew I was less likely to talk if I were in the middle of working and someone wanted to pull me away from that.

Stopping outside his door, Jack rapped his knuckles on the wood. A moment later it opened.

In his mid-forties, Tim Snyder was a thin man with iron-gray hair at his temples. Wire-rimmed glasses framed pale gray eyes. Tiny lines fanned out from their corners, indicating a man who liked to laugh.

Right now, though, those gray eyes looked at us with concern as Jack raised his badge and introduced himself.

"Professor Snyder, I'm Detective Fiore with the Carter County Sheriff's Department. This is Delaney Fowler. May we come in and talk to you for a few moments about Ella Kerns? It won't take long."

"Of course." The man's expression cleared slightly in understanding, and he stepped back to motion us inside. "Have a seat. Please." He waved us toward the worn, upholstered chairs in front of his desk.

Thanking him softly, I moved to the one closest to the far wall, which left me partially hidden by the computer monitor. That was fine by me. As Jack said, I was here to observe. Mostly.

Professor Snyder rounded his desk and sat down. "What can I do for you? I'm happy to answer whatever questions you have. Ella's death has shaken the entire department. She was a talented student."

I studied him, knowing Jack would ask me my impression of the man later. He seemed genuine. His gaze was steady, not shifty like Theodore's had been, and his expression seemed open and polite.

"I'll cut right to the chase. We've received a tip that you and Ella had a disagreement a few weeks ago. Tell me about that."

Professor Snyder's mouth tightened ever so slightly in irritation. "Students disagree with professors daily. That's hardly unusual. It was a minor issue."

"Right, but you were yelling loud enough to be heard from the hallway. That sounds like more than just a minor disagreement."

Snyder's gaze shifted from Jack to me, then back again, his mouth pressed into a tight line. I crossed my legs and looped my hands over my knee, hoping to appear like a friendly ear and not like someone digesting and studying his every word and move.

"Ella was upset about a project submission," Snyder finally said.

"Upset how?" Jack asked.

"She accused me of favoritism." The professor's jaw flexed faintly. "She believed another student's work was... not possible."

My eyebrows rose slightly.

"Not possible, how?" Jack asked. "Like, computer-generated, or something?"

That would make sense. AI art was all the rage in some circles.

"Not exactly, no. The assignment required students to create a multi-layer composite—a blended photograph, if you will—using practical darkroom techniques. No digital manipulation. The skill level required is advanced but it's not out of the realm for any of my students in that class."

"And she believed someone cheated?" Jack asked.

"In a way, yes. She believed someone submitted work that wasn't theirs. Or, at least, not completely. In her opinion, the student's use of lighting consistency, grain structure, and burn patterns were beyond what they had demonstrated previously."

The what? "Grain structure?" I asked before I could stop myself.

Jack shot me a quick look.

I rolled my lips in and sent him a quick doe-eyed look of apology. I'd broken the cardinal rule and asked a question.

Professor Snyder continued, oblivious to the silent conversation that just passed between me and Jack. "Film leaves fingerprints, and students develop habits. They have particular exposure choices and contrast preferences. Ella argued that this particular piece didn't match the student's prior portfolio."

Jack tipped his head slightly. "And you didn't agree?"

"No. While I agreed it was an improvement to hi—to the student's abilities, it didn't feel out of the realm of what could be considered natural growth."

I narrowed my eyes a fraction at the professor's slip of the tongue. Had he been about to say "his" instead of "the student's?"

"Ella disagreed with me. Quite vocally, I may add. I admit, I raised my voice, but it was in an effort to shut down the conversation. I had already tried several times much more quietly."

His gaze moved between us, the expression in his eyes earnest and without artifice. "Ella was an excellent student. Driven and meticulous in her work. She strived to be the best."

"Do you think she was jealous of the other student?" I asked. Jack would just have to deal with me asking questions. This was important to the conversation, and there was no guarantee he would ask that.

"No. She didn't get jealous when someone did better than she did. She just got more competitive. In this case, I think what upset her was the perceived lack of integrity."

He leaned forward. "I don't know what you heard or who it was from but let me be clear. I did not dismiss her without recourse. I told her if she could bring me concrete evidence that the student's work was not their own or did not follow the guidelines of the assignment, then I would take action. Academic misconduct allegations are serious business. It can ruin a student. But I simply could not take action on a hunch. It would harm them, and me, to do so."

For a second, Jack's dark gaze pinned the professor's, assessing him. "Tell me about your reaction to the news of Ella's death."

I blinked, my brain scrambling to follow the abrupt shift in the conversation.

Professor Snyder seemed to have a similar problem. He straightened in his seat, surprise flashing in his eyes before a sadness took hold.

"Her death was devastating," he said quietly. "I've never lost a student before, and I've been teaching almost twenty years. She was…" He paused, the sadness in his eyes making its way to his mouth, turning the corners down. "She was a light. Every day, she came in with a smile, excited to learn." His frown turned quizzical, and he tipped his head. "Except for the last week or so before she died."

Jack's gaze sharpened. "How so?"

"I'm not sure." Professor Snyder lifted a shoulder. "She just seemed… quieter? Less smiley?"

"Was this before or after your argument?" Jack asked.

"Before. She died two days after that." He looked away, a muscle ticking in his jaw. "I don't know what you're thinking, detective, but whoever killed her, it wasn't me. I hope you find them, though. I can't think of a single reason Ella deserved to die."

I couldn't, either, but someone thought there was one.

"Who was the student she accused of cheating, professor?" Jack asked.

"I'd prefer not to say. Like I said, allegations of academic misconduct can ruin a student. Even if nothing is ever proven."

I glanced at Jack, wondering if he would let that stance stand. If the student had truly cheated, it was motive.

"Did you inform that student she had concerns?" Jack shifted in his seat.

"No." Snyder shook his head. "I would never betray a student's confidence that way." He raised a finger. "I did, however, remind the class as a whole to be sure they weren't taking shortcuts and were working alone."

"Did any of your students, particularly the one Ella accused of cheating, seem more upset than the others about the reminder?" Jack continued.

"Not really, no."

There was a quick knock on the door.

I glanced back to see a student peeking in through the small window.

Jack rose and held out a hand. "We won't take up any more of your time. Thank you for speaking with us, professor."

"You're very welcome." Professor Snyder shook his hand. "If you have any other questions, please reach out." He took a business card from the holder on the desk and held it out.

"Thank you." Jack took the card and slid it into his pocket.

I stood and followed Jack to the door, offering the professor a quick smile.

Muttering a quick, "Excuse me," to the student waiting in the hallway, we headed out.

"What did you think?" Jack asked as we walked side-by-side down the hall. "Was he telling the truth?"

"I think so, yes. He didn't seem shifty or like he was trying to hide something. He didn't even really show any guilt over not taking Ella's concerns more seriously."

"I noticed that. He didn't even want to entertain the idea a student cheated without some sort of proof."

I weighed the consequences of cheating against murder. It didn't seem plausible it could be the motive for her death, but I'd heard of crazier reasons. "Why didn't you push him for a name?"

"Because he isn't the only one who can give that up."

"Theodore?"

Jack made a low, non-committal sound. "Maybe. I was thinking of a few of her other classmates. Ones she was close to who don't have a reason to want to get the charges against them reduced."

"Oh. True. He'll say a lot that doesn't mean much to sway a judge."

"Exactly. It'll also be hard to convince a jury what he says is true when his integrity is already in the toilet, even if it is. I need someone without a checkered past."

I tucked the corner of my mouth between my teeth, thinking about how we could get that information. "I could talk to Allie again and see if she knows who might be able to help."

"That's a good idea, but I'll talk to her. You don't need to be any more involved in this."

Mouth flat and my eyebrows dipped in a perturbed frown, I cast him a quick, annoyed glance. "I don't know why you insist on denying my help. I get answers. Plus, I'm already here." I gestured around us.

"Because it's dangerous, Delaney. I've made peace with the idea that I'm a target, and I've trained for it. You haven't. It's a lot easier for someone to get to you and harm you than it is me. What we're doing today—it's not going to become a thing."

I huffed. "I'll be fine. I pay attention to my surroundings everywhere I go. I'm a woman, after all. Murderers of college students aren't the only danger out there for someone like me."

"But it's one less you have to worry about if you keep your nose out of this."

I rolled my eyes. "Of all the—" I cut myself off, turning to stare at the main door as we walked right past it. "Where are we going? That's the exit." I stopped to point.

Jack, now several steps ahead, gestured to the atrium just beyond us. "To the photography exhibit."

My confused frown turned curious. "Oh? I didn't know there was one."

"And that's why I'm the detective, Delaney. There was a flyer on Professor Snyder's bulletin board. There have also been several up and down the hallway. Plus, the banner." He pointed to the six-foot-tall, free-standing banner positioned near the wall to the left.

"Oh." I chuckled. "I guess so." Maybe I could do a little better job about paying attention to my surroundings. To be fair, though, I usually did when I was by myself. Jack's presence made me feel safe, so I focused more on other things than on what was around me.

With a wry smile, he tipped his head toward the atrium. "Let's go."

We wandered into the room, immediately dwarfed by the tall ceiling. Sound echoed in the cavernous room, making it feel like there were more people milling about than there actually were.

"Are we looking for anything in particular?" I sent a quick glance at Jack as we entered the maze of temporary walls covered in photographs.

"Just patterns."

"Patterns? Of what?"

"Names."

Ah. I knew what he was getting at. We were looking for someone who excelled—possibly because they cheated.

So, I paid attention to the creators. There were several who showed up a few times, including Ella. Jack jotted down names as we went.

"Oh, I think these are the composition photos Professor Snyder was talking about." I paused next to a panel. They were all similar in structure, but still very different. Some of them were definitely better than others.

Ella's was spectacular. But so was one that surprised me.

Theodore Alcorn's.

Twenty-Seven

I was proud of myself. I lasted roughly eighteen hours before I broke my promise.

Well, I guess it wasn't really a promise, because I never promised anything. Jack hauled me into the photography exhibit before he could extract that from me.

But now that I had some time to think and mull over our conversation with Professor Snyder, as well as the details of the case, I had questions I wanted answers to, and waiting on Jack wouldn't get them. He might not even know which questions to ask.

Adding the last petal to the buttercream flower I was working on, I set the piping bag down and wiped my hands on a towel. Reaching for my phone, I paused the music and found Allie Kerns's name in my contacts.

I left it on speaker and picked up my piping bag again. Baking helped me think and stay focused.

After five rings, it rolled to voicemail.

"Hey, Allie. It's Delaney," I said after the beep. "I just had a question about Ella's classmates at the college and if she was close to any of them. If you could give me a quick call back, that would be great, thanks."

Tapping the screen with a knuckle to end the call, I frowned. Well, that was a bummer. Hopefully, I wouldn't have to wait too long for her to call back.

Lucky for me, I had things to keep me busy.

Grabbing another square of parchment paper, I put a dab of frosting on the flower nail and started in on another rose. These were for an anniversary cake. I was almost done and then I could add them all to the cream-colored, single-tier, round cake sitting in the fridge.

I had just started adding flowers to the cake when my phone rang.

It was Allie.

Answering, I put it on speaker. "Hey, there. Thanks for calling me back."

"Oh, sure. Sorry I didn't answer before. I was cleaning and didn't hear the phone ring."

"That sounds exciting for a Friday morning."

She chuckled. "I have to work all day and all weekend and this place is a mess. I haven't touched it since Ella—" Her voice broke suddenly, and she paused. "Anyway, it needed cleaned," she finally finished.

That made total sense. Doing normal, everyday tasks would be the last thing I think I'd want to do if one of my sisters died.

"I'm glad you called, though," Allie continued.

"Oh?"

"Yeah. While I was cleaning the guest room, I found a piece of paper behind the nightstand. Something Ella wrote, but it doesn't make a whole lot of sense to me."

I frowned at the phone. "What's on it?"

"Photography notes. But not about class or any of her projects. She just wrote, 'How did he blend double exposure with shadow layering without the edges ghosting?' She also wrote, 'Lighting doesn't match previous projects.' and, 'Why that picture?'"

I heard some rustling. "Do you know what that means?"

My heart thundered in my ears. Was this the evidence Ella needed for Professor Snyder? Or just perhaps her thoughts on what made her suspect cheating? "Maybe. Is that all it says?"

"No. Down in the corner, she wrote, 'Talk to Snyder,' and underlined it twice. I think that's one of her professors."

"It is," I murmured, chewing on my bottom lip as I thought about who the "he" in the note could be. "Allie, were there any classmates Ella was particularly close to? Ones she might confide in about things?"

"Hmm… maybe? I know she was pretty good friends with a girl named Sarah. She talked about another one too. Kenadie, I think her name is."

"Okay. Do you know last names?"

"No, sorry. Why did you want names, anyway?"

"It kind of has to do with that note. I don't want to say too much. That's more up to Detective Fiore to disclose, because I'm not sure what all he wants to get out. He needs to see that paper. Can you take it to him before your shift?"

"Can I give it to you to do that? I don't really have time to run to the police station until Monday."

Jack would most definitely want that information before then. "Sure, that's fine."

"Great. Can you meet me at the coffee shop around eleven? That's when my shift starts."

I glanced at the clock on the wall. It was just after ten. "That's not a problem." I had just enough time to finish this cake.

"Okay, I'll see you there. Thanks."

"Yep, bye."

"Bye." She hung up and my phone went dark.

Time to kick it into gear. There was no telling how long I would be at the station, talking to Jack, and I wanted this cake off my plate, no pun intended. This was my last special order to finish before I focused solely on Daphne's wedding.

Time flew off the clock as I placed flower after flower on the cake. I put the last flourish to the "Happy Anniversary" text as the hour-hand finally ticked to eleven o'clock.

Straightening, I admired my work, smiling at how perfect it looked. I did good with this one. Pink and lavender flowers cascaded down the side and around the rim. A flowing, minty-green script filled the top, not a wiggle in the lettering in sight.

Smiling, I popped it into a box, then in the fridge. The couple's daughter would be by tomorrow morning to pick it up.

With a quick slap at the wall to turn off the lights, I hurried up the steps, slipping into my jacket as I exited the building. It was chilly today. I hoped it warmed up some next weekend, or we were all going to freeze during Daphne and Morgan's ceremony. At least the reception would be inside a heated tent. Daphne didn't want to move the ceremony in there, though, unless it rained. She wanted to look at the lake when she pledged forever to the man she loved.

I couldn't say I blamed her. The lake was a lot prettier than the blah white wall of the tent.

I made the short drive downtown and found a place to park near the coffee shop. The wind gusted as I shut my door, going straight down the collar of my jacket.

With a soft squeal, I yanked the zipper up, then locked my car. I was glad I was meeting Allie at the coffee shop now. A tall, hot latte would be coming back to work with me. I wasn't acclimated to the cooler weather yet.

Hurrying down the sidewalk, hunched into my jacket, I turned into the coffee shop. The smell of freshly-roasted coffee assailed my nostrils, bringing a smile to my face. There wasn't much better than the smell of fresh coffee.

I scanned the area behind the counter for Allie but didn't see her. She must be in the back.

"Hi. What can I get you?" the young woman at the register asked.

"I'll take a white chocolate raspberry latte, please."

"Hot or iced?"

"Definitely hot," I said with a quick smile.

The girl grabbed a cup and wrote on the side with a marker. "Can I get a name, please?"

"Delaney."

She added that to the cup, then totaled up my order.

"Is Allie here?" I held my card over the reader to pay.

The girl looked up with a frown. "Not yet. I think my boss is going to call her and make sure she didn't forget she had a shift. She's not usually late."

Alarm bells clanged in my head, but I pasted a smile on my face. There were now people in line behind me, and I didn't want to hold them up. "Okay. Well, if she comes in before I leave, can you tell her Delaney's here?"

"Sure."

"Thank you." I stepped to the side to wait on my drink.

My smile died as I found a place against the wall to wait, a concerned frown taking its place. She should be here. Hopefully, her car didn't break down or something on the way to work, and she was just running late for some benign reason.

I kept my eye on the door while I waited, hoping she'd pop in, a bit frazzled, but with a smile.

"Delaney."

The same girl who took my order called my name and held out my drink.

With another polite smile, I thanked her and took it, then hurried back to my car, but not because it was cold outside this time.

My headlights flashed once as I unlocked the car. Quickly sliding inside, I set the cup in the holder and started the engine. I would just pop over to Allie's apartment and make sure everything was okay. During our conversation outside her parents' house a couple of weeks ago, she mentioned she lived in the new apartment complex in town. There was only one that fit that bill. Hopefully, if I managed to follow the same route she took to work, I would find her if she was broken down on the side of the road somewhere.

But eight minutes later, I pulled into her apartment complex without seeing a single car on the side of the road.

I slowed, staring up at the three-story buildings. There were three of them and they formed a horseshoe shape around the main parking lot. I didn't know which unit, or even which building, was hers.

Crap.

But I did know her car. That would at least give me a place to start.

At little more than a creep, I rolled through the parking lot until I spotted Allie's red Ford sedan. Finding a visitor's spot, I parked and got out and walked toward her car.

"Oh, heck yeah." On the parking block in front of her car, stenciled in black paint, was her unit number, "Bldg 1, 307."

I looked at the building directly in front of me. Was this building one? Did that mean the third floor?

Scanning the façade of the gray-sided building, I noted a brown plaque near the entrance to the covered staircase that wound its way up the middle of the building, doors coming off it like spokes on a wheel. It contained unit numbers for the three floors: 105 – 108, 205 – 208, and 305 – 308. I was in the right place.

Jogging toward the covered breezeway, I paused as a man emerged from the shadows.

He glanced up, and I couldn't stop my gasp of surprise.

It was Leo Stanhope.

What was he doing here?

Recognition flared in his dark eyes when he spotted me. His step quickened and his gaze dropped as he hurried down the last few stairs and hung a left toward the parking lot. In seconds, he was inside an old gray truck and backing out of his parking space.

My eyes narrowed. Was that a *numbered* parking space?

Waiting until he was out of sight, I walked over to look at the parking block where he'd been parked.

It was. Building 1, unit 205.

Odd.

Allie never mentioned he lived here. In fact, she'd told me about how she insisted Ella come stay with her after she broke up with Leo so he couldn't find her.

How weird would it be if none of them knew he lived in Allie's building?

But why wouldn't Ella know he lived here?

I didn't have answers for that, but I knew who might.

Allie.

Turning around, I jogged back toward the breezeway and headed up the stairs.

By the time I reached the first set of steps leading from the second floor to the third, I was wishing I spent more time in the gym and less time in the kitchen and had to slow down. If the zombie apocalypse ever hit and I had to run up more than one flight of stairs to escape, I was screwed. My legs were burning. So were my lungs.

Reaching the landing, I paused for a moment to suck in a couple breaths. After Daphne's wedding, I needed to haul the weights out of the closet and download some exercise videos. This was pathetic. Outrunning the zombie apocalypse up at least three flights of stairs was a must.

Scanning the doors surrounding the landing, I found Allie's in the corner on the left.

I walked over and knocked.

No answer.

And no noise behind the door, either.

I tried again. "Allie? It's Delaney. Are you in there?"

When I still didn't get an answer, I tried the door. It was probably locked, but just on the off-chance—

The knob turned easily in my hand.

Well, crap.

My heart did a little flip in my chest as I pushed the door inward.

It only opened about a foot before it hit something.

I poked my head inside.

"Oh! No!" The words left me on a sharp gasp.

On the floor, just inside the door, lay Allie. Face down, with one arm beneath her and the other above her head, her feet and legs blocked the door. Scattered past her on the carpet were the contents of her purse. She had her keys clutched in her fingers.

Squeezing through the doorway, I scurried around her prone form to her head. "Allie?" Kneeling beside her, I reached out to brush her hair back.

That's when I noticed the blood in her hair.

"No. Oh, no. No, no, no, no. Oh, don't be dead. Please, don't be dead."

With gentle fingers, I brushed her blonde locks away from her neck and pressed my fingers below her ear, feeling for a pulse.

A soft thump bumped my fingers.

"Oh, thank goodness. You're alive. Okay." The wave of relief that rushed over me made my head feel fuzzy. I sucked in a breath to steady myself.

Hands shaking now, I took my phone from my pocket and called for help. The conversation with the dispatcher was a bit of a blur. All I could think was why target Allie? Why now? What did she know?

Over and over, the thoughts cycled through my mind. Even when the paramedics showed up and I answered their questions, even on the drive to the hospital behind the ambulance, I couldn't help but wonder who wanted both Kerns sisters dead.

Twenty-Eight

"You know, I would say I'm surprised to see you here, but I'm really not."

The tired male voice I knew so well brought my head up from where I stared at the book I'd pulled up on my phone, trying to pass the time while I waited on news about Allie's condition. I tried to feign a smile of welcome but just couldn't muster one.

The sour expression on his face eased a little. He sat down next to me. "How are you holding up?"

I lifted a shoulder and turned off my phone screen, putting it face down in my lap. "Okay, I guess. Better than her family." I tipped my chin toward Allie's parents across the waiting room. Dave stood at the window with a deep-set frown in place, arms tightly crossed and his back stiff as he looked out at the busy parking lot. Paige sat in a chair a few feet away, dabbing at her eyes with a tissue as she stared off into space. They just looked shell-shocked.

Jack glanced their way, studying each of them for a moment. "Yeah. They're understandably upset."

"You talked to them already?"

He nodded.

"Oh." How had I missed that?

"So, what happened? Why were you at her apartment?"

I flicked my gaze to him, then down for several beats before I met his eyes again. "I called her."

That knowing stare, the one that said he disapproved, appeared. "I told you I would talk to her. You didn't even give me a full day."

"I know, but I just—" Pausing, I wet my lips and shook my head. "It was eating at me, and she knows me. I figured we could have a friendly conversation, then I could pass the info along and let you do the deeper digging. It was only supposed to be a phone call." I held up my hands, striving to look innocent. "I swear."

"Okay. Then how did you end up at her place?"

"She was cleaning right before I called her, and she found a paper behind the nightstand in the room where Ella stayed in the days before her death. It had notes about the kid she thought was cheating."

Jack's gaze sharpened, the stare of disapproval disappearing. "Did Allie tell you what it said?"

"Something about exposure and layering without ghosting. I don't remember exactly. She also wrote to tell Snyder in one corner. I don't know if this was the evidence he wanted, or if those were her notes from before, when she first brought him her suspicions. I also asked Allie about Ella's friends, which was the entire purpose of my phone call. She mentioned two. A girl named Sarah and another named Kenadie. She didn't know any last names."

"All right. None of this explains why you went to her apartment."

"She asked me to bring you the note, because she had to get to work, and she had a busy weekend ahead. We thought it would be faster if I grabbed it and brought it to you. I had time."

That stare returned. "What you should have done was call me, and I would have gone to her and collected it."

Again, I shrugged. "It wouldn't have mattered." I looked toward the corridor. "She'd still be back there, unconscious." I turned back to him. "Actually, she could be in a worse state. You might not have gone over there until much later."

He blinked twice, then continued, ignoring my comment. "Do you know what happened to the note? Did you see it anywhere when you found her? I didn't find anything like that on the scene."

"No, but it might have been on her person."

"Okay. I'll check with the medical staff."

"Jack, there's something else." Leo's dark eyes and the flash of fear in them when he saw me flitted through my mind.

"What?"

"I saw Leo Stanhope at Allie's apartment complex. He was leaving as I was arriving. He came down the stairs as I approached."

Jack's expression darkened, giving him an air of danger that sent a shiver up my spine. I was happy that the emotion behind that look was not directed at me.

"Did he say anything to you?" he asked, his tone curt.

"No. He got in a gray pickup that was parked in a spot for Building 1, Unit 205, though."

He repeated the number quietly, then nodded. "I'll look into it. I don't think he lives there. The address I have for him is a single-family home."

"Do you really think he could have done it? I mean, Allie said he had a temper, and the way he acted at the grocery store proves that, but is he really a murderer? Poison is a lot different than getting angry and bludgeoning someone."

"Yeah." Jack tipped his head, that midnight gaze studying my face as he thought about that. "It is."

Soft buzzing erupted from his jacket.

"I'll look into Leo's movements, track down the friends Allie mentioned, and see if the staff here have that note." He fished his phone from his pocket. "You go home, or to work, or somewhere safe and keep your head down. Theodore Alcorn made bail and Leo's still out there. If either one of them is the culprit, well, you've certainly made yourself a nice target today." With one last pointed look, he stood, answering his phone. "Fiore."

Through narrowed eyes, I watched him walk away, phone pressed to his ear. Did he really need to point that out quite so bluntly? I didn't want to think about that.

All I wanted to think about was who had motive to want either sister—or both—dead. Someone was angry enough about something to lace Ella with cyanide and to hit Allie over the head hard enough to leave her unconscious and bleeding on her apartment floor.

But who?

Twenty-Nine

ould that clock tick any louder?

I aimed a glare at the analog clock to my right. It wasn't that quiet in here. I shouldn't be able to hear it.

Puffing out my cheeks, I looked down at my phone again and tried to focus on my book. I'd already read the same paragraph four times and still couldn't remember what it said. I should probably do what Jack suggested and go back to work, but I couldn't bring myself to leave until I knew Allie was okay.

"Family of Allie Kerns?"

My head shot up.

Allie's mother, Paige, flew to her feet. "Yes?"

Her husband, Dave, was instantly at her side.

"Is our daughter okay? Can we see her?" Paige took a step toward the young female doctor.

I stood, too, even though I wasn't family. Jack, who had stayed because he wanted to talk to Allie once the doctors okayed it, came up beside me.

"I'm Dr. Fishbaugh." The young woman directed her attention to Dave and Paige. "Your daughter is awake and talking, but she's a little confused about what happened and where she is. She took a pretty serious blow to the head and has a concussion. Thankfully, the CT scan didn't show any evidence of a bleed on her brain." The doctor held up a hand. "Now, hopefully, that won't change, but for now the scans look stable."

Paige visibly wilted. "Thank goodness. Can we see her?"

"Yes. If you'd like to follow me, I'll take you to her."

Bending down, Paige scooped up her handbag.

Jack raised a hand. "I'm Detective Fiore with the Carter County Sheriff's Department. I need to speak to Ms. Kerns." He turned to Dave and Paige. "I'll give you a few minutes, first, before I invade, though. Take your time."

Dave offered Jack a weak smile. "Thank you. I appreciate that." Taking Paige's hand, they followed the doctor out of the room.

"Can I come in with you?" I asked after they disappeared. "I know you want to question her, but I really just want to see for myself that she's okay." I wrapped my arms around myself, thinking about the fear that punched me in the gut when I found her. "Seeing her like that…" I paused and shook my head, swallowing back the lump that formed in my throat. "I was so relieved when I felt her pulse."

His expression softened. "Sure. I won't even ask you not to ask any questions."

I chuckled. "Good, because I didn't plan to stay silent."

We sat down again to wait. I didn't even bother trying to read again. Focus was impossible with the current state of my whirling mind. I wanted to not only see with my own eyes that Allie was all right, but to find out what happened. I had so many questions.

Did she know the person who did this?

Was it a burglary gone wrong?

A random weirdo who didn't know anything about her and was just looking for something to steal or money to feed a drug habit?

Thankfully, I didn't have to sit around wondering for too long. A nurse popped in about ten minutes later to tell us the family was ready for Jack to speak to Allie.

We headed down the corridor, deeper into the ER. They'd yet to move Allie to a room upstairs. I hoped she wouldn't have to stay overnight but had my doubts. I'm sure her parents would love nothing more than to take her home and fawn over her, but the doctors probably wanted to monitor her for worsening concussion symptoms. She was unconscious a long time, and I knew some brain bleeds could be slow and not show up right away.

The cubicle door slid open with a near-silent whoosh when the nurse grasped the handle and pulled.

I let Jack lead, stepping in just behind him.

The lump reformed in my throat as I took in Allie's slight form under the stark-white hospital blanket and even brighter white bandage surrounding her head.

Glassy blue eyes turned to us.

I tightened my jaw muscles, holding back the urge to gasp as I got a good look at her face. She didn't look much better than when I found her. Just awake. Her skin was nearly the same color as her bandage and dried blood smeared the side of her face and streaked the blonde hair hanging beneath the bandage.

"Hi Allie." Jack walked closer.

I shuffled toward the foot of the bed to lay a hand over her leg under the covers. "How are you doing?"

"My head hurts, but I guess I'm okay." Allie's gaze landed on Jack. "What are you doing here?"

His brows twitched in a silent frown.

"She's still a little confused," Dave said. "We keep telling her what happened, but she keeps forgetting some of the details."

"Ah." Jack nodded once, then turned back to Allie. "Just do your best to answer questions, okay?"

Her head bobbed an affirmative.

"Do you remember what happened at all?"

"Sort of. I remember getting ready to leave. I had my purse. And my keys." She looked past Jack, her eyes unfocused as she struggled to remember. "I opened the door." Her gaze reconnected with his again. "He was there. And he pushed me back inside." She stopped, pressing the heel of one hand to her temple.

"Don't think too hard." I squeezed Allie's leg. "It won't help and will just make everything worse."

"I'm okay. It's just a blur, you know?"

Jack let a beat of silence pass before continuing. "What happened after he pushed you?"

She frowned. "After who pushed me?"

My gaze connected with Jack's.

"You were attacked at home, honey." Paige patted her daughter's hand.

Allie's brows twitched, then the clarity returned to her gaze.

Jack repeated his question.

"I stumbled, then screamed at him to leave," Allie replied quietly. "But he didn't. He grabbed my arms and shook me."

"Did you recognize him?" Paige asked.

Allie glanced at her mother. "No."

My eyebrows rose. She didn't recognize him? Well, that ruled out Leo.

"Do you remember if he said anything?" Jack asked.

"Um…" Allie's eyebrows drew down into a deep vee. "He—he asked what Ella told me. I asked him what he meant, but he just screamed in my face to tell him what she said."

"How did you end up with the head wound?" Jack motioned to the bandage on her head.

The confused frown returned for a moment, then she raised the same hand that she'd pressed to her temple to finger the gauze. "He got frustrated with me, because I couldn't answer him, and he pushed me again. I must have hit something. I don't know what."

I did. The entryway table. There had been blood on it. Allie was lucky her head wound wasn't much, much worse.

"Is there anything you can tell me about your attacker?" Jack asked. "I know you said you didn't know him, but did you see his face?"

"I… um…" She pressed a hand to her temple again. A fierce wince pinched her features, and she moaned softly.

"I think maybe you'll need to continue this another time, detective." Paige laid a hand on her daughter's arm.

"Of course." Jack backed off. Reaching into one of his many pants' pockets, he withdrew a card and handed it to Dave. "Allie, if you think of anything else, or if you feel up to talking again, give me a call, no matter the time."

She offered him a fragile, weary smile. "Okay."

Giving my arm a nudge, Jack tipped his head toward the door.

I nodded. "Allie, you take care." I turned my attention to her parents. "If you guys need anything, please call. I'll help however I can."

"We will," Paige said. "Thank you for finding her and getting her help."

"Of course. I'm glad I was there." Waggling my fingers, I stepped toward the door. "Take care."

I followed Jack into the hallway.

"Well, unless Leo paid someone to terrorize Allie, you can cross Leo off your list."

"Maybe."

"Maybe?" I frowned. "Why maybe? She said she didn't recognize him. She'd know Leo."

"It's like you said, maybe he paid someone."

My nose wrinkled and my lips flattened. "I doubt that. Everything I've learned says he doesn't have two nickels to scrape together."

Jack made a low, non-committal sound.

"So, if not Leo, who? Would she recognize Theodore?"

"I'm not sure. I do know this wasn't random."

"No, definitely not." But if not Leo or Theodore, then who? Who else would have motive?

He scrubbed his hands over his face, leaving behind a weary expression. "I agree Leo's not likely, but I'm going to dig into him anyway. Him and Theodore. And whoever else even gives off a hint of suspicion. Do you need a ride? Did you come in the ambulance with Allie?"

"No. I drove. But thank you."

He nodded once, his attention already shifting to other things. "Okay. I'll walk you out."

"Don't you still need to track down the note Allie found?"

"I will." He motioned me forward.

Thankful his earlier ire with me seemed to be forgotten, I didn't argue and let him lead me outside.

"Where did you park?" He paused at the edge of the sidewalk, peering out at the sea of cars.

"Over there somewhere." I gestured to the left.

Jack stepped off the curb.

"You don't need to walk me to my car, Jack. I'm a big girl."

"Humor me. Two women have been attacked in this case for what they know. Everyone in town knows you like to stick your nose in things you shouldn't, so I'd like to keep you from being the third."

I wanted to be mad about the busybody comment, but the note of genuine concern in his voice held my tongue. I didn't want to end up as the third victim, either.

So, we wove through the rows of cars to my bright blue SUV. The lights flashed when I unlocked it.

Jack opened the driver's door. "Keep your head on a swivel, please. If anything feels strange, get the heck out of there and call me."

"I will."

He stepped back so I could get in, then shut the door.

I started the engine and fastened my seatbelt, but he didn't move. He was much too close for me to drive away. Hitting the window button, I rolled the window down.

"You have to move so I don't run over your toes."

"Lock your doors. As soon as you get in the car. Don't wait for the automatic thing to kick in when you drive off. Close door, hit lock button. Every time. Got it?"

A bit irritated at his high-handed tone, I raised a hand high, one finger extended, then poked the lock button. "There. Happy?"

"No. Because I don't think you're really taking this seriously."

"I am, but you don't need to be so tyrannical. I will be vigilant and keep my phone handy. Stop worrying about me and go find who put Allie in the hospital and murdered Ella." I jabbed a hand toward the building looming over the parking lot.

Jack's intense stare didn't change, but he did take a step back. "Be careful."

"Yep." Hitting the window button, I rolled it up, then put the car in reverse. Once out of my space, I only cast one glance in the rearview mirror at Jack.

He was still watching me.

Should I be more worried?

His actions said yes. But I was learning that Jack was much more cautious than I would ever be or ever had been.

Nearing the parking lot exit, I forced my thoughts off Jack and onto where I should go. The church to work would be the obvious choice, but I needed a clear head to decorate. I could just bake, but I didn't need the overstock.

I glanced at the clock.

It was just after three.

Tapping my fingers on the steering wheel, I made a split-second decision.

Thirty

Darcy lived in a cream-colored single-story cottage with sage green trim that reminded me of something that came out of a kid's fairytale storybook. Situated on a little over an acre just outside of town, she'd turned the lawn into a lush, blooming garden, which, obviously, aided in it looking like a fairytale house.

I turned into the drive and parked, glad to see James's car wasn't there. I quite liked the man, but I needed my sister to myself for a bit.

Hopping out of my car, I walked up to the front door and rang the bell. Hopefully, she was home and hadn't run errands after school.

My worries were short-lived when the door swung open.

"Hey." The welcoming smile on Darcy's face quickly turned into a concerned frown. "What happened?"

"Allie Kerns was attacked." I pushed past her and into the house.

"Is she okay?" Darcy pushed the door shut and led me into the living room.

"She'll be fine with a little time." I perched on the cream sofa.

Darcy sat in the floral-print wingback chair across from me. "That's good. I don't think you came here, though, just to tell me Allie's been attacked."

"No. I came to ask if you could try to get a little information about the students in one of Ella's photography classes."

Darcy's brows twitched into a small frown. "What kind of information?"

"Stuff about their skills. Allie found a note Ella wrote. She thought someone was cheating on an assignment. There was something in the note about ghosting and layers. I don't have it, so I can't tell you exactly what it said. All I know is she was suspicious about the quality of the work in relation to their abilities, and she wanted to tell Professor Snyder." I held up a finger. "Jack and I talked to him, by the way. He couldn't tell us much, except that she brought him her suspicions, but she didn't have any proof, so he didn't do anything."

"Was the stuff in the note proof, then?"

"I don't know. I never saw it. Allie read part of it to me over the phone, but I'm not a photographer, so I don't know what any of it meant, or even remember exactly what she said."

"You can't be any more specific?"

My mouth flattened, and I looked past her to stare out the window as I tried to recall what Allie said. "Not much. There was something about ghosting and edges. And the lighting. Ella wrote that the lighting didn't match past projects."

"Hmm..." Darcy rolled her lips in, a thoughtful frown dipping between her eyebrows. "That's not much to work with, but it gives me a little something, I suppose." She leaned to the side slightly, reaching into the pocket of her leggings and producing her phone. "Let's call Tim and ask him—"

"No." I held up a hand. "We asked him about who Ella thought was cheating, and he wouldn't give up the name. I don't think he will without a court order or more evidence."

Darcy paused, her finger hovering over her phone screen. "Okay..." She rolled her lips in again, thinking. "I could try—"

I interrupted her again. "I have a better idea."

"Oh?"

Standing, I motioned for her to get up. "Let's go look at the student photography exhibition."

"The exhibition?" Darcy frowned as she stood. "How will that help?"

"You can look at the pictures and maybe identify some of their techniques. That should help jog my memory, and just maybe we can figure out who Ella thought was cheating."

A quick smile spread over Darcy's face. "That's not a bad idea. Okay, let's go."

The trek to the college was a quick one. Darcy lived closer than I did, so we were soon pulling into a visitor's spot and heading into the building that housed the photography program.

It was much busier in the middle of the day than when I was last here, even with part of the building roped off for repairs.

Breezing through the main doors, we entered the atrium and the student exhibition.

"So, which photos are we looking at?" Darcy eyed the rows of panels.

"Ones from Snyder's class." Waving a hand at the sea of exhibited work, I wandered in, heading for the group of images Jack and I looked at yesterday.

"Here." I paused in front of the ones I thought were right. "These."

Darcy stopped next to me, then took a few steps back, surveying the photographs. "What did you want me to tell you?"

"I guess what techniques the students used." I needed her

to say something that would ring a bell, so we could dig a little deeper.

With a nod, Darcy started with Ella's pictures of Fernwood and the surrounding area, explaining the layering process she used. The moment she muttered "double exposure" I remembered more of what Allie said.

"That!" I snapped my fingers and pointed at Darcy. "What you said about double exposure. Ella wrote down something about how he blended double exposure with shadow layering and didn't get ghosting."

A smile lifted Darcy's mouth. "Now we're cooking. Okay." She turned back to the pictures, studying them with an even deeper intensity.

"I would say Ella's, this one, and…" Her gaze roved over several photos, and she stepped down to a different panel. "This one. They show the most refinement and likely used that technique. All the others have some element of ghosting or used a different method to achieve a similar result."

Once again, Theodore Alcorn was on the list. The third name, Scotty Adams, I didn't recognize.

Gaze lifting, Darcy glanced around. "Let's find some more of Mr. Alcorn's and Mr. Adams's work."

I followed her through the exhibit. Several times, she paused, studying a photo, then moved on without a word. After we'd walked through the entire exhibition twice, I finally grabbed her arm and stopped her from walking through a third time.

"You have to have some thoughts by now, Darce."

"I do, but I want to look at something again."

She had a look on her face that told me she was puzzling something out. "Okay…"

Darcy took off, beelining to a photo from a different class. She stared at it for several seconds, then looked at me. "What do you see?"

Immediately, I frowned. "What do you mean? Does this use the techniques Ella mentioned? It's a picture of the lake."

"It is, and it does. But do you notice anything familiar?"

Frowning harder, I stared at her for a second before turning to the photo. Tipping my head, I studied it more closely. "Darcy, I don't know anything about photographic techniques. I'm not—" My words abruptly stopped, and I stepped closer as it clicked. The images weren't just similar; they were exact copies. "That's—" I pointed at the photo and looked at my sister. "It's the same."

She nodded. "There's no way anyone else could have taken this picture. Someone used Ella's photographs and passed them off as their own."

Thirty-One

This time, I did the smart thing, and I called Jack instead of marching down to Professor Snyder's office. I even rooted my feet to the floor at the entrance to the exhibition. Thankfully, it didn't take him long to arrive.

"Okay. Time to stop being cryptic. What did you find?" His low, whiskey-toned voice was no-nonsense. Enough so, that I held back the quip that sprang up about his lack of proper greeting.

"Something interesting. Well," I glanced at Darcy, "Darcy found it. But it's obvious enough that even I see it."

Jack held out a hand toward the exhibition. "Lead the way."

He didn't need to tell me twice. I unstuck my feet from the floor and headed into the atrium, not stopping until we were in front of Ella's photographs.

"Take a good look at these."

The beginnings of a confused frown furrowed his forehead. "What?"

I rolled my eyes and huffed. "Just look at them."

He sighed and pinched the bridge of his nose. "Delaney, I'm in no mood to play games."

"There's no game, Jack," Darcy said. "You need to look at these pictures to understand the next ones."

His frown turned more curious. Finally, after studying our faces for several seconds, he nodded once and looked at the photos. "Am I looking for anything in particular?"

"No. Just take in the pictures."

"Okay." His eyes roved over the images for a few moments before he turned to us. "Now what?"

"This way." Motioning him to follow, I headed deeper into the exhibit, pausing in front of the pictures Darcy pointed out earlier.

"Look at these now."

That curious and slightly perturbed frown still on his handsome face, he peered at the photos. "What am I looking for?"

"Check out the setting." Darcy gestured to the central photograph in the display of the lake. The image was black and white.

Jack leaned closer. "I don't get it. It's the lake."

"It is, but it's a specific part of the lake." I pointed out the houses and the boats moored along the shoreline. "These same homes and boats were in Ella's picture collage."

He lifted an eyebrow, incredulity all over his face. "One, how do you know that? And two, so what? It's a public waterway."

"That section isn't." I jabbed a finger at the photo. "And we"—I waved a finger between myself and Darcy—"know that, because we grew up staring at that view." It was the same view I'd admired just a few short weeks ago at Daphne's bridal shower. It was seared into my brain.

I turned my finger back to the picture. "That image was taken from the inn's private dock. You can only gain access if you have the code or if someone from our family invites you out there. Earlier this summer, Scarlett asked if Ella could use the dock for pictures. Of course, we said yes. No one else from the photography program could have gotten that particular shot except her."

Jack's gaze sharpened. The curious frown he'd been sporting morphed into something more intense. "You're sure."

"Yes," Darcy and I said in unison.

Taking his phone from his pocket, he snapped a quick picture of the display, which included the student's name: Malcolm Brookings. "Do either of you know this student?"

We both shook our heads.

"How about whether Ella would share her pictures with another student?"

"I doubt it," Darcy replied. "Submissions for grades have to be original works, unless it's a collaborative assignment. Then, both students' names would be listed." She gestured to the name tag. "Ella's isn't on this, but it's definitely her picture."

"All right. Let's go find Professor Snyder and Professor…" He leaned in to look at the tag, which included the professor's name below the student's. "Garner."

Together, the three of us set off out of the atrium and into the main hallway.

"Do we know where they are at the moment?" I asked. It was the middle of the day. They could be anywhere, even at home.

Jack waved his phone. "I asked the university for copies of the staff's schedules." He thumbed open the screen. After a minute of scrolling, he clicked the button on the side, darkening it, and shoved it back into his pocket. "They're both in class."

"Oh." My nose wrinkled. "I guess we need to wait, then."

He scoffed. "No. This is a murder investigation. I wait for no one." With that proclamation, he walked off down the hall.

I shared a look with Darcy and shrugged. "You heard the

man. Murder waits for no one." I gestured toward him, motioning her to go first.

She chuckled. "I guess not."

Picking up our pace, we hurried after him until we caught up. Taking a detour around the hallways roped off from the lab fire and following the signs for the temporary classroom assignments, we quickly located both Garner's and Snyder's classes.

"If you want to get Professor Snyder, I can talk to Dr. Garner." Darcy tipped her head toward Garner's classroom.

"That's fine. Bring him out here, but don't tell him what's going on. Just tell him it's urgent. If he asks for more information, mention my name."

Darcy nodded and stepped away.

Jack wagged a finger at me. "Stay here."

At my nod, he turned away, disappearing into Snyder's classroom.

Moments later, he reappeared with an annoyed Professor Snyder. Darcy emerged from the other classroom about the same time with Professor Garner, who looked more curious than annoyed.

"I'm sorry to take you both away from class, but I have some questions," Jack said. "Would you follow me, please?" Not waiting for a response, he turned, heading for the atrium again.

Darcy and I traipsed along behind.

"What is this about?" Professor Snyder asked.

"I'd like to know that as well," Dr. Garner said.

"It's easier to show you." Jack kept walking.

I bit back a smile as Professor Snyder huffed. This was partly of his own making. If he'd told us who Ella accused of cheating, we might have answers already.

But we might also be barking up the wrong tree, so I was actually glad he'd been reluctant to name names.

Re-entering the exhibition, Jack took the same route we did and showed both men Ella's picture first.

"Take a good look at Ms. Kerns's work. Soak it in." Jack gestured to the photo collage. "Pay particular attention to the lake shots."

The professors took turns studying the image.

"Did you get a good look?" Jack's gaze bounced between the two.

They both nodded.

"Good. Let's go this way." He pointed down the aisle.

The five of us wound through the displays, stopping in front of Malcolm Brookings's black and white shots.

"Now look at that one." Jack tapped the frame around the picture.

Again, the professors took turns looking at it.

"I'm not sure I understand the issue." Dr. Garner peered over the top of his glasses at Jack. "It's just a picture of the lake. So was Ms. Kerns's photograph."

"It's not the setting. It's where it was taken at the lake." Jack looked at Darcy and me. "According to these two, this image"—he tapped the frame again—"and the one Ella took are from their family's private dock. Only Ella had permission to be there. So, either Mr. Brookings trespassed, or he stole Ella's picture."

Professor Snyder muttered a soft curse.

Dr. Garner stepped closer to the photo, peering at it more closely. "You know, I thought at the time he submitted it that it was a step up in quality for him." He looked up at Jack. "But it never occurred to me that he cheated. I just thought someone gave him some tips or the lessons from class finally clicked. Some students just take longer to bloom."

"How did he get it, though?" Snyder asked. "They don't have any classes together, do they?" He glanced at his colleague.

Dr. Garner shook his head. "I don't think so, no. But all the students share the main photography lab. If Ella left her negatives unattended, he could have made copies." He turned to Jack. "We have records of who goes in and out of the lab. They have to swipe their student IDs."

"Can you get me the logs?"

Dr. Garner nodded. "Yes. Let me go back and dismiss my class, then I'll be happy to help in any way I can."

"Is Malcolm Brookings in your current class?"

Garner's expression turned thoughtful, then suspicious. "Actually, he should be, but he didn't show up."

"No?" Jack raised an eyebrow. "Interesting." He tipped his head toward the exit. "Okay. Let's go."

My thoughts whirled as Darcy and I trailed behind the three men. Why didn't Malcolm show up today of all days? Or had it been several days since he was there? Why would he steal Ella's photos? His couldn't have been that terrible.

Unless they were.

Maybe he'd been in danger of flunking out of the program and saw an opportunity to bump up his grade.

In any case, there were a lot of questions surrounding Malcolm Brookings and his actions. Hopefully, we were finally on the right track to solving Ella's murder.

We had to be. What else was there about her that would lead someone to kill her?

Thirty-Two

The lab access logs told an interesting story.

Professor Garner had been efficient in pulling the records, and within the hour, we were staring at the proof. Jack spread the printouts across the table in the small conference room he commandeered at the university. Darcy and I leaned in from either side.

"There." Jack tapped a line on the page. "Malcolm Brookings accessed the photography lab at ten-forty-seven p.m. on September third. Ella Kerns signed in at six-fifteen that same evening and signed out at nine-twelve."

"So, he went in after she left." I traced the columns with my finger. "How long was he there?"

"Signed out at eleven-nineteen. An hour and a half."

"That's more than enough time to duplicate negatives," Darcy said. "Especially if he knew where she kept her things."

Jack flipped to another page. "He did this at least four other times over the past six weeks. Always after she left. Always late at night when the lab would be mostly empty." He sat back, crossing his arms. "The question is whether he just stole her photos or whether he killed her to keep her quiet about it."

My stomach tightened. Academic fraud was one thing. Murder was a whole different conversation. Why would he kill for a better grade?

"Is he already on academic probation or something?" I asked.

"Actually, he is. Dr. Garner mentioned that when he gave me the logs. One more failing grade, and he was out of the photography program."

"Did he happen to say what Malcolm's backup plan was if that happened?"

"No. I doubt it was anything the kid really wanted to do for the rest of his life, though, you know? You flunk out of college, and you're stuck working a dead-end job for minimum wage, unless you can get into a trade school, or you get lucky."

I couldn't disagree with that. "Do you have an address for him?"

Jack shot me the look. The one that said he knew where I was going with that, and the answer was that it was none of my business. His next words confirmed it.

"Don't even think about it."

"I wasn't going to go knocking on his door." I held up my hands in defense. "I was just curious."

"Sure you were." He gathered the printouts into a neat stack. "I'm going to find Mr. Brookings and have a conversation with him. You two are going home."

I huffed, pulling a perturbed face. I didn't want to go home. I wanted to go with him to talk to Malcolm.

Darcy pulled her phone from her pocket and glanced at the screen. "I need to get going, anyway. James and I were supposed to have dinner together." She aimed a pointed look my way that clearly said she was ready to leave, and I was her ride.

Dang it. I was hoping she'd back me up and argue we should be in on the conversation, since we were the ones to break the case open. Again.

"Good." Jack turned to me. "And you?"

"My car is here. I drove, remember?"

"I remember. I also remember you have a habit of not doing what I ask."

I simply arched an eyebrow, refusing to acknowledge the correctness of that statement.

He studied me for a beat. "Go home. Work on Daphne's cake. Do not—" He raised a finger, wagging it in my direction. "Do *not* go looking for Malcolm Brookings."

"I don't even know what he looks like." Though I was sure I could find that out if I really tried.

"Good. Let's keep it that way." He tucked the stack of papers under his arm and walked out of the conference room. At the door, he paused and looked back. Something in his dark eyes softened. "Thank you. Both of you. What you found today was critical."

A rush of warmth flooded my chest. Jack didn't hand out compliments lightly. "You're welcome."

After he disappeared down the hall, Darcy turned to me with a knowing smile. "He likes you."

"Stop."

"He *really* likes you."

"Darcy."

She raised her hands. "I'm just stating facts." Her phone buzzed and she looked at the screen. "James is at my house, wondering where I am." She typed out a quick message then slung her purse over her shoulder. "Are you ready?"

"I guess," I said on a sigh.

Darcy chuckled. "Don't sound so disappointed. I'm sure you'll find other opportunities to play detective."

I let out a quick snort as we exited the conference room. "Hopefully it's for something much more mundane. Like who ran through Lucile Prosser's flowerbeds. I've had enough of murder."

"Me too."

"But tonight, at least, I plan to behave."

"Yeah?" Darcy glanced at me as we left the building, headed for the parking lot.

I nodded. "Daphne's cake won't decorate itself, and I only have a week to finish. Less than that, actually, since there's so much else to do before the wedding next weekend." I was also more rattled by Allie's attack than I cared to admit. The image of her crumpled on the floor, blood in her hair, kept replaying behind my eyes like a movie I couldn't shut off. Someone was willing to hurt people to protect a secret. A secret that might have started with stolen photos. That part boggled my mind. Who would murder someone over a stolen picture?

The drive to Darcy's, then home was uneventful, if a little tense. Jack's advice to keep my head on a swivel and my own anxiety over the day's events meant I gave every vehicle we passed an extra-long look. Could they be Malcolm Brookings? Or was there a different faceless and nameless killer out there that I'd passed and didn't know it?

By the time I pulled into my driveway and saw my cat, Millie, sitting in the front window, watching for me, I was tenser than coiled springs on my garage door.

Normally, I got out as the garage door closed, but this time, I waited until it was down all the way before I shut off the engine and released the locks. I wasn't taking any chances.

Gathering my things, I got out and went inside.

Millie chirped and wound between my ankles, instantly easing my anxiety.

"Hi, sweet girl." Bending down, I let my bag drop to the floor and scooped her up, burying my face in her soft, calico fur. She purred, leaning back to lick my face with her sandpaper tongue.

For a few moments, I just stood there in my entryway, holding my cat and letting the day's events settle over me, processing the chaos of my Friday.

Once I felt like I could function without jumping at the slightest sound, I headed for the kitchen, where I set Millie on a barstool and grabbed my apron. I probably should have gone back to the church to work, away from my cat, but I could keep the flowers contained and Millie off the counter.

Grabbing the bleach spray and a clean rag, I wiped down the counter, then washed my hands and set to work. The hundreds of gum paste flowers I needed for Daphne's cake wouldn't make themselves.

I was three petals into my seventh peony when my phone trilled from my bag where I left it by the garage door. For a moment, I debated just letting it ring, but with everything that had been happening lately, I figured that probably wasn't the best idea.

Setting down the flower and my tools, then snatching a hand towel from the stack on the corner of the island, I wiped my hands and hurried over to retrieve the device.

The ringing grew louder as I removed it from my bag. A quick glance at the screen showed Jack's name.

My heart did that stupid little flip it always did when his name popped up.

Then a confused frown made my eyebrows dip. What could he be calling about?

Just before it rolled to voicemail, I answered. "Hello?"

"Malcolm Brookings wasn't at his apartment." Jack's voice was clipped. Professional. Whatever warmth he'd shown at the university had slid back behind that cop mask he'd perfected. "His roommate says he hasn't been home since yesterday."

"Yesterday? Also, why are you calling to tell me this? I thought you wanted me to stay out of it."

"I do." There was a slight pause, then I heard a beep of car doors unlocking. "But as I've said, you've proven useful, and I could really use a sounding board."

"Oh." A giddiness bloomed in my belly, spreading warmth through my torso. It was nice to know Jack thought I was useful and not a nuisance.

"Anyway, to answer your first question, yes. No one has seen Malcolm Brookings today."

A chill skittered down my spine. "That's not a coincidence."

He did that hum thing, and a beat of silence passed. "Maybe. I've got a BOLO out on him, in any case. If he's still in the area, we'll find him."

"What does he look like?" I asked, not because I intended to go looking. I'd learned my lesson and had no desire to end up in the same boat as I did with the last murder case I got involved with—no pun intended. I did, however, want to know who to slam the door on if he showed up at my house.

Jack hesitated, then sighed. "Five-ten. Thin build. Dark hair, usually messy. Wears glasses. Mid-twenties."

I repeated that to myself, trying to match it anyone I'd see before. No one sprang to mind.

There was another detail that came to mind though. "Have you had any luck with tracking the man James saw arguing with Ella at Scarlett's shop? Didn't you say you tracked him on surveillance cameras to a gray sedan?"

"I did, yes."

"Could that have been Malcolm? I know it wasn't Leo. He drives a truck." I thought back to the conversation we'd had about the man James saw. My shoulders slumped as dismay filled me. "Wait. James said the guy was older. Fifty-ish with silver-blond hair. That's not Malcolm."

Silence. Then the soft clatter of a keyboard.

"Jack?"

"Give me a second." More clicking came over the line. "Well, crap."

One of my eyebrows winged upward. "What?"

"His vehicle registration shows a 2019 gray Honda Civic sedan."

My grip on the phone tightened. "Okay, but still… James said the man he saw was older. It wasn't Malcolm."

"No, but…" Jack's tone shifted, the gears turning almost audibly.

Silence stretched over the line.

"But what?" I finally asked.

"But it could match a family member. One who maybe borrowed Malcolm's car."

That was an interesting theory. "Who, though? A father? An uncle? And why? Wouldn't they have their own vehicle?"

"Possibly. Maybe theirs was in the shop." Rustling came over the line, then the sound of a car starting.

"I'll look into it. Stay put, Delaney. I mean it."

"I'm elbow-deep in gum paste. I'm not going anywhere."

"Good." Another pause. "I'll call you later."

"You better," I grumbled. Otherwise, I'd hunt him down tomorrow and demand answers. He couldn't loop me in and then not keep me in the loop.

A soft, surprised chuckle rumbled through the phone. "I will. Lock your doors."

"They're locked."

"Good." He bid me goodbye, then hung up.

I stared at my phone for a long moment before a slow smile crept over my face.

He said he'd call.

I looked forward to it.

Thirty-Three

Saturday morning dawned bright and cold. Frost clung to the grass outside my kitchen window as I sipped my coffee and reviewed the last of my to-do list for Daphne's wedding.

The cake was coming together beautifully. The deep crimson fondant was smooth and flawless, and the cascade of gum paste peonies, roses, and dahlias in shades of cream, pink, and dusty mauve looked stunning against it. Delicate aqua piping and gold leaf accents would tie it all together once I added the buttercream detailing on the morning of the wedding, when everything was fresh.

Carol arrived at the church at our usual time. The scent of her coffee preceded her through the door.

"Morning." She held out a thermos. "You look tired."

"Thanks." I took the thermos and poured myself a cup. It was miles better than the stuff I normally brewed. "It's been a week. And thank you for coming in today. I know it's not one of your normal days to work."

"Of course. It's no problem. I know how busy you are with this wedding."

Carol's expression turned serious as she tied on her apron. "I heard about Allie. The news is all over town. Is she okay?"

"She will be. She has a concussion, but no brain bleed, which is a miracle." I took a sip of coffee and let the rich, dark roast warm me from the inside. "Jack has a suspect."

Carol's eyebrows rose. "For Allie's attack or Ella's murder?"

"Possibly both. A student named Malcolm Brookings. He was stealing Ella's photographs and passing them off as his own. Darcy and I figured it out at the photography exhibition."

"Seriously?" Carol's mouth dropped open, and she paused, reaching for the flour canister. "Someone killed that girl over *photos*?"

"That's what we're trying to figure out. The cheating alone seems like a stretch for murder, but Jack thinks there might be more to it. Malcolm's been missing since the day Allie was attacked." I set down my coffee and reached for the flat of eggs I'd pulled out of the fridge earlier. "There's also this mystery man James saw arguing with Ella at Scarlett's shop. Jack hasn't identified him yet, but he thinks it might be a relative of Malcolm's."

Carol was quiet for a moment, measuring flour into a mixing bowl. "You know, Morris mentioned something the other day I forgot to tell you."

"Oh? What?"

"He said a guy came around the logging office a few weeks back, asking about Leo Stanhope. Wanted to know his schedule and where he'd be at certain sites. Morris thought it was strange, because the guy didn't work for the company, and Morris had never seen him before."

My pulse quickened. "What did the guy look like?"

"Morris said he was older. Probably mid-fifties. Light-colored hair. Fit, like he worked outdoors."

My hand stilled on the binder. "Carol, that sounds like the same man James described."

Her eyes widened. "You think so?"

"I do." I reached for my phone. "I need to call Jack." I needed to do that, anyway. He'd never called me back last night, like he said he would.

"Delaney." Carol set down her measuring cup and gave me a look I hadn't seen from her before. It was the same look my mother gave me when she wanted me to really listen. "Be careful with this. I know you want to help, but someone already put Allie in the hospital. I don't want to see you end up there again, either."

The sincerity in her voice—the genuine worry—made me pause. "I know. I'm just passing along information. That's all."

She held my gaze for another beat, then nodded. "Good. Now call him, then help me figure out how to make these cinnamon rolls look like roses. I saw a video online, and I think they'd be adorable for your menu."

I couldn't help but smile. Carol was coming into her own, and it was wonderful to witness.

I dialed Jack's number. It rang three times before he picked up.

"Fiore."

"It's me. You forgot to call."

His low chuckle eased some of my ire at his lack of communication yesterday evening.

"It was late by the time I got home, and I figured you were in bed already. I didn't want to wake you. I know how early you get up."

Okay, that was kind of sweet.

"I didn't have too much to report, really, except to say I caught up with Leo Stanhope and asked him why he was at Allie's apartment complex. He's pet-sitting."

"Pet-sitting?" My eyebrows shot up.

"Yep. I spoke to his friend, who verified his story. I think you're right, and Leo isn't our guy."

"Well, I might have a different avenue for you to go down."

A soft sigh came through the phone. "Of course you do. How did you manage to gather *more* information at this early hour?"

"Don't be like that. This is good." I put him on speaker, then relayed what Carol told me about the man who'd come to the logging office asking about Leo.

The silence on the other end stretched long enough that I tipped the phone to look at the screen to make sure the call was still connected.

"Jack?" I glanced at Carol, whose eyes shifted from the phone to me, then back again.

"I'm here. I'm thinking."

More silence filled the air waves, which I felt a need to fill. "The description matches the man from the surveillance footage at Scarlett's shop. If this person was asking about Leo's schedule, that suggests he wanted to know when Leo would and wouldn't be at certain locations. Like Ella's apartment."

"Maybe." His voice had gone low and distant. Another long pause came over the phone line before he spoke again. "If Malcolm's father or another relative was involved, maybe gathering intel or even delivering the cyanide, then Malcolm may not have acted alone."

"The cyanide." My mind raced back to the invoices Allie found in Ella's things. That was it! "Jack, the work orders Allie brought you—the ones for cyanide from the logging company. Whose name was on those?" I could not for the life of me remember the name on it.

Jack sucked in a sharp breath. "Why didn't I think to check that?" Self-censure rang through his low grumble.

I heard papers rustle, then he muttered a soft curse.

Carol and I shared another look.

"The name on the cyanide invoice is Conrad Brookings. He works for a pest control company that contracts with the logging operation. He has access to cyanide-based fumigants." A grim edge sharpened his voice, then typing came over the line. A moment later, Jack muttered another curse. "He's also fifty-six-years-old, five-eleven, has silver-blond hair, and he's Malcolm Brookings's father."

My free hand gripped the edge of the counter. "He's the man James saw."

"I think so. And I think he's the one who attacked Allie. She said she didn't recognize her attacker. She might know Malcolm but probably not his father."

Everything clicked into place with perfect precision.

"Malcolm stole Ella's photographs to pass off as his own," I said. "Ella caught on and went to Professor Snyder, who asked for proof. Without his negatives, she probably couldn't give concrete proof, so she started documenting the discrepancies, like the note Allie found. Malcolm must have realized she was onto him and panicked. Jack, I bet either his father stepped in, or he helped Malcolm poison Ella."

More details fell into place as I mused aloud. "Conrad Brookings had access to cyanide through his pest control work. Likely, he went to the logging company asking about Leo's schedule"—I waggled a finger, looking at Carol—"probably to make sure Leo wasn't around when he went to Ella's apartment. Or..." My finger stopped, aimed toward the ceiling, and I paused for just a second as another thought struck me. "It was to frame him. He argued with Ella at Scarlett's shop, maybe trying to convince her to drop the accusation. When she wouldn't back down, he poisoned her, but he needed a fall guy. The boyfriend who works for the same company he's contracted to for pests would be perfect. And when Allie started finding Ella's evidence, he went after her too."

"I agree your theory is plausible, but we can't speculate," Jack said. "I need evidence."

I rolled my eyes. Of course he would play the evidence card.

"I also need motive for why he would poison her," he continued. "I get that Malcolm would be expelled from the university for his actions, but that's not the end of the world. It doesn't equate to murder in most people's eyes. A jury would think the same thing, and a good defense attorney would hammer that home."

"Well, what did he stand to lose if Malcolm got caught?"

Before Jack could say anything, the answer hit me. "The invoices!"

"What?"

"The invoices Ella had. They were for cyanide." My gaze met Carol's. Her wide eyes told me it had clicked for her too.

"Right. And? We know this," Jack said.

"Were they for more than what he would need to do his job?"

Jack groaned. "Are you sure you're not looking into a second career as a detective? I haven't reconciled his chemical usage against his workload, but I will now." He sighed. "I bet you're right. And if Conrad found out she got a hold of those invoices, that would be a strong motive to shut down her mission to prove Malcolm was cheating."

"Yep. It put undue attention on him and whatever he was doing with that cyanide. Do you know how she got them? I don't think you ever told me."

A quick beat of silence passed. This time, though, he didn't leave me hanging.

"Leo said they were in a pocket of one of his sweatshirts. We found one of his shirts in the belongings she took to her sister's. She must have scooped it up with her clothes without realizing it."

Voices in the background of the call drew his attention for

a moment. I heard him mutter, "I'm coming," before he spoke into the receiver again.

"I need to go. I'm gathering a few colleagues, and we're going to go see about having a chat with the elder Mr. Brookings. His home address is about forty minutes from here."

My heart thudded against my sternum as the knowledge he could be walking into a dangerous situation hit. "Be careful."

"I will. You too. If anything happens—"

"I'll call you or 9-1-1. I don't plan to go anywhere for a while. Carol and I have too much work to do."

"Good. I'm glad you're staying put. I'll call you later." There was a short pause. "I mean it this time."

A quick huff of air escaped on a silent laugh, but my smile was short-lived. "Jack?"

"Yeah?"

"Catch him." Ella deserved justice. So did Allie.

"I plan to." The line went dead.

I set my phone down, my hands trembling slightly. Not from fear this time, but from the overwhelming feeling that we were finally close to letting Ella rest in peace.

Carol appeared at my elbow. "Well, that took a turn."

I turned to her, a fierce smile pulling at my mouth. "I think we just helped solve a murder."

An answering grin spread across her face. "Does this mean I get a raise?"

A deep, belly laugh burst free from me, releasing a good deal of the tension I'd been holding onto for a while now.

Wiping at the moisture on my cheeks, I shook my head. "You haven't even worked off the cake yet."

"Details." She waved a hand and turned back to her cinnamon rolls, still grinning. "Details."

Thirty-Four

C arol left around four. I stayed another two hours, losing myself in making more flowers for Daphne's cake, using it as a distraction so I wouldn't think about Jack and what he might be walking into.

And why he hadn't called. I hoped it was because he was busy booking Conrad and Malcolm into jail, but I feared it was because he or someone else was hurt.

Or worse.

I failed miserably at keeping my thoughts off what was happening, but the flowers turned out great.

My phone rang just as I was sliding the last tray of flowers into the fridge. Jack's name lit up the screen, and my heart lurched into my throat as I snatched it up.

"Hey. Are you okay?" I crossed my fingers and said a quick prayer he would say he was.

"I'm fine." He sounded tired. And frustrated. "They weren't there."

"What?" I relaxed my hand, but my forehead wrinkled with a frown.

"The house was empty. Both vehicles gone. We canvassed

the entire neighborhood. No one has seen anyone at home since yesterday."

My stomach sank. "They ran."

"Looks that way. I've got a BOLO out on both of them as well as Malcolm's car and Conrad's blue F-150. If they're still in the area, we'll find them."

"And if they're not?"

"Then it gets harder, but not impossible. We have enough for arrest warrants. The sheriff sent their info to the local news stations. Their faces will be everywhere by morning."

I leaned against the counter, pressing my fingers to my temple, then winced as I hit the spot that was still sore from the explosion. "I'm sorry, Jack."

"Don't be. We're closer than we've ever been, and that's because of you and your persistence. I just need a little more time." A beat passed. "Where are you?"

"Still at the church. I'm about to head home."

"Okay. Watch yourself."

"Head on a swivel." I saluted to no one and smiled.

"It better be. Because if the Brookings haven't left town, well, everyone knows who's been helping the police."

My mouth flattened. "You're such a joy to be around, you know that?"

"Just keeping it real, Delaney. Text me when you get home, so I know you made it, all right?"

"Fine. Okay."

"I mean it, Delaney."

"I know you do." And I did. Despite his gruffness, I knew he cared now. I would do as he asked. Causing him extra worry wasn't something I wanted to do. He had enough of that from other sources.

"Go home. Get some rest. I'll keep you updated."

"Thank you for calling. I know you're busy."

"I told you I would." The faintest warmth crept into his voice, softening the edges of his brusque tone. "Be safe."

"You too."

We hung up, and I gathered my things, turning off the lights as I climbed the stairs. Outside, the evening air had turned cool, carrying the scent of woodsmoke. Leaves rustled in the light breeze, the sound a little more brittle than just a few weeks ago as they changed colors. Fall was truly upon us.

A smile toyed with my lips as I glimpsed the fading sun on the horizon. The sky was rapidly turning a deep indigo above the last streaks of orange and pink.

I locked the church door, then walked to my SUV, keys already in hand.

Hearing Jack's voice in my head to lock the doors as soon as I got in, I poked the lock button the moment the door shut.

The engine turned over with a quiet rumble as I pushed the start button, and I pulled out of the gravel lot onto the main road after buckling up.

The drive home was only about fifteen minutes. I took the long way tonight, not because I was looking for trouble but because the route along the lake was prettier and I needed the peace the view brought. My thoughts were a jumble, and so were my emotions.

I felt the tension ease from my shoulders as I rounded the bend and the lake came into view. The waning sun was behind the mountain, but there was enough ambient light to turn the water to liquid pewter. It shimmered as the breeze rustled up tiny waves on the surface.

Taking a deep breath, I held it for just a moment, then let it out, letting the peacefulness invade my body. I loved living here and couldn't imagine ever being anywhere else.

Five minutes from my house, though, my peace evaporated. Passing through the stretch of road that wound past the old lumber mill, I saw it.

Just a flash, but it was enough to make me slow down and pull over.

I bit my lip, glancing in my rearview mirror. Was that really what I thought it was?

Twisting in my seat, I looked over my shoulder. I'd pulled up too far and couldn't see it from here.

"Your brain is probably just playing tricks on you," I muttered as I performed a three-point turn in the middle of the road. "I mean, what are the odds there's a gray Honda Civic parked behind the mill?"

But as I approached the mill again, slower this time, and from the side where the car was parked, I realized the odds were greater than I thought.

Because sitting amongst the overgrown bushes alongside the mill office and partially behind the old rusted-out blue dumpster was that very car.

"Well, crud."

My pulse spiked. I gripped the steering wheel tighter and forced myself to keep driving at the same speed, not wanting to alert anyone who might be watching.

A snort escaped. Like I'd done by turning around and driving by again in my bright blue car?

Once I was past the mill and around the next bend, I pulled onto the shoulder and fumbled with the infotainment system to pull up my phone contacts. Tapping Jack's name, I waited as it rang through the car's speakers.

Jack answered on the second ring. "Hey. Are you home?"

I could hear the slight smile in his voice and hated to dash it. "I think I found Malcolm's car." My voice came out steadier than I felt. "It's at the old lumber mill on Amherst Road. The one that's been shut down for years. The car is parked behind the office building, like someone tried to hide it."

Silence. Then the sharp click of a car door. "Are you sure it's a gray Civic?"

"Yes. I couldn't see the plate, but it's definitely a gray Honda, and it's newer. Jack, there's no reason for anyone to be parked back there. That place has been abandoned for at least two years."

"Where are you now?"

"About a quarter mile past the mill. I turned around when I passed it because I only caught a glimpse the first time and had to be sure. I'm pulled over now, out of sight."

"Stay there. Actually, better yet, go home. But don't pass the mill again." His engine roared to life in the background. "I'm at least ten minutes away, but I'm calling in backup. Hopefully, they'll be there faster. Do *not* go back."

"I won't." I wasn't crazy. Or suicidal. People with weapons for protection could handle the murdering scumbags holed up at the mill.

"Delaney." The single word held a note of warning, and I knew he thought I might try to be a hero.

"I said I won't. But I'm not leaving."

He growled. Actually growled.

"If they leave, you won't know which way they went," I argued. "At least with me on this side of the mill, I can tell you if they pass me."

A beat of silence passed.

"Okay, fine. Stay. But keep your head down. If they pass you, *please*, for the love of God, do not follow them."

"Direction of travel only. I will stay parked."

"Thank you." A siren whooped a few times in the background before he must have silenced it. "Stay on the line with me."

I did my best to relax into the seat, then sat in the growing darkness, watching my mirrors. Minutes ticked by, my anxiety rising as the seconds passed. Jack's steady breathing and the sound of him coordinating with dispatch anchored me to reality, so I didn't spin off into a sea of "what-ifs."

Then headlights appeared in my rearview mirror. Not from the direction of town. These were coming from the direction of the mill.

"Jack. Someone's coming from the mill."

"What kind of vehicle?"

I squinted into the mirror as the headlights grew closer. "Truck. Dark color. It's—crap. Jack, I think it's an F-150. It might be Conrad's truck." It must have been further back than Malcolm's sedan, where I couldn't see it from the road.

"Or it could be some random person driving down Amherst. That's a popular vehicle. Duck down. Don't let them see you, just in case. The first marked unit is only about a minute away."

My gut screamed at me that it wasn't a random person. That it was, in fact, Conrad Brookings.

And he was about to drive away, out of sight. If he got to the highway, he could disappear in any direction.

"Delaney, silence is not golden in your case. Whatever you're thinking—"

"He's going to get past me." I shifted my SUV into drive and cranked the wheel, pulling forward and angling my car across the narrow two-lane road. It wasn't a perfect block. There was a sliver of space on the lake side, but the shoulder dropped off sharply toward the water. He'd have to slow down significantly to get around me without toppling over the edge. I might not stop him, but I might slow him down enough for that deputy to arrive.

Tires screeched on the pavement.

I glanced out my window. Headlights filled my vision and the truck fishtailed slightly as the driver attempted to stop. I let out a soft squeak.

"Delaney?"

"Please stop, please stop, please stop," I muttered.

The headlights grew larger as the truck got closer. I squeezed my eyes shut and braced for impact. "Oh, God," I whispered on a squeak.

"Delaney! Talk to me. What's happening?"

Bright light filled the interior of my car. I cracked an eyelid open to see the pickup stopped just feet away.

Relief flooded my veins, making my limbs heavy. But just as quickly, that feeling disappeared when the driver's door opened.

"Oh, crap," I muttered.

Jack cursed. "Would you please tell me what's going on?"

"I, um…" I swallowed hard, getting rid of the lump that formed over my vocal cords. "I blocked the road. With my car."

"You did *what*? Of all the crazy…" He stopped and heaved a heavy sigh. "Stay in your car. Do not get out until the deputy or I reach you."

"No worries." I shrank into the center console as the truck's driver's side door closed, revealing a middle-aged man of average height with silvery-blond hair. "But just so you know," I said to Jack. "I was right. It's Conrad Brookings."

I tried to meld and become one with the console as he approached my window. In the background of my phone call with Jack, I heard the crackle of Jack's police radio and his response, but I couldn't make out what he said. Hopefully, he was informing his backup of the current situation.

"Lady? Are you crazy? Why are you blocking the road? Move!" He swept an arm out as he peered inside.

I just shook my head.

He leaned closer. Shadows swam around his face as his proximity to the car obscured some of the light from his head-lights. The hard glimmer in his eyes shone clear and bright, however.

"What is your problem?" He smacked the window. "Move your car."

"Oh, Jack," I whispered. "You need to hurry."

He didn't answer, so I took that to mean he was concen-trating.

"Hey!" Conrad smacked my window again with his open hand. "Lady, come on. What's your deal?" He yanked on the door handle.

Thank goodness I had not only manually locked my doors but changed the setting so they unlocked upon exit and not upon parking. I didn't pick up enough speed with my maneuver to block the road to re-engage them automatically.

The flutter of blue and red lights blinked off the trees and filled the growing darkness.

I sat up and looked through the passenger window.

Not one, but two sheriff's cars pulled to a halt behind me. A deputy exited each one, but they stayed behind their doors for cover.

"Conrad Brookings! Put your hands up and get on the ground now!" one of them yelled.

Conrad's fists clenched and unclenched at his sides. A muscle ticked in his jaw and a wildness entered his eyes. Eyes which darted between the deputies and the lake to his left, calculating.

"Don't do it, Brookings," one of the officers warned.

Jack's truck roared around the bend and came to a rocking stop behind the two cruisers.

At the appearance of a third cop, the fight leached from Conrad. His shoulders slumped and his head drooped. Slowly, he raised his hands.

In seconds, both deputies and Jack had moved forward and quickly cuffed him.

I sagged against the steering wheel, my forehead resting on my clasped hands. My heart hammered so hard I could hear it in my ears.

"Holy. Cow." I blew out a breath, getting a handle on my frayed nerves, and lifted my head.

Jack had advanced on Conrad's pickup. Movement from the passenger seat caught my eye.

Malcolm.

Weapon raised, Jack ordered him out of the vehicle.

The passenger door opened, and Malcolm stepped out without resistance. Jack had him cuffed and marching toward the rest of us in less than a minute.

With both men secure, I shut off my car and got out.

Jack's gaze roved over me, but I hadn't a clue what he was thinking. That impenetrable cop mask was back on his face.

He marched Malcolm right past me to the first of the two cruisers. After a quick search of the young man's pockets, he read him his rights. When Malcolm refused to talk, Jack put him in the back of the cruiser and shut the door.

The two deputies had Conrad leaning against the hood of my car as they searched his pockets and mirandized him.

Jack walked up, his gaze fixed on Conrad. "Did someone read you your rights?"

"Yeah. I want a lawyer."

"That's fine." Jack's head bobbed once. "I'm happy for you to sit in holding for a while." He turned to one of the deputies. "He have anything on him?"

The man shook his head. "Just ID and some cash."

"Okay. Take him and his son back to the station. I'll be there in a bit. I want to meet the crime scene crew at the mill."

"Sounds good." The deputy grasped one of Conrad's arms. "Let's go Mr. Brookings."

My gaze followed Conrad and the deputy to the second cruiser. When I turned around again, Jack's eyes were fixed on me.

The cop mask had slipped.

Relief, a healthy dose of exasperation, and something deeper warred for prominence in his dark eyes.

For a long moment, he just looked at me. That muscle ticked in his jaw as he weighed words in his head, and his dark eyes held mine with an intensity that made everything else around us fade to nothing.

"You blocked the road," he finally said.

My cheeks heated. "I had to do something. Letting them get away..." I trailed off and glanced toward the lake for a moment. "It just wasn't an option."

"You could have been killed. What if he hadn't stopped in time? Or he'd had a weapon?"

I lifted a shoulder, not sure what to say. "None of that went through my mind. I just knew he couldn't get away."

Jack stepped closer until he was close enough, I had to tip my chin up to look him in the eye.

"You're impossible, you know that?"

"But would you really want me to be any different?" I arched an eyebrow.

Those luscious lips that looked like they'd been sculpted by one of the master Italian sculptors curved upward ever so slightly. "Probably not, no."

"Then it's all good. I didn't even get a scratch this time, and you got your bad guy." I glanced past him at the cruisers. "Bad *guys*."

He crossed his arms, his expression relaxing. "Are you sure you're okay?"

"I'm fine. A little rattled, because well..." I motioned to Brookings' truck that was just a few feet from my driver's door. "But I'll be fine. Like I said. Not a scratch." I held up my hands, turning them one way, then the other.

He rolled his eyes, but an amused smile ghosted over his mouth.

Then he straightened and looked back toward the truck. "There's a camera case in the cab."

My gaze snapped to the pickup. "Ella's cameras?"

"Maybe. Could be Malcolm's, but considering it's purple and blue tie-dye, I doubt it." His eyes followed mine. "There's also a bunch of chemicals in the truck bed. I bet one will match the cyanide used to poison Ella." He turned back to me. "I hate that you were here, but I can't argue with the result. So, thank you."

A quick chuckle escaped me. "I'm going to remind you of this every time you tell me to stay out of things now."

"Oh, I'm sure you will." He grinned, then nodded toward my car. "Go home. For real this time. I'll be at the station most of the night processing them."

Home sounded amazing. I was done playing crime fighter. "Okay." Hopping into the driver's seat, I reached for the ignition, then paused. "Jack?"

"Yeah?"

"Will you call me? When you're done? Even if it's late. I don't care what time. I think…" My voice trailed off, and I stared through the windshield for several beats as I gathered my thoughts into words. "I think I just need to know it's all really over."

Something shifted in his expression. A tenderness invaded his features I'd never seen before.

"Yeah," he said quietly. "I'll call."

Thirty-Five

T his time, Jack kept his word and didn't let me sleep.

I was curled up on the couch with a blanket and Millie in my lap, deep in dreamland, when my phone rang.

My heart skipped, then pounded against my sternum at the noise. Millie flew off my lap, equally startled.

Blinking rapidly to clear the grittiness of sleep from my eyes, I reached for my phone on the end table.

Jack's name appeared.

"Hey," I said, answering on the fourth ring.

"Hey." His voice was tired but warm. "I'm sorry if I woke you."

Pushing against the back of the couch, I sat up, coming more awake by the second. "You're fine. I did ask you to call no matter what time."

He chuckled softly. "You did. I listened this time." A yawn overtook him. "Sorry. I probably shouldn't have and just went home to bed."

"Well, I'm glad you didn't do that. I sat down on the couch, thinking I'd wait up just a little bit, and I fell asleep. You saved me from waking up with a stiff neck."

"I'm glad I could be of service." He yawned again.

"So, is it really over? Did you find what you needed to make charges stick against the Brookings?"

"Yes. Both of them have been booked. Malcolm had a change of heart when we got back to the station, and he was away from his father. Conrad lawyered up, but the evidence speaks for itself. His prints match some partials from Ella's apartment that we couldn't identify before. Allie's attack might still be a hard sell to a jury, but I'm hoping forensic evidence will place him at the scene. Our crime scene unit found foreign DNA under her nails. Both men will have theirs compared to it."

"Good." Millie jumped back onto the couch, and absently, I stroked her soft fur. "Did you break the news to Ella and Allie's parents?"

"Yes. They're relieved, but also back in the throes of grief now that they have a face and a name to attach to their anger. I think it'll take some time for them to fully move on, but in the end, I think they'll be fine. They have each other to lean on."

"Yeah." Millie headbutted my hand, purring up a storm. "Does Scarlett know?"

"Not yet. I figured you could break the news to her. She is officially off my suspect list."

I chuckled. "About time."

Another beat of silence settled between us. Not uncomfortable, just a moment of quiet as the conversation shifted.

"Delaney?"

"Yeah?"

"What I said that one day about you being a distraction..."

My heart kicked up a notch. "What about it?"

"I didn't mean it the way it sounded. Or maybe I did, but not in a bad way." He paused, and I could picture him running his fingers through his thick, black hair as he tried to figure out what to say. "You make it hard to focus, and in my line of work, that can be dangerous. But it's not because you're a nuisance. It's because—" He stopped. Blew out a breath. Started again. "It's because I care about what happens to you. More than I probably should, considering the way you like to get involved in my cases."

Warmth bloomed in my chest and spread outward, tingling all the way to my fingertips. "Oh." I couldn't make any more words form. I was both too tired and too flummoxed by the idea Jack found me distracting in a good way to say more.

He let out a breath that was half laugh, half exasperation. "I basically tell you I find you appealing and all you can say is, 'Oh?'"

My laugh was fuller this time. "I'm too tired for midnight confessions."

The low rumble of his laughter filled my ear, adding to the warm feeling already flooding my body.

"But for what it's worth," I continued, "you're a distraction for me too."

"Oh, yeah?"

I could hear the smile in his tone.

"Yeah." I tucked my legs under me, grinning. "A really annoying one."

He laughed. A real laugh this time. Low and rich and warm enough to make my toes curl.

"I mean, do you know how annoying it is to have a man tell you he'll call and he only has a fifty-percent success rate?"

"I would call us even, or even say I'm winning, because I constantly tell you to not get involved, but yet you still do," he countered.

I hummed a non-answer, unable to argue there.

"So." He cleared his throat. "After the wedding next weekend, when things calm down. Would you want to grab dinner? Just the two of us."

My heart, which had calmed down from my abrupt awakening, picked up speed again. "Are you asking me on a date, Detective?"

"I believe I am."

What? Was he serious? Darcy and Daphne had both said they thought Jack liked me, but as much as I'd wanted that to be true, I never thought it was. Apparently, I should have listened to them.

"Delaney?"

"I'm here. I just…" I cleared my throat. "Um, I'm—You really want to go on a date with me?"

His soft huff of a laugh tickled my ear. "I thought that was obvious from the distraction comment. Yes. I would like to take you on a date."

"Oh."

Just say yes, Delaney.

"Yes." The little push from my inner self was all I needed. "I'd like that. Very much."

"Good. We can talk more about it at the wedding, if you want. Or I can call you."

That comment brought me out of my spin-cycle of emotions and made me chuckle. "Considering your track record, the wedding sounds good."

He groaned softly. "I'm never living that down."

"Eh, maybe." I shrugged and smiled, adjusting the phone. "Once you've improved your record to, say, ninety-five percent?"

"Oh, a goal, huh? I'm a goal-oriented person, so challenge accepted. But in the meantime, save me a dance at the wedding."

Dance? With Jack?

My entire body heated at the thought of being so close to him. I fanned my face. "I will."

"I look forward to it. Now get some sleep. Not on your couch."

My expression softened. "You too."

"I plan to sleep like a rock now that this case is solved."

We said our goodbyes, and I hung up the phone. Setting it on the cushion beside me, I scooped up Millie and held her close, grinning like an absolute fool.

I had a date.

With Jack.

An actual, bona fide, real date.

Holy cow!

I let out a squeal and stood.

Millie chirped and squirmed, wanting down.

"Sorry, Mills." I gave her a quick scratched behind her ears, then set her on the couch. "Let's head to bed, yeah?"

She blinked her golden eyes at me, then with another chirp, hopped onto the floor and trotted toward my bedroom, as if to say, *It's about time.*

I couldn't agree more. In more ways than one.

THANK YOU SO MUCH for reading *Baked Goods and Bad Blood*. I hope you enjoyed it. Book 3 in the series, *Crimson Cake and Conspiracies,* comes out in September 2026, so stay tuned. E-book pre-orders are available on my website: https://ashleyaquinn.com/fernwood-mysteries-ashley-samuels To stay up-t0-date on all the happenings in Fernwood, be sure to follow me on Facebook @ashleysamuelsbooks

About the Author

After spending most of her adulthood moving around the U.S. and Europe, Ashley has settled in the wilds of South Dakota with her husband, two kids, and a menagerie of pets. She started writing in her teens and never stopped. Her first novel, a romantic thriller under the pen name Ashley A. Quinn, debuted in 2016, and she has since published more than twenty books. When not writing, you can find her with her nose stuck in a mystery thriller or binge-watching British TV dramas and reality shows. She is an avid baseball fan and also enjoys growing all the things in her garden and book-binding.